TATTOOS
&
TEACUPS

ANNA MARTIN

Dreamspinner Press

Published by
Dreamspinner Press
382 NE 191st Street #88329
Miami, FL 33179-3899, USA
http://www.dreamspinnerpress.com/

This is a work of fiction. Names, characters, places, and incidents either are the product of the author's imagination or are used fictitiously, and any resemblance to actual persons, living or dead, business establishments, events, or locales is entirely coincidental.

Tattoos & Teacups
Copyright © 2012 by Anna Martin

Cover Art by Shobana Appavu bob@bob-artist.com

ISBN: 978-1-61372-590-0

Printed in the United States of America
First Edition
July 2012

eBook edition available
eBook ISBN: 978-1-61372-591-7

To the fair city of Edinburgh,
my summer home,
thank you for the inspiration.

PROLOGUE

ONCE, when I was on a trip to New York City, I stopped to watch a group of hip-hop dancers who were performing in the street. I was fascinated by the brash colors and thumping beat of the music, and the tricks and flips they performed with apparent ease. Although I stood back in the crowd—there were two or three people in front of me—I couldn't help but be both impressed and intimidated as one of the dancers walked right up to the person in the front row, throwing his arms wide out to his sides and pushed his chest almost right up to the other man's, shouting, "Boom!" Right in his face!

The sheer gall of the dancer made me smile, even as my stomach flipped at the idea of such confrontation. Much to my surprise, the other man, not the dancer, just laughed and made some funny noise in the back of his mouth, like he was rolling his Rs, and the dancer seemed to take this as encouragement to perform a backflip from standing, to the raucous approval of the assembled crowd.

Chris made me feel like that. Intimidated, and a little impressed. He was the same as that dancer in so many ways: loud, colorful, swirling into my life with a loud "Boom!" and disappearing just as quickly. Like those hip-hop dancers, though, I was left with the simmering feeling that I'd experienced something completely new, and I was irrevocably changed for it.

PART
ONE

CHAPTER ONE

SEPTEMBER on the Northeast coast was a colorful affair. In private, I still say "colourful" (with the added "u") as a way of reminding myself never to succumb to the Americanisms that plague my day-to-day life. Despite the months that had melted into years since I had left my native Scotland, I liked to maintain a grip on my heritage and a certain amount of decorum when it came to correct spelling, punctuation, and grammar. It may sound dull, but I assure you, I am not. I just appreciate the correct use of the English language.

I was sixteen, actually, when we left Edinburgh for New Hampshire. Sixteen years in Scotland, sixteen in America. The summer of my thirty-second year on this planet had made me feel itchy, like it was time to move again. Time to go somewhere new, do something different or find a new path for myself, maybe.

It was unlikely, though, the chance of moving. My career was settled, and I was starting to be appreciated for my knowledge and expertise in my field. I was invited to events and conferences and lectures to talk about my research into the work of Rudyard Kipling and his impact on colonial society. I sometimes repeated these lectures to glassy-eyed third-year college students, although I doubted many of them appreciated what I was trying to impart to them. None of them ever submitted my suggested essays, anyway.

The routine settled around me without me even really noticing; my apartment—my flat, and my cat, and my car, and my work all had their allocated slots, and I was happy, so was there any point in changing anything? I was lonely, though. The cat did something to ease the heartache of coming home to an empty flat, but he wasn't anything more than a tuna-stealing companion. And wasn't that just a lie.

On the love front, I was painfully bereft. And had been for longer than I would have ever, ever admitted. When we'd moved to America—Mum, Dad, me, and Jillian—I'd just completed my Highers, the qualification sat at age sixteen in Scotland that permits a child of that age to leave the education system if they so wish. I was essentially stuck in no-man's-land, unable to do anything in the States without a high school education but having already finished my schooling according to my home country.

Since Jilly would also be going to the local high school, I agreed to go on the pretense of being there as her moral support. In fact, Jilly was more than capable of taking care of herself and quickly took advantage of her years at gymnastics club back at home and insinuated herself into the cheerleading squad. The other children at the school seemed to go through phases of either mocking my accent or revering me for it.

In a world where fitting in was everything, coming out simply wasn't a possibility.

College was supposed to be my saving grace, a place where I could stand proud as a gay man and embrace love, life, and another man without fear of repercussions. The truth was something slightly different. Although there was an LGB society on campus (they had yet to add the T) it was headed by a frankly terrifying lesbian and the only men there seemed to be flamboyantly gay, and they scared me even more than the overtly macho men that surrounded me in my dorm.

I kept promising myself, *Next year will be different. Next year you'll find someone.* But I never did. Jillian blamed it on me not getting out enough. So did my friends. The sad fact of the matter was, I'd labeled myself unlovable, a static, stoic bachelor, and myself and Flea, my scruffy cat, were doing quite well on our own, thank you very much.

And then? *Boom.*

"FOR next week," I called out over the sound of people grabbing bags and shoving hastily scrawled notes into them, "please read *The Man*

Who Would Be King for me! We are leaving poetry behind for the time being."

My response was a general muttering, which I took to be acceptance. The required reading list for my course was adequately prepared well in advance to give my students ample time to become familiar with the material, but it was always worth reminding them.

It was my last class of the day; a serendipitous glitch in the college's lecture programming system meant that by 2:00 p.m. on a Friday, I was finished for the week and could start my weekend early. Not that I ever did. My position allowed me to demand a nice office, and after three years they finally granted it to me. I was young to hold such a prestigious position but not above abusing it.

The only downfall was the long trek across campus in between the Literature building, where I worked, and the History building, where my office was located. I could have moved into the Literature building, naturally, if I were to give up my nice office. So the walk was good exercise.

I kept the room decorated in a style Jillian referred to as "grumpy old man", and it suited me down to the ground. One wall was dominated by a large bookcase, which I filled, delightedly, with secondhand books and copies of volumes I kept in my personal library at home. I had a lovely wingback leather chair kept behind an antique desk I'd found at a flea market and a long, comfortable sofa I rarely used except to nap on sometimes when I'd been at the campus from dusk 'til dawn.

After dumping my briefcase and notes on an increasingly perilous pile of stuff on the corner of my desk, I settled back to start reading through the e-mails that had accumulated in my absence. They were filled with the usual rubbish: students pleading for extensions due to the death of their granny/ dog/ second cousin in Peru, an invitation from my mother to Sunday lunch, messages to the whole faculty asking for our cooperation in the "Clean Up The Campus" campaign, and one from my friend Adam with the question:

The Boat or The Bird?

I laughed and sent an e-mail back: *The Boat, for sure.*

There was a pub that we liked just off campus called the Ship where they served good beer and better food. On campus there was a bigger bar that the students drank in too, called the Two Magpies. We'd nicknamed the bars in an attempt to hide from our students where we'd be drinking on any particular night. Unfortunately, someone overheard one of our conversations, and now the nicknames had entered the general student consciousness.

I worked solidly for a few hours, making progress through the pile of work on my desk, and looked up at the clock in surprise when Adam knocked on my door at five.

"Hey," he said, sticking his head around the door. "You ready to head out?"

"Yeah, nearly. Come in a minute." I gestured him inside.

Adam flopped down on the couch, making himself at home while I saved everything and packed up all I'd need for the weekend.

"This place is a dump," Adam opined.

"It is not a dump. It is organized chaos," I corrected him.

Adam snorted with laughter under his breath. He wasn't a lecturer, Adam. He worked in the campus theater as a working technician. From the bright lights of Broadway to the dusty spotlights of the college auditorium, his career had taken a bit of a downturn, but he'd wanted to move his young family out of the city and into the suburbs. I liked his laidback, easygoing nature, characterized by a lolloping gait caused by his six-foot frame.

"Come on, beer's waiting," he huffed as I finally stuffed the last of my papers into my briefcase.

"I'm coming."

"That's what he said."

"Adam, don't be crude."

He knew about my sexuality and occasionally made fun of me for it, not in a cruel way, just the way friends do. He asked me once if I found him attractive. I said no, I didn't go in for redheads.

My ancient, rusting Buick was something else that often caught the sharp end of his witty tongue. It was a remnant of my own college days, and I liked the familiarity of the heap of junk, even if it did cost me more to keep running than it was worth. I drove over to the Ship with the windows down, pretending to us all that there was warmth left in the air when in reality, autumn was creeping in fast.

I HAD been persuaded, against all my better judgments, to stay at the Ship far longer than I had originally intended. Once we were past the point where I could reasonably drive home, it was actually embarrassingly easy to keep me there, teetering on a barstool as we debated the perils of American "football."

"Now rugby," I said, slapping an emphatic hand down on the bar. "There's a real man's sport. None of this namby-pamby padding you Yanks all wear."

"Your accent comes out when you're drunk, you know that?" Adam said.

"Aye," I agreed. "That it does."

"Aye," he parroted.

A light hand tapped me on the shoulder. I whirled around too quickly; the world blurred before my eyes before fixing on a young blond man.

"Can I help you?" I asked him, trying to suppress the Scottish aggression in my voice.

"Sorry," he said, a slow, easy smirk spreading across his face. "Thought you were Gerard Butler there for a minute."

"Butler!" I yelled. "Bloody Gerard bloody Butler is the bane of my bloody existence!" My wild gesticulating had caused me to spill some of my pint down my shirt, a fact I was made aware of as the amber liquid seeped through to my skin. "And he's about ten years older than me!"

"Sorry about this," Adam said, leaning over me, slurring his words. "He gets rowdy when he's drunk."

"I can see that," the boy said. He hopped up onto the barstool next to mine and gestured to the barmaid. "Do you have a name?"

"My name," I said, pulling myself up to my full (seated) height, "is Robert Andrew McKinnon. The second. Who the hell are you?"

"Chris. Christopher Jacob Ford. The only. I like your accent."

Adam collapsed into giggles, and I took his hand to shake. His brightly colored, vividly tattooed hand.

"Ah, everyone likes my bloody accent," I sighed into my pint glass.

"He says 'bloody' a lot when he's drunk," Adam helpfully supplied. "Hey, are you gay? Robert is, and he hasn't gotten laid in ages."

"Adam!" I exclaimed and shoved his shoulder. He fell off the barstool.

I didn't apologize—he deserved it—but I did buy another round of drinks while he loped off to the bathroom. To the loo. To the bloody loo.

"So," I said to Christopher Jacob Ford, emboldened by my display of brute masculine force, "are you gay?"

He smirked at me in a way I should have interpreted as "yes." In a way, once upon a time, I would have interpreted it as "yes."

"If you wanna know," he said, pushing a neat white card across the bar to me, "call me."

I lifted the card to my face. It had ten numbers and the characters *C.J.F. (1)* printed on it in neat handwriting. I tucked it into my wallet for later.

I WOKE up the following morning with a ball of fluff on my head and another one forming between my teeth. On trying to move I discovered two things: the ball of fluff on my head was Flea, who indignantly dug his claws into my scalp as I tried to dislodge him, and the ball of fluff between my teeth was certain impending death.

Hangovers enhanced my sense of melodrama.

I crawled out of bed, where I'd sprawled to sleep, facedown, wearing one sock and my shirt and tie. Nothing else. Walking to the bathroom (I refused to crawl, even though that was clearly the better option), I tried to use the power of positive thinking to will myself back into consciousness. It didn't work, but the steaming-hot shower, painkillers, two glasses of water, and committing an act of self-love all went most of the way toward fixing it.

Just after I'd finished shaving and dressing in my favorite blue jeans and plaid shirt, the intercom buzzed. I didn't have time to comb my hair before answering it, which annoyed me greatly.

"Haven't you done enough already?" I barked at Adam as his grainy, grey face appeared on the little screen.

"Thought you might like to join me and the family for breakfast," he said with a jovial smile. I huffed and buzzed him in.

"I do have other friends, you know," I said as he let himself in through the front door I'd apparently forgotten to lock the night before.

"I know you do," he countered. "But by my reckoning, you'll be like a bear with a sore head this morning, and a good breakfast will go miles toward fixing it."

I mumbled and grumbled and pulled on shoes, combed my hair, and found a nice sweater vest to go over my shirt.

"Are the kids coming?" I asked.

"They're already in the car. As is Marley. Waiting for you."

"All right, all right," I muttered, taking the hint. Glanced in my wallet and winced at its contents, or lack thereof. Frowned at the little dog-eared card that had been tucked in behind my driver's license. Left the house as Adam smacked me around the back of the head to hurry me along.

Marley is Marlene, Adam's equally tall, exceptionally beautiful wife whom he got pregnant while she was dancing in *Romeo and Juliet* and convinced her to give up the high-pressured, super-slim world of ballet for motherhood in the suburbs. Two children later and I think they're the happiest couple I'd ever met.

"I'm seeing Chloe later," I said as I climbed into the backseat of the car, between Tia and Charlotte at their request.

"Good, you don't see her enough," Marley said as she leaned through the gap between the front seats to give me a kiss.

The first time I went out with Adam's family, I felt like a third wheel, intruding on personal family time that I had no right to intrude on. That soon passed, though. Marley was too warm and loving for me not to warm to her, and other friends joined us often enough.

As we settled into our table at the diner, I pulled my wallet out again, determinedly looking for that bloody card. While inspecting it further, Adam began to laugh.

"I'm glad you hung on to that," he said, still chortling.

"What is it?"

"Some guy gave you his number."

It came back to me in flashing, still images: a young blond man, pushing Adam off his barstool, tattoos. *"If you wanna know, call me."*

"Oh crap," I muttered, dropping my head to the table, making the girls laugh.

"Let me see," Marley said. I passed her the paper without lifting my head. Her fingertips threaded through my hair and gently massaged my neck. "What does C.J.F. brackets one mean?"

"It means," I said, summoning the shards of my dignity and sitting up again, "Christopher something-beginning-with-J Ford, or Frost, or… no, I think it was Ford, the first."

"And only," Adam helpfully supplied.

"Yes. The first and only."

"Are you going to call him?"

"No!" I exclaimed. "Absolutely not. He thought I was Gerard Butler."

Marley winced in sympathy. She knew Butler was older than me and that I hated the comparison. Especially when people said, "Oh, I thought you would have been about the same age…."

"Butler is rather dashing, though, Robert. You should start taking it as a compliment. All the girls like him."

"Yes, well, I'm not particularly interested in having all of the girls liking me."

Tia looked up from where she'd been stirring her orange juice with a straw. "Uncle Robert, why don't you want all the girls liking you?"

"New topic of conversation!" Marley said loudly and enthusiastically, clapping her hands and smiling brightly. Adam leaned over and whispered something in Tia's ear, making her frown, then violently start stirring her juice again. I suspected he'd told her the truth.

The waitress came shortly after that and took our orders.

THAT evening I settled down with an Indian takeaway meal and tried not to think of Chris and his number and the paper that was burning a hole through my wallet into my ass cheek. Arse cheek. Eventually, as I was cleaning up the kitchen, I removed the slip of paper from my wallet and stuck it to the fridge with a magnet shaped like a tomato. I stared at it for long moments, wondering what the hell I was going to do with it.

I CLOSED my eyes and dialed his number blind, letting the beeps tell me that I was pressing the right numbers. I gritted my teeth as it rang. Felt like I was going to throw up.

I cleared my throat. "Hello, um, Chris? This is Robert."

"Mm. Robert. Robert, Robert… oh! Gerard Butler."

This was a bad idea. "Yeah."

"Hey! I was hoping you would call."

"Oh. Well, I did. How are you?"

"Good, man, I'm good." The sound of him rummaging around. It sounded like he was still in bed. It was nearly two in the afternoon! I was calling from my lunch break! "What are you doing?"

"I'm actually just on my lunch break."

"Cool. Wanna meet for a beer later?" My heart leaped.

"Yeah. Yeah, that sounds good."

"Awesome. Well, I've got your number now. I'll text you when I move."

"Okay. I'll speak to you later, Chris."

"Yup. Later."

Then he hung up. I stared at my phone for long moments, in complete shock. I had a date. On a Tuesday night. I slammed my laptop shut and raced across campus to try and find Adam.

THERE was no time after my last class of the day to go back to the apartment and change, so I was forced to go out still dressed in my suit (although I did take off my tie and leave it in the car, with my jacket. It was an attempt at casualness at which I fear I failed.)

I had received a text from Chris saying that he'd gone to a coffee shop; I was relieved it wasn't another bar after our last encounter. I parked just a few doors up and compulsively wiped my hands on my thighs a few times, trying to dispel the nerves that were gnawing at my stomach. I hadn't been on a date in… too long.

Chris stood as soon as I walked through the door and waved me over.

"I was starting to worry you were going to stand me up," he said, teasing.

"Oh, no, I would never do that," I said. "I got caught up at the office. I'm sorry."

"No worries," he said, flashing me his boyish grin and settling back into his deep leather chair.

I bought him a refill and me a decaf in an effort to calm my nerves. The hot liquid scalded my tongue as I sipped at it, forcing me to hide my grimace of pain.

"Where do you work?" Chris asked as I sat back in my chair. I carefully returned my cup to its saucer.

"I'm a professor, actually, at the university."

"Oh yeah?" He sounded interested. "What do you teach?"

"Colonial literature, with a particular emphasis on Kipling. Please tell me you're not a student."

Chris laughed easily. "I'm not a student, Rob."

"Robert," I corrected automatically, then cringed. "Sorry."

"I had an uncle called Robert," Chris said, waving off my apology. "He was a pervert and an alcoholic. Rob sounds… younger."

"I don't generally let people use that as a nickname."

"I'd gathered that."

"I suppose I could make an exception for you."

I was treated to another smile. To see it again, the concession on my name was nothing.

"And you?" I asked. Sipped still-scalding coffee. "What do you do?"

"I'm a percussionist," he said.

"A drummer?"

Chris frowned, rolled his eyes, and threw his hands up in the air. "No, not a drummer, a percussionist."

"I'm sorry," I apologized.

"It's fine. Well, to be fair, I do own a drum kit. But I also work freelance for orchestras and symphonies and all that shit too."

"Wow," I said, impressed. "How long have you been doing that?"

"Drumming? Since I was eight. I started on everything else when I realized how much money there was to be made doing all of the highbrow shit as well. I'm in a band," he added, bragging, but it suited him. "Yeah. That's how we ended up here. We've been on tour for about a year and a half."

"Where did you come from?"

"Florida, originally," he said, leaning forward to collect his mug from the table and stretching the thin white T-shirt he was wearing tight over his back. "Moved about some when I was a kid, ended up in Tallahassee, where I met the guys. We played out the South over a period of a few months, then decided to get on the road."

"Where have you been?" I asked. "Sorry—I don't mean to bombard you with questions, I'm just interested."

"Nah, I don't mind," he said, smiling again. "I'm an arrogant little shit, I like talking about myself. We hit most major cities on the East Coast on our way up here. Atlanta, DC, Baltimore, New York... then Boston, and here I am."

"Boston isn't nearly as impressive as where you've been before," I said, trying to phrase the next question not like a question at all.

"Ah, John's sentimental," Chris said. "Our strings man. He grew up here and wanted to come back, play some gigs, catch up with people he used to know. We'll be here for a few months yet."

"Sounds good."

"Can I ask you something?" Chris asked, and I nodded. "How old are you?"

"Thirty-two," I said.

"Oh. That's not so bad."

"You're going to destroy me if you say you thought I was older." I could feel a telltale flush creeping up the side of my neck.

"No, not exactly," he lied. "Just... you're really cute, Rob, you know that?"

"No I'm not," I mumbled, flushing even more.

"Ah, maybe you just need someone to tell you it more often."

I nodded and fiddled with my coffee cup. "Why?" I blurted out.

"Why what?"

More blushing. "Why me?"

He laughed—not at me, it wasn't malicious, but almost as if he was mocking my naïveté. "You're interesting," he started, leaning forward on his elbows. "I've got to admit, I think the accent is very sexy. You're… strong-looking. Composed. I like that."

No one had ever pulled me apart like that before, highlighting what I was sure were my faults and turning them into compliments.

"And it doesn't bother you that I'm… older?"

"What, by nine years? No, it's nothing."

"Really?"

"Sure. Look, Rob, I like you, but I'm guessing you have a problem with me, and that's cool, I promise."

"No, no." I scrambled for some kind of control over the conversation. Did I ever have it in the first place? "I do, I mean, I like you too, but I just… I don't know how…. Oh, shit."

Chris's frowning softened. A smirk tugged at the corners of his mouth. "You're really not very good at this, are you?"

I lowered my hands from my face. "I'm really not."

"I'd like to see you again."

"I'd like to see you too. Would you like to come out to dinner with me on Friday night?"

He smiled again and scratched behind his ear, exposing a long line of colorful tattoos up his inner arm and sneaking under the edge of his T-shirt. "Sure. Sounds good."

"Excellent." I smiled and let out a long, relieved breath. "I'll call you when I've made reservations."

"Do people still make reservations?" he asked. "I thought they only did that in the movies."

It took a moment, but I realized he was teasing. "Fuck off," I told him, surprising myself. "You need reservations to go to nice restaurants. I'm not going to take you to Wendy's."

"Fuck off," he said right back, laughing too. "I've been to nice restaurants before. Do I need to dress up?"

"No," I said, desperately trying to think of a nice place to take him. "Just be yourself."

"My usual self won't get served in fancy places," he said.

"We'll be fine." I stood, stretched, and smiled. "It's been good seeing you again, Chris."

He stood too. "You too. I'll speak to you soon."

It was too early for kisses, or even a brief hug, and the low table was between us, making it hard to lean over, anyway. A handshake was too formal. In the end I smiled again and left, the knot in my stomach starting to make its presence known once more.

CHAPTER
TWO

I DECIDED on a Chinese restaurant for our date, mainly because it was one of my favorite places to eat, and also because who doesn't like Chinese food? I felt more nervous than I'd been in years, probably because I hadn't been on a date in years. Even the normally tedious task of dressing myself became something nerve-wracking. I pulled nearly every item of clothing out of my closet, discarding one thing after another before settling on a pair of worn jeans and a white shirt, and a pair of comfortable boots. I wanted to take my glasses off, and get a haircut, and change all sorts of things about the way I looked. It was a frantic phone conversation with Marley that settled my nervous stomach, her reassurances that Chris already liked who I was and that I didn't have to change for him.

Although I offered to pick Chris up from his place, he just asked for the address of the restaurant and said he'd meet me there. Still, I was early and parked a block or so away, hovering by the entrance to the restaurant and trying desperately to not look like someone who had just been stood up.

I did not expect Chris to pull up on a motorbike. The rational side of my brain, the dominant part to the point where I didn't realize I even had an irrational side, disapproved. The newly discovered irrational side shot a hot thrill to the base of my spine.

"Hey," I called as he pulled off the helmet. Thank God he was wearing a helmet.

I wasn't sure if Chris had dressed up or dressed down for the occasion. Clearly I hadn't seen enough of him yet. It was the "yet" that sent another little thrill through me. He was wearing wool pants, dark charcoal grey, almost black, and a soft, soft blue cotton shirt, loose at the throat and with the sleeves rolled up, displaying his brightly tattooed forearms. It was stuck somewhere between formal and casual, and I wanted to reach out and touch him.

"Rob," he said with the slow, confident grin of someone who knows how amazing he looks. His stride across the sidewalk was long and casual, and he came right up close to me, leaning in and brushing his lips over the corner of my mouth. I reached out blindly and grabbed his upper arm, loving the strength apparent in his lean muscles.

I desperately wanted to take his hand as we entered the restaurant, but I didn't know how open he was with his sexuality and I didn't want to make him uncomfortable. It became clear pretty quickly, though, that he was happy to be affectionate in public.

As I gave my name to the hostess, he placed his hand on my lower back, only lightly but enough for me to feel its solid heat through my shirt. I could feel the erratic beat of my heart in my chest, knowing that I'd not felt this way for a long time, and the last time it had taken months for me to get to a place where I was this confident in someone else's presence.

I felt him inhale from behind me, breathing in the scent of my cologne. Fuck if this man wasn't going to drive me to distraction. But as we were led to our table, he dropped back, out of respect to other diners or to make me feel more comfortable, I didn't know. I never asked.

I wondered if Chris was the sort of person who expected me to order since it was our first official date, but he seemed quite happy to accept the menu from our server and asked me what was good here, so I guessed he was independent enough to make his own decisions— when it came to what he ate, at least.

"Are you vegetarian?" I asked.

He laughed shortly. "No. You think I got a body like this without a healthy amount of protein in my diet?"

The little wink at the end of his sentence made me smirk right back at him and wonder exactly what was his main source of protein. I had the impression if I were to ask him, he would almost certainly tell me "meat."

"Do you like sweet and sour?"

"Mm."

The woman who took our order was tiny, and her shiny dark hair fell in a sleek crop to her neck. When Chris asked for a beer, I followed his lead this time and hoped the alcohol would soothe my nerves. Normally I'd drink wine but was slightly fearful of appearing prissy. And beer was fine.

"So how long have you been in Boston?" I asked as our drinks were delivered.

"Um," he said. "About ten days?"

"Really?" I said with a laugh.

"Yeah. Lexi—Alexis, she's backing vox and rhythm guitar—she arranges where we're going to stay in each city. Since we're planning on being here a bit longer than we normally camp out, we got a house this time, down over on Mansfield?"

"I know it," I said.

"Yeah. I told you before that John went to college here, so we knew we'd stop by for a while. His grandparents are here too, so I applied for a guest spot with the symphony and got it."

"That's pretty great."

"Thanks."

"So Alexis and John, they're in the band with you?"

"Yes. And a guy called Danny too. We play under a couple of different names. Ice on the Tracks for our own stuff, and sometimes Dark Side of the Spoon."

"Pink Floyd?" I said, laughing.

"Yeah. We don't just cover Floyd tracks, but it just so happened that one of theirs was the first song we learned to play as a group. John came up with the name, and it sort of stuck."

"Are you any good?"

A platter of starters arrived then with soup, and we took a few minutes to rearrange things on the table to make room for it all.

"We've got a gig the weekend after next," Chris said, looking up at me from under his pretty blond eyelashes. "You should come."

"I'd like that," I said.

Our conversation was smooth and natural as we talked about the area and the various things there were for a newcomer to explore, weighing these against the naturally beautiful sights of touring this part of the world and the cities along the East Coast that we'd both visited. Every little thing he told me about himself I savored, piecing the nuggets of information together to start to build a more three-dimensional picture of this most interesting man.

"Tell me about your family," I said after our starters had been cleared and the main course was served.

"I'm the middle child of five," he said with a wry grin. "Two older brothers and two younger sisters."

"Wow."

"Yeah. And my youngest sister is only nine. My mom and dad had a surprise when Molly was born 'cause I was twelve at the time. Then they had Brianna two years later."

"They know you're gay?"

He raised an eyebrow at me and smirked in what I was starting to learn was an often repeated gesture. "My mother likes to tell the story of how I told her at eight years old that I was going to marry a boy, because girls were 'gross'. It was probably a bit young to be coming out of the closet, and neither of us mentioned it again, but since I was eight, it's sort of just been understood in my household that I'm not straight."

"That's amazing," I said softly.

"Are your folks not cool?"

"Not really."

"That sucks," he said sympathetically. "Come on, I've given you the lowdown on my family. Spill."

"Well," I said, and took a mouthful of really good fried rice. "I have one sister. Her name is Jillian, but we call her Jilly. She's two years younger than me."

"Married?"

"No, she says she doesn't have time for a boyfriend. She works in advertising. My parents moved us over here when I was sixteen; my father was working for an international shipping company in Edinburgh, and they have offices here too. My mother never worked."

I fiddled with a napkin on the table as Chris cocked his head to one side, clearly interested in my story.

"My mother, ah, she's a complicated woman. They don't really accept me."

He shrugged. "So fuck 'em," he said. "My band are my family. Even though my folks are okay with who I am, if I was their only son, things would probably be different. The fact that both my older brothers are married and having kids means they can afford to have one son who breaks the mold."

As we finished the meal, our conversation turned to music, and we surprised ourselves and each other by having very similar tastes. I found great pleasure in being able to impress him by having seen some of his favorite bands live and was equally impressed by his wide and extensive musical knowledge, although that should really have been expected.

When Chris excused himself from the bathroom, I paid the check without his knowledge so he wouldn't try and split it with me. I didn't have any problems with equality. In fact, I couldn't imagine a relationship working without it. Instead I merely held the belief that since I had been the one to invite him to dinner, I should be the one to pay.

The table was cleared by the time he returned, and I had his jacket brought over for him.

"Thanks," he said in a soft voice as he shrugged it on.

I led him from the restaurant and turned to him in the cool night air, struggling for the words to keep this going for just a little bit longer.

But Chris spoke first. "I had a really nice time tonight."

I had to stop him somehow, so I blurted out the first thing that came to mind.

"Would you like to come back?" I asked, desperately nervous. "To see my place?"

He smiled, warm and easy. "Of course. I'll follow you, since I've got the bike with me."

I nodded and chewed my bottom lip. "Okay."

"Hey. Rob." I met his eyes and watched as he reached up, tugged my bottom lip from between my teeth. "If you're not okay with this, then it doesn't matter, I promise. I can come back another time."

"No, no," I said. "I want you to."

I tried to drive slowly, to give him a chance to follow me but not so slowly that he thought I was a total loser. It was a difficult balance to try and maintain. He parked up under the glow of a streetlamp, and I admired his self-awareness.

On a completely impulsive move, I reached for his hand as we silently walked up to my apartment block. Chris didn't say anything, just slid his warm, dry palm against mine and curled his fingers to fit in between my own.

I lived on the second floor of the building and had developed a habit of taking the stairs, only because the elevator so often smelled of stale bodies and spilled milk for reasons I could never quite fathom. Chris let me take the lead, and I got the impression he was checking out my ass, not that I was bothered by that. Not at all.

"Here," I said, holding the door for him as he entered the flat. I moved quickly to flick on the lamps in the main room that the front door opened on to, preferring their soft light rather than the harsh, industrial feel of the overhead light.

"Nice place," Chris said as he shrugged out of his jacket. I got the impression he really meant it, he wasn't just trying to be polite.

Flea jumped down from where he'd been hiding on top of a bookcase, purring loudly and winding his way around my feet.

"You want feeding, hmm?" I said to the cat as Chris bent down to scratch under his chin.

"What's his name?"

I grinned. "Flea."

He cocked an eyebrow at me. "Seriously?"

"Yeah. Chilis?"

Chris laughed. "That's actually awesome."

"Thanks," I said, walking through to the kitchen. Predictably, Flea followed me, still meowing. Chris followed too.

"Does he mind that you live on the second floor?"

"Nah," I said and dumped cat biscuits and water in his tray and left him to it. "He gets in and out through the kitchen window. I couldn't keep him in if I tried. Luckily for me he isn't much of a mouser."

When I turned back from the cupboard, Chris was so close I almost startled. Almost. He had what was becoming a familiar smirk on his face as he took another step closer and, with a hand on the counter either side of my body, effectively trapped me in my own kitchen.

Our height difference was only a couple of inches, if that. Nevertheless, I liked the way he tilted his head up to me as he ran his nose along the edge of my jaw.

"I want to kiss you," he said in a soft voice that belied the straining tension elsewhere in his body. In his arms! His arms were all tense from pressing against the counter and… oh fuck.

I nodded, and Chris closed the short distance and pressed his lips to mine. I was expecting him to be rough, to demand and then take, but he was whisper light as his soft lips skimmed over mine, then caught my bottom lip between them.

I was sure he could feel my racing heartbeat as I deepened the kiss, wrapping my arms around his lower back to keep him pressed close to me. Tentative tongues flicked out to taste the other, and I could feel Chris smiling, not mocking me but just enjoying this slow, easy kissing.

It was totally unlike me, but Chris was totally unlike me in general so I figured I should just go with my instincts, so I insinuated my hands under the edge of his untucked shirt to skim over the hot, smooth skin of his lower back. At this, one of his hands left the counter and curled around the back of my head, threading through my hair and angling our kisses so he could reach deeper. Find more.

Chris hummed and ran his hand down my body, blatantly cupping my ass, but I didn't mind. He rocked his hips against my own, and I didn't mind that, either. Never before had there been that spark with someone, cliché as it sounds, but he ignited something in me and made me feel something that I hadn't been sure I was capable of feeling.

When he moved and placed wet, gentle kisses on my neck, I may have whimpered. When his hand went to the buckle of my belt, I hesitated for the first time since he'd started kissing me.

"Let me," he whispered.

It was fairly terrifying to let him slide leather through metal and metal through denim, over and over until my jeans were open and his hand, warmer than I was expecting, slid into my boxers.

My fingers curled around the edge of the unit behind me as he took a firm grip on my cock and stroked it with firm, even strokes.

"You're not circumcised," he said as he ran the pad of his thumb over the head of my cock.

"No," I croaked. Then again, "No. It's, ah... it wasn't that common in Britain in the seventies. Still isn't, as far as I know. Do you mind?"

It was fairly impossible for me to hold an actual conversation while he did that, and I was appropriately proud of the achievement.

"Not at all," he said. "I'll take a closer look later."

His lips and tongue and teeth attacked my neck and throat as he worked me, teasing me, torturing me with softness and hardness combined, lust and power and submission. I wanted him. I needed him.

Then his fingers pushed deeper into my boxers to gently graze against my scrotum.

"Don't," I said, my hand shooting out to grab his forearm.

I wasn't ready to explain, and my expression must have conveyed that to him. Chris took my hand off the arm that was still half buried in my underwear and placed it on his own back, took a better hold of my cock, and put his lips on mine.

My fingertips stroked the back of his neck as our kisses grew sweeter. He was still pushing me toward orgasm, there could be little doubt about that, but there seemed to be a different reason for it now.

When I grunted the word "Close," he seemed to understand, and the movements of his hand increased until I was crying out, spilling over his hands and into my own underwear. Chris was hard too, I could feel it against my thigh, but he moved back and shook his head when I reached for him.

"Next time," he said softly, bringing our lips together again.

In the ensuing silence between us, little sounds started to make themselves known: the cat scratching at his post, the television from the apartment above mine, the clanking of water in ancient pipes.

"I don't think I've come in my own underwear for years," I mumbled against his neck.

He laughed, a soft, throaty sound. "It's a very underrated activity, coming in your underwear."

And when he looked up at me, my heart dropped to my stomach.

"Do you get a day off during the week?" Chris asked as I ran my fingers through his hair.

I shook my head.

"If I don't have lectures, then I hold seminars and a creative writing group too. And I have quite a heavy teaching schedule."

"How come?"

"Because I'm good?" I said with a smile and a shrug. "I teach because I love it," I said, and he turned his head to kiss the side of my neck. "I didn't want to work in a high school where half of the kids don't want to be there. All of my students chose my courses, and I love mentoring them."

"I bet you're a great teacher."

"I finish early on a Friday, though," I said, dismissing his compliment. "If you want to come over, I'll cook dinner."

"I'd like that."

I was aware that it was late, that he wasn't going to stay the night, and that making plans to see each other again in less than a week was probably his cue to leave. I didn't want him to, though. There was a moment when I thought about asking him, but it seemed inappropriate somehow.

"Can I text you?" he asked as I showed him back through to the hallway.

"Yeah," I said. "I'll have to remember to put it on silent during my classes now, though."

He laughed and reached for the door. "I had a really good time tonight," he said and reached for my hand. I let him tug me close and kiss me gently. Then, while my eyes were still closed, he let go. I heard the front door click shut, then a few minutes later the roar of his motorbike.

Realizing I wanted to watch him leave, I dashed over to the window just in time to see him pull away.

Never before had I been this close to having something with someone. Chris was so different to me, in every possible way. And despite the handful of relationships I'd had before, Chris was different from all of them too.

"THERE'S not a lot to tell, so far," I said to Marley, lying my pants off and hoping that the distance the telephone call was creating was enough for her not to be able to tell.

I selected a butternut squash and added it to my cart.

"I don't believe you," she said frankly. "Have you had sex yet?"

"Not that it's any of your business, but no."

A pair of red peppers.

"I still don't believe you," she said. I had to admire her persistence, but then again, when it came to gossip, Marley was practically an expert at wheedling it out of me.

"Don't, then," I said, forcing nonchalance into the words as a bag of potatoes signaled the end of the vegetable aisle.

"What's he like?" she demanded in a brisk, no-nonsense tone, and I couldn't help but smile. Her method could use work, but there could be little doubt about how much Marley cared.

"Young," I said with a touch of guilt.

"I know that," she said with a sigh. "Tell me something else."

"He's intelligent," I said. "More than I gave him credit for. And he has this amazing sense of self, like he's entirely comfortable in his own skin and he doesn't need anyone else's approval. I like that about him."

"How big is his cock?"

"Marlene," I said. "I'm scandalized. I have no idea. And even if I did, I wouldn't tell you."

"Liar."

"Fairly big," I admitted. "I've not had a decent grope yet so officially the jury's still out."

A small blue-haired lady was squinting at me with a murderous expression in the bakery aisle, so I made a swift change of direction, loaf of bread in hand, and headed for the deli. It seemed logical.

Over the phone line, I heard Marley sigh with happiness. "I love having a gay best friend," she said. "And you're finally living up to the high standards I set for you."

"I'm so pleased you've finally managed to fit me into a check-box category," I said sarcastically.

"Oh, don't get your panties in a twist," she said airily. "When can I meet him?"

"When he's something more than a nice guy who I've seen a couple of times? I haven't met any of his friends yet, Marley. We're taking it slow."

"Why the hell would you want to do that?"

"Because… because I actually like him, okay? I don't want this to be another one-date-wonder situation."

She was silent for a beat too long, then sighed dreamily. "You're such a romantic. When are you seeing him again?"

"Friday night," I admitted. "I said I'd cook so I'm trying to get some groceries in."

"And wine," she added. "Don't forget the wine."

"Lots of wine."

"Yes. Then if the entire date goes to shit you can just get drunk, get naked, and masturbate."

"A regular Friday night in!" I said chirpily.

"Make sure he's good to you, Robert," she said, her tone suddenly changing to serious. "I don't want you to get hurt."

"I won't," I said. I appreciated the gesture, but really, she was worrying about nothing. "I'll fill you in on the gossip as and when I have some."

"Appreciate it."

"Tell the girls I said hi."

"Will do. See you soon."

By the time Thursday rolled around, I'd managed to work myself up into something akin to blind, breath-stealing panic.

The flat—and the cat—were given an unprecedented spring clean—even though it was September—in my haste to distract myself from my own thoughts. The place was... modest. It was never supposed to be my home; I'd bought it out of necessity. Being close to the university, it made my commute blessedly short, and it was the perfect size for a single man such as myself. The realtor had described the kitchen as quaint, cozy, bijoux—utter bullshit, of course. The place was tiny. Just enough room to back up against the refrigerator and receive oral sex, my brain helpfully supplied. To fight the memories of two nights before, I forced myself to stay in the bijoux room and tidy, rearranging my cupboards and cleaning out my salad drawer. Defrosting the freezer. New grocery list. Cat food. Milk, bread, beans. Condoms.

Shit!

The vacuum cleaner did a job on the carpets and another on the sofa, digging out stray cat hairs and banishing them to the swirling vortex of Dyson-made doom. Fear made me poetic. I rearranged my bookshelf. (Twice.) Considered the Dewey decimal system and discarded it in favor of good old-fashioned alphabetical. By author and genre. Therefore, *Anthropology* by Darren Abraham started my collection. I gave up when my brain told me to keep Kipling together but my new system demanded that poetry, novels, and short stories be separated.

Moved to the bedroom. Changed the sheets. Decided that I needed new sheets, ones without floral patterns that I'd inherited from my mother. Opened my wardrobe. Sank to the floor, clutching my chest as the spasms of a panic attack gripped me.

I thumbed speed dial on my phone and prayed that my mother wouldn't answer.

"McKinnon residence," Jilly chirped.

"Jill," I said. "I need to go shopping."

CHAPTER
THREE

"So, WHAT are we looking for?" Jilly asked. Her arm was threaded through mine as we navigated the mall, stopping frequently to peer into windows at tiny-waisted, large-breasted mannequins with milky, unseeing eyes. They reminded me of something out of *Dr. Who* from my childhood and, due to that connotation, freaked me out.

"I need some new linens," I said in my most airy, offhand manner. "And some new clothes."

"You're seeing someone," she said, her eyes alight with excitement as she spun me around. I blushed. She squealed and danced on the spot. "You are! Tell me about him."

"I'm telling you nothing," I said. "We've only been on one date. I'll tell you more if it goes any further."

She pouted but acquiesced. "Clothes shopping? For you? Well, it happens so rarely we should make the most of it."

"I buy new clothes," I protested, stung.

"Yeah, a new corduroy jacket to replace your last corduroy jacket. You're such a cliché."

"I need jeans," I said, ignoring her. "And shirts. And maybe a new sweater."

By the time we sat down for lunch, burgers sitting like kings on unfolded wax paper and shiny golden fries split between us, I had spent nearly three hundred dollars. On clothes. We hadn't gotten to the linens yet. I was desperately not thinking about the money lest it cause another panic attack.

"Please tell me?" my sister begged. Her eyes widened, and her lower lip was thrust out in a parody of childish begging. Which had always worked on me.

"He's nice," I said, giving in. "He makes me feel… I don't know. Younger. And so much older than him at the same time."

"Are you?"

"What?"

"So much older than him."

I sighed heavily. "Somewhat."

"Ooh," she said, grinning. "A younger man. You old dog, Robert."

"He calls me Rob," I admitted, swirling a fry in blood-red tomato ketchup.

"And he still has his balls?"

I snorted with laughter. "Apparently so. I haven't gotten a good look at them yet, I'll admit."

"Yet?"

"Yet. I've said too much. Don't tell Mum, for God's sake."

"I won't."

She wouldn't. We were far from close, Jilly and I, but we had the shared experience of being uprooted from our home at a young age and being forced to relocate to a new, scary environment. She had adapted much better than I had. Being younger had its advantages, as did her naturally extroverted nature.

I paid for lunch, treating her since she'd helped—there was no denying that—with the shopping.

The only thing left was for me to actually call him so all the effort was worthwhile.

In lieu of making a call, I diverted my attentions via a barber's.

"Trim?" I was offered.

I wrinkled my nose. "A little bit shorter than normal?" I posed it as a question, leaving room for mocking if my suggestion was stupid.

"Sure," my barber, Alfred, said. He was closing in on seventy-five, at least, and refused to retire until his son returned from his tour in Iraq. Only then, Alfred claimed, could he close up shop. And who was I to challenge his superstitions?

The satin-smooth cape was tucked around my neck, and as the first curls of my hair dropped to the floor, my phone buzzed in my pocket, causing me to nearly leap out of the chair in shock.

"Gracious, boy, what on earth was that?"

"Just my phone," I said, sitting back down, blushing furiously. "Sorry, Alfred."

I pulled it out from under the voluminous cape and opened the text message.

Hey.

From Chris. Just one word. And a smiley face comprised of semicolon, hyphen, and close brackets signs. Oh. A winking face.

Hey.

I sent a message back. Waited.

What are you doing?

Getting my hair cut.

Alfred asked, "Who are you sending messages to like a teenager?"

"A friend," I said, ducking my head.

"Oh, come on, boy, I've known you too long for you to be embarrassed. Tell me about her."

Her. Her her her her her. Female. Er, no.

"There's nothing to tell," I said honestly. Sort of honestly. There was nothing to tell about a "her."

"I know when not to push," he said, remaining aloof.

He didn't push, to his credit, and I tipped him well for keeping his nose out.

My phone beeped again in the car.

Are we still on for tonight?

My heart hitched in my throat.

Yes, I am if you are?

I hesitated, my thumb hovering over the Send button for long moments while I contemplated the possible ramifications of my actions, closed my eyes, and pressed down.

There was no way I could drive until I had heard back from him. The mist of rejection hung heavy in the car, swirling around the air freshener and clogging up the rearview mirror. In an attempt at distracting myself, I pulled down the visor and checked out my hair in the little mirror, turning my head from side to side to get a better look. It was okay. Shorter at the sides than I'd worn it in a long time but still longer on the top and at the nape of my neck, folding back nicely from my forehead and held there with viscous gel that gave it a dull shine.

The phone beeped.

Sure. What time should I come over?

I took several deep, cleansing breaths.

Is 7 okay for you?

Yup. I'll bring a movie.

With that decided, I swung by the supermarket on my way back to the flat to pick up the last of the groceries I'd need. Then spent a further twenty minutes roaming the aisles, trying to decide what on Earth to cook. I wasn't a particularly bad cook, but I wasn't Gordon Ramsey and never would be. I could make lasagna… nice, tasty, inoffensive lasagna. And ciabatta bread—not garlic. Just in case.

Popcorn, that rare Saturday-morning-pictures treat from my childhood, now readily available "pop in the bag" style, was added to my basket. Though I would mourn the loss of the sweetened kind we preferred in Scotland, I had nevertheless adapted to the buttered version here in the States. It would be ready, freshly popped in a bowl, for either pre- or post-dinner consumption.

The rhythmic task of preparing the food calmed me somewhat; it was a focus for my scattered nerves, which were being soothed by my favorite album by my favorite band, my cat's namesake. Flea wound his way around my legs, crying for attention as I simmered the sauce. I scooped him up and gave him a tickle under the chin, then the catnip that was all he'd really wanted in the first place.

When the doorbell rang, I was freshly showered, the food smelled good, and the new shirt I'd bought with Jilly did, I'll admit, look good. Better. Better than the last time he'd seen me.

I opened the door with a smile.

"Hey."

"Hey," he said, leaning in to kiss me quickly. To my absolute disgust, my stomach fluttered at the gesture. Such a fucking girl. "This is for you."

He was holding out a bottle of wine, a nice bottle by the looks of it, an Italian merlot that would be lovely with the lasagna.

"Perfect," I said. "Thanks. Come in. Make yourself at home."

"Thanks."

I watched, all attempts at surreptitiousness failing miserably as he stripped out of his leather motorcycle jacket and boots, hanging the former on the coat hook and setting the latter down next to the door. Neatly. I was in love.

"I made lasagna, I hope that's okay."

"Sounds good," he said. "Smells better."

There was a glint in his eye that I recognized from the first night we'd met, something dark and humorous, dangerous, maybe, intensely… intense. Like a private joke he was unwilling to share. I cocked an eyebrow at him, questioning. He was still smiling as he took a step toward me again, bracing his palms flat on my chest as he leaned up and in for another, slower, sweeter kiss.

I let my fingertips feather through his hair; the lightness of it surprised me, as if the pale strands were somehow less substantial due to their lack of color.

"What was that for?" I asked as we broke apart.

Chris shrugged. "Because I wanted to."

I couldn't argue with that.

The dining table—such as it was; it only sat two people—had been set already, and I'd stuck a candle in an old bottle and let it burn down low. A little corny, maybe, but nice. I directed Chris to a corkscrew and wineglasses as I served up and placed a large bowl of salad on the table between us.

Fortune or fate had us sitting at the same time.

He raised his glass, the smirk back on his face, and I clinked mine against it.

"To…." I let my voice trail off, letting him finish the toast.

"To dashingly handsome Scotsmen and their sublime taste in men?" he suggested.

I laughed. "And to rather beautiful young percussionists who know how to flatter."

"I'll drink to that," he said.

For all of my concern that the spark between us would have fizzled out, I needn't have worried. He was still charming and funny and sweet; the conversation flowed between us like the wine from the bottle, which eased the conversation along nicely. It was only when the candle started to flicker, having burned down to nearly the end of the wick, that I noticed the time. We'd long since cleared away the plates and sat down again, hands cupping the bowls of our wineglasses to bring the rich liquid to body temperature. Our bodies were angled together over the table; the ledge dug into my stomach, but I wasn't going to lean back. When he moved, I mirrored his actions. When I tilted my head to the side, he followed suit.

"Tell me about Scotland," he said.

I smiled sadly. "I haven't been back in a long time."

"How come?"

"It's a long way away. I don't really keep in touch with my family over there anymore, not past the annual exchange of Christmas cards, anyway."

"Do you miss it?"

"Some days," I said, sipping the wine. "I miss… the driving rain." I laughed. "You've never seen rain until you've seen Highland rain. And the sense of history. Everything is so old."

"I'd love to go there one day."

"A lot of Americans do," I said. "It's very picturesque. All, you know, cobbled streets and medieval churches. Hundreds and hundreds of years of history and development and change. It's easy to get lost. I heard once that Edinburgh defies all laws of geography and physics inasmuch as when you go somewhere, you go uphill. And when you take the same route home, you go uphill again. It's true."

Chris smiled and reached over for my hand. I let him take it. He stroked my wrist with his thumb for a moment, and then I flipped his hand over to reveal the bright skull tattoo.

"Tell me about this?" I asked.

"It's a Day of the Dead skull," he said. "It's a Mexican Catholic tradition, honoring those who have passed. This one was for my best friend; he died of meningitis when we were seventeen."

"I'm sorry."

He shrugged. "He was the one who got me into playing music. I wanted it on my hand so I could see it every time I play."

"What about the others?" I asked, gesturing to his bare arms. Once again, Chris had rolled his sleeves up to his elbows, showing off the collection of tattoos dotting his forearms.

"Oh, they look pretty," he said, smirking again. He allowed me to turn his arm over, inspecting the stars, the roses on his elbows, knuckle dusters (of all things), swallows and a ship and an erotically twisted mermaid.

"Siren," he corrected me when I asked. "She's not a mermaid, she's a siren. A warning to men at sea: don't get too close."

"There are many ways to interpret that statement," I said, laughing.

"And so you should," he agreed.

"Are there more?" I wondered, thinking under his clothes.

"There are."

"Can I see them?" I asked.

"I'm sure you will," he countered. Winked. "I'm guessing you don't have any?"

"Oh, God no," I said. "My mum would kill me."

Chris laughed, open, genuine laughter that crinkled his eyes and shook his chest. "Mine isn't too fond of them. She likes this one, though."

He pulled his shirt aside to reveal a heart and a banner with the word "Mom" on it.

"Very traditional," I said, smiling.

He hummed in agreement. "I like the old Americana style. It's so bright and vibrant."

"Like you," I said without thinking.

The smirk returned.

"There's something else you should probably know," I said, taking his hand and tracing the brightly colored skull on the back of it with my fingertip. I didn't pretend to understand why he would want tattoos, but they were undoubtedly beautiful.

"Okay. Go on."

"I, uh…." How to explain Chloe? "I have a daughter."

My fingertip stopped its gentle stroking to give him a chance to pull away if he so wished. He didn't. "Oh." Chris turned to me with an amused grin. "You had sex with a girl?"

I felt the heat rising in my cheeks. "Yeah. Once."

"Now that's a story I need to hear."

Sighing, I settled back into my chair. "Once upon a time, there was a confused young man and a very pretty girl."

"Uh-oh," he interrupted. "I think I know how this one goes."

I laughed, relieved at his easy acceptance so far. "Maybe. Luisa was a very good friend of mine from high school. We went out on a couple of dates with friends, but I didn't come out properly until I got to college. I didn't want to humiliate her."

"Understandable," Chris said. I scowled at him. He mimed zipping his lips.

"The first Christmas we came home from college, she asked if I was sure. About liking boys. And I said yes. So she asked if I'd ever slept with a girl before. And I said no. So she said how could I be sure if I'd never done it before? So we did."

"You got it up for her?"

"Yeah. Not saying it was easy, but I did it."

"Close your eyes and think of England," Chris said seriously.

"Exactly. So, when we came home again for spring break, she told me that she was pregnant, and I asked her if it was mine, and she hit me. Gave me a black eye. Then I had the humiliating task of telling my parents that yes, I'm still sure I'm gay, but I managed to knock Lu up anyway and now I'm literally and metaphorically screwed."

Chris frowned and turned our hands over, taking mine in his. "What did you do?"

"Luisa had the baby in the summer between freshman and sophomore year, then went straight back to classes. Chloe was raised by her maternal grandparents for a few years while we both finished our education. Then the three of us tried to live together for about a year, but that was a complete and utter disaster, so I took a teaching position here."

"Where does she live now?"

"Lu or Chloe?"

"Both. I'm guessing they're together."

"Oh, yeah, of course. Lu got married about four, no, five years ago now. Chloe has a little sister and another brother or sister on the way."

"And a stepdad."

"I don't mind so much about that," I mumbled. "I'm not the best father in the world."

"Why not?" Chris demanded, looking upset for the first time since I'd started the conversation. "You made her, you should take responsibility for her."

I nodded slowly. "I know that. But Chloe is nearly fourteen, Chris. She doesn't like anyone these days, least of all an absent father figure. Mike is good for her, I know that, he's a great dad."

"Does she know you're gay?" he asked.

"I don't know. Maybe. Probably."

"Well, that clears that up," he said sarcastically.

"I don't know," I repeated. "Luisa may have told her. I certainly haven't. She has enough problems to deal with without adding her absentee father's sexuality into the mix."

"Would you introduce her to me?" he asked. I felt that this was some kind of test. How serious was I about our relationship? Serious enough to mix boyfriend and daughter?

"Yes," I said. "If you would like to, of course I will."

He nodded. "Okay."

I excused myself to the bathroom and let him wander around the rest of the flat. When I came out, he was studying a painting of a church near where I grew up.

"Is this Edinburgh?" he asked. I nodded, going to him and wrapping my arms around him from behind.

"I used to be able to see that church from my old bedroom. I loved the gargoyles. They were all over the building, snarling and screaming at you."

"Do you write?" he asked, turning in my arms. I shook my head. "You should," he insisted. "You have a way with words."

"I've written a lot of research papers," I said, correcting my previous statement.

"That doesn't count."

"I've been working on a book for a long time," I admitted. Walking backward to the sofa, I kept my arms around him, bringing him with me. "It's still in the writing process."

"What's it about?" he asked, then huffed a breath as we slumped into the cushions.

"Kipling," I admitted. "It's not a biography, or a critical analysis of his work, but it has elements of both."

"Maybe I'll get to read it someday," he said softly.

"Maybe."

"I'm giving a lecture next week on scansion and meter," I said. "It's similar to what you do: rhythms and beats and flow and pace."

"In poetry?" he asked.

"Yes," I enthused. "Kipling was a master. He crammed so many beats into one line. It's sort of like…." I searched for the comparisons to music that I'd used years ago, trying to find another level for my students to connect to. "In four-four timing, you have four beats in a bar, right?"

"Right," he agreed.

"But the melody over the top of a four-four bass line may have many more beats in it."

"That's pretty normal, actually," Chris said. "It's the skill of the percussionist to be able to play different rhythms with each hand and foot."

"Exactly," I said. "So, okay, you've probably heard the phrase 'the female of the species is more deadly than the male'."

"Yeah…."

"Even though that line has," I counted them on my fingers, "fourteen syllables, metrically, it has four beats. Four bass-line beats."

He thought it out, and I let him get it in his own time. "I think I get it."

I tapped it out for him, repeating the phrase until he heard the stresses on the beats.

"All speech has natural patterns. And in poetry, there's hundreds. But Kipling really knew how to manipulate meter and shove as many unstressed beats into a four-stress-beat line as possible."

"It sounds complicated," he said.

"It is," I agreed. "But here's where our worlds collide. I spend hours poring over poetry, finding the stressed and unstressed beats, working out the rhythms and how that changes things, how it affects the music of the poem."

"And this is your lecture."

"Part of it," I said, smiling. "You should come along."

He raised an eyebrow at me. "Seriously?"

"Yeah," I said, an attempt at nonchalance. "I'd like to hear your opinion. There's always a seminar afterwards."

"I never went to college, Rob," he said. "I doubt I'd have anything interesting to say."

"That's why I'm interested in your opinion," I argued. "Because you don't have an academic viewpoint, you have a musical one. That's going to be completely different to what my students are used to hearing."

He leaned in and kissed me on the nose. "I'll think about it."

I beamed at him.

"But if I come to your lecture…."

"Go on," I encouraged him.

"I have a gig booked with a local theater company. They're doing *Aida*. Would you come?"

"Yeah," I said. "I'd like that."

I glanced at the clock on the wall; in all the time we'd spent talking and eating and more talking, it had crept up to midnight. It was a do or die moment—I could ask him to stay, or we could end the night here.

Despite my hormones (those long-forgotten friends) screaming at me to ask him to stay, I had some old romantic notion of wooing this man. I wanted to date him, to do things properly. It would be too easy to take advantage of the spark between us and act on it, letting it ignite a fire that could too easily burn out.

I turned and found Chris's lips, kissing him slowly, letting the spark smolder between us until we were both angling for more. He broke it off with a laugh, then nuzzled into my neck and kissed the delicate, oh-so-sensitive skin there.

Then he stood, maybe understanding what I was thinking, that the anticipation we were building was delicious and should be savored. I stood too and kissed him again, then silently followed him back to the front door.

"The lecture is on Wednesday afternoon," I said. "If you want to come, just let me know and I can give you directions."

"I'm not sure of my schedule, but I'll be in touch," he promised.

I sighed heavily, and my fingers twitched to touch him again as he layered back up in his leathers. Chris kissed me again before he left, the heavy motorcycle gloves clumsy on my face.

"Night," he murmured.

"Good night," I echoed.

After I'd locked the door behind him, I closed my eyes for a brief second, allowing myself to bask in the thrill of whatever this was, then crossed to the window to watch him swing a leg over his bike and roar off down the street.

CHAPTER
FOUR

I DIDN'T own a tuxedo, so I had to go down to the hire shop that Marley had given me the details of. Chris had laughed at me when I'd said where I was going, then told me in a low voice that he couldn't wait to see me in it. He, of course, already had a tux for occasions such as this. I couldn't wait to see him, either.

I left the shop with a suit bag over my arm and butterflies in my stomach. It was only an evening at the opera. I'd been once before with my mother, so I knew what to expect, but the added complication of Chris made the experience new and strange in a wonderfully welcome way.

He texted me just as I was parking the car. Unsurprisingly, he was smoking around by the stage door. His dark-suited figure glowed in the light from a window high above him and I only noticed his nervous energy as I approached.

"Hey," I said softly, placing my hand on his upper arm.

"Hi," he said shortly. Threw the glowing butt of the cigarette away, for my benefit, I knew that.

I caught his hand as he brought it back to his body. Turning his palm over, I studied the smooth, even color of his skin. Chris caught my expression and smiled.

"Makeup lady got to me," he said by way of explanation. "They don't mind what I look like on the street, but there's a certain level of decorum around here. They covered up the one on my chest as well, just in case the color shines through under the lights."

I nodded as if I understood, but deep down it bothered me that that little, vibrant part of him was being covered up. Chris watched me, frowning, as I pulled a handkerchief from my pocket and rubbed at the thick layer of makeup that obscured his tattoo. The white came away with an orange smudge, and a small patch of red was then visible, just by his thumb.

Chris's frown relaxed into a smile, and I lifted his hand, pressing the softest kiss into his red ink.

A tinny voice rang out over a metal speaker bolted to the outside wall. "Ladies and gentlemen of the orchestra, this is your call to the stage, please, your call to the stage. Thank you."

"I need to go," he said apologetically. I let go of his hand and nodded again.

"Me too. I'll see you after." My eyes darted to the stage door, where a bored-looking man read a newspaper, studiously ignoring us. I leaned forward and brushed my lips over his. "For luck," I explained.

Chris nodded and kissed me back, then disappeared back into the theater.

I had to rush back around to the front of the building; the usher on the door scowled at me, and I knew I'd left it too late to be admitted to the auditorium. I could already hear the orchestra tuning up. I was in luck, though, and the ticket that had been reserved for me was a private box, so I could sneak in without disturbing anyone else.

The view from the box was obstructed, and I couldn't see the whole stage. I did, however, have a perfect, uninterrupted view right down onto the rhythm section. Chris walked through a door that probably couldn't be seen from the auditorium, not looking up and going straight to his instruments, touching each of them in turn, checking that they were in the right places.

Only then did he look up, searching for me. I didn't ever find out if he saw me, leaning eagerly over the balcony, trying desperately to catch his eye; just then the house lights started to dim, and I was forced to sit back to watch the show.

Not that I actually paid attention to anything that happened during the performance. My eyes were fixed on the man in the black suit, his face furrowed in concentration as he flipped page after page of sheet music and watched the conductor for cues. It was hard to correlate this intense, serious musician with the wild, laughing man I'd come to adore.

At the end of the first act, I went to the bar and ordered a whiskey, neither enjoying nor tasting the liquor as I sipped at it absently. I wanted to know what Chris was doing backstage. If he was outside chain smoking—that was the most likely scenario—I knew I didn't have time to race around the side of the building to go and see him. Not if I wanted to be back in my seat again for the beginning of the second act.

The rest of the show passed in a blur; I enjoyed the music, but I was anxious, edgy to see him again, to be able to praise him and thank him for sharing this side of himself with me.

He'd called me on Tuesday night to apologize because he wouldn't be able to make it to the lecture the following day, and I tried not to be too disappointed. The band, who he had rehearsal responsibilities with, were half of his source of income, and they needed to rehearse and promote like crazy to build up anticipation for their upcoming gig.

I also had a feeling he was afraid of not fitting in at the university, even though he wouldn't say as much. His earlier confession about not excelling in school had touched me, in a way; I'd always taken my academic success for granted, studying came easy to me, and I had a genuine interest in my subject that fueled my career.

My line of work certainly exposed me to others who weren't as lucky. My students were not easy to categorize, and doing so was often a fruitless task. There were those who were forced into taking my subject by the parents who were funding their education. Those who saw it as an easy ride. Those who took it because they were good at it, or perceived it as a good career move, or because they didn't know what they wanted to do with their life and English was a solid base from which to move forward.

Chris didn't fit into any of those categories, and although he was clearly successful in his own career, he hadn't followed a traditional academic path.

As I took my seat for the second act, I resolved to spend more time paying attention to the actual music and less time making goo-goo eyes at the man in percussion. That resolution lasted about twenty minutes before I gave in and learned my first lesson when it came to the combination of Chris and music—that he was utterly captivating.

There was a little crease in his forehead as he split his focus between the sheet music and the conductor, his concentration never seeming to waver. As for the music itself, well, I'd never really been able to find my thing when it came to classical music. There had never been a hallelujah moment when it had all started to make sense, not like when I was given a book of poetry by a stuffy old aunt and spent an entire weekend absorbing it aged just fourteen.

Still, I could understand the passion if not the subject matter, and Chris had passion in droves.

A fair explosion of rapturous applause broke my reverie, and I joined in, surging to my feet alongside those either side of me. Even though common sense told me Chris wouldn't be able to see out into the audience with the bright stage lights shining in his eyes, I still let myself indulge in a silly fantasy that he could see me.

I had no idea what post-concert etiquette was as far as going backstage to meet him was concerned and, as such, let the crowd surging for the exit carry me out onto the street. The night was still fairly warm, and by the time I'd extracted myself, he was there, waiting for me on the steps to the building.

"How did you get out here so fast?" I asked, placing my hand on his upper arm to get his attention.

It worked—he whirled around with a smile on his face and shrugged. "None of the kit is mine. I just had to grab my bag. Do you want to go for a drink?"

The words came out in a rush, and I realized that he was nervous. Nervous for my reaction.

"Chris," I said. "You were wonderful."

He ducked his head and blushed. "Thank you. Drink?"

I nodded, and he led us down the street, past where I could see fellow audience members drinking champagne in wine bars, to a smaller bar that almost reminded me of the hole-in-the-wall pubs that were abundant in Edinburgh.

"Let me get you one," I said as he reached for his wallet.

"I'll get the first round."

I nodded and took a moment to look around.

The bar was narrow, probably only a few meters from one wall to the other, although it stretched back quite a way, with little tables and booths dotting the walls. The patrons drank whiskey in short tumblers or pints of dark ale and wore hats made of the same tweed fabric as the upholstery in the booths.

"I can't believe I've never been here before," I said softly as we waited for the barmaid to come down our end. "It's great."

"One of the horn section told me about it," Chris said. "Nice, right?"

"Very," I agreed.

We both ordered beers, and I heaped praise on him, much of which he neatly deflected. I was surprised. Chris had struck me as a man confident in himself and his achievements. Both bottles were drained at almost the same time, and I knew that if I was going to drive home, I shouldn't drink a second.

"When will I see you again?" I blurted as I walked him back to his car.

"Soon, I hope," he said softly. "I think you're fascinating."

I winced. "Is that a good thing?"

Chris bit back a smile and wet his lips as his cheeks strained not to break into a full-fledged grin. Then he reached out and cupped my cheek in his palm.

"Yes," he said. Then he kissed me. I was too stunned to properly kiss him back, a point that made me furious once he'd pulled away.

He was two steps toward his bike when I regained my senses enough to grab him by his wrist.

"Chris, wait," I said. "Should I call you?"

He nodded, that same amused expression dancing across his features.

"Yeah."

"Okay."

"Okay. Good night, Rob."

"Night," I said vaguely.

He pulled his helmet from where it had been locked to the back of the bike and pulled it on, then kicked it into action and pulled into the traffic. After a moment I forced myself to move. I'd been standing on the spot, probably frowning and definitely staring after him.

It was creepy.

On the drive back to my flat, I debated with myself on whether or not the night counted as a date. I didn't think it did. There had not been any flowers, for one, and I was a great believer in the significance of flowers being sent to someone I was dating. They were not just for women.

Then again, he had kissed me before we parted ways. A kiss, especially the sort of kisses that Chris was capable of dishing out, was not the sort of thing one took lightly. Warm breath and the flick of a hot tongue against the seam of my lips…. Yes, that was definitely a date-type kiss.

Maybe I was over-thinking things. Heaven knows it wouldn't have been the first time.

On reflection of my previous sexual and romantic partners (this did not take very long), Chris was easily the most sexual of the lot. Yet we'd not made any further strides toward being intimate with each other, not since he'd stroked me to orgasm in my kitchen.

Opening the fridge and reaching for the cream still brought a hot flush of pleasure and embarrassment to my cheeks.

I resolved, as I passed over the cream and selected milk to go in my tea, to send flowers to him the next day.

There was a little florist that I passed on my way to work, and I headed there rather than to one of the larger commercial places. Despite their small size, the shop had a large and beautiful range, and it took me more than a few minutes to decide whether or not I wanted to send a message hidden in the blooms.

My instinct was to go bright and varied and unusual; birds of paradise or tiger lilies, maybe. But on contemplation they seemed too brash and not romantic enough. I'd passed over the roses on my first sweep of the store, but a closer look revealed a selection of dark pink flowers, still in their buds. They weren't red, or baby pink, not too obvious and slightly unusual, and the meaning was clear.

I signed my name on the card but nothing more and drew Chris's card from my wallet, still with his *C.J.F. (1)* written on the back of it, to give his address for the delivery.

His response, when it came later that afternoon, was everything I'd been hoping for.

No one has ever sent me flowers before. They're beautiful. Thank you.

It gave me the confidence to keep a semi-regular conversation going between us over the following few days, nothing too intense or serious but enough that we got used to a light banter back and forth. It was just text messages, no actual conversations, but his good night message every night made me smile. Slowly but surely, he was creeping into my life.

THERE could be little doubt that I was fairly terrified about meeting Chris's friends. If it wasn't bad enough that I was so much older than all of them, I couldn't help but feel that they were so much cooler than me. They were in a rock and roll band, for goodness' sakes. Chris made it easier on me by taking me to the house one night after I'd finished work and cooking me dinner. The others were out when I arrived and clearly had their own evening routines, which continued despite my presence.

I met Danny first: a tall, olive-skinned, lanky man with bright eyes and an easy demeanor. He said hi, grabbed an apple from a bowl on the counter, and disappeared. A few minutes later, music started on one of the upper floors.

Alexis, or Lex, as she introduced herself, and John were next. They seemed at first to be an odd pair to me. She was small with vibrantly red hair and creamy pale skin, and bright blue eyes that she lined heavily with makeup. He was clearly the more laidback of the pair, wearing flip-flops and khaki shorts and a fleece sweatshirt. His thick, light brown hair was a mass of curls, and he wore a scruffy beard. I liked him on sight.

"He's only a few years younger than you," Chris said after they, too, had moved on. "John. He's going to be twenty-nine next week. Are you coming to his birthday?"

"When is it?" I asked.

"Next Friday night."

I nodded. "Sure."

The party was being held at the house, and I had no idea how the little group had amassed such a large quantity of friends and acquaintances in such a short amount of time. I arrived with whiskey as a gift and beer to drink and wimped out, calling Chris when I arrived instead of going to the door. Even though it was only 9:00 p.m., the party seemed well underway.

When I saw him appear on the porch, I climbed out of the car, surprised and oddly pleased when he took off from the porch with a jump and a run to launch himself into my arms. I caught him, laughing, and kissed him deeply.

"I missed you," he said when we broke apart. It had only been a few days since we last saw each other.

"Come on inside," I said. "You'll freeze out here without a coat."

Again, Chris surprised me by holding on to my hand as we navigated the party, introducing me to people he knew from the symphony or fans and groupies that they'd already picked up during their short time in the area.

John and Lex were in the kitchen. He seemed pleased with the whiskey and made room in the fridge for the beer.

"I'm hiding this," he said, holding up the whiskey. "Otherwise it'll get destroyed tonight."

"Good plan," Lex told him, and he kissed her lightly on the top of the head before heading back to their room.

The entire evening had the feel of one of the dorm parties that I rarely took part in during my own college career. Most of the guests were of the right age, and even if we were spared drinking games and beer bongs, that was made up for with all of the horrendously drunk, skimpily dressed young ladies in attendance.

One couldn't help but admire the way Chris easily and confidently deflected the attentions of those girls, and in such a way that they didn't even know that they'd been brushed aside as easily as an irritating yet beautiful moth. Even as I struck up conversations with his friends, his eyes kept meeting mine across the room, little flickers to make sure he knew where I was.

His protectiveness was just endearing enough not to be annoying.

I'd just finished giving John instructions on how to get to the steakhouse that served some of the best beef and barbecue in the whole state when Chris sidled up to me and slipped his hand in mine. I looked down at him with a smile, amused enough to give him a little kiss on the lips when his pout demanded it.

"Come with me," Chris said, tugging at my hand.

"See you again," I said to John. He nodded, lips pressed together in amusement as if he knew exactly what Chris was up to. In all likelihood, he did.

I followed him through to the hallway, where it was slightly quieter. Chris stopped short and turned to face me.

"We need to have sex," he said, a slightly desperate look on his face.

"We will," I said. "I thought we agreed to take it slow, though?"

"Rob." Chris spoke my name reverently and stepped forward to take my face in his hands. "Rob, you're amazing. You're possibly the most amazing man I have ever met, and certainly the most amazing man I have ever dated. You are sweet and kind and loving and funny and so adorable, and the sex could be absolutely fucking terrible."

"You're really worried about this, aren't you?" I said, amused.

He dropped his head forward to rest against mine. "Yes."

"Come on, then," I said, taking his hand once more and lacing my fingers with his.

"Come on what?"

"Come on home with me." Something about this man infused me with confidence.

His eyes widened comically. "Are you serious?"

"Yeah," I said lightly, more than a little amused. "I like sex, Chris. I'm pretty sure I'm going to like sex with you. And now," I leaned in and lightly bit the end of his nose, "I have something to prove."

His response was to rock his hips forward so his pelvis bumped into mine, emphasizing the hardness he was concealing in his jeans and the need he had for me. I took his hand and led him through the house, stopping by the closet at the front door to find my coat.

"Do you need to bring anything with you?" I asked before we left.

"You've got condoms? And lube?"

"Yes."

"Then I'm set," he said.

Because I could, I kissed him hard. This was no teasing little brush of lips on lips but a promise of what he could expect from me.

I wasn't too surprised when he groped me for most of the journey as I drove across town to my flat. I managed to swat his hand away every time he went to undo my fly, but this wasn't a sufficient deterrent for him to stop rubbing my groin through my jeans.

Chris was clearly a little buzzed, but I didn't want that; too much alcohol left me with a numbness rather than energy, and for this I wanted to have all my mental faculties firmly in place.

The last time Chris had been in my home, he'd been in my bedroom, but only because it was the only way to access the single bathroom in the flat. I guessed he hadn't lingered because when I showed him through again, he took his time wandering around, looking at the little bits and pieces that transformed the place from somewhere where I laid my head at night to my home of the past four years.

Still, I wasn't really one for collecting things, "dust collectors" as my mother called them. As far as personal items went, I had books; stacks of books on nearly every possible surface. The most precious thing in my room was the one Chris homed in on, almost as if he knew or understood its value.

He was incredibly careful with the small frame that held a picture of me and my daughter, taken a few days after she was born. There were photographs taken in the hospital, but I'd never liked them. There was a clinical, depressed, slightly desperate edge to them all. We were only nineteen. Our parents were furious with us. I was overwhelmed.

When we were allowed to take her home, things only got worse. Chloe was a colicky, fussy baby almost from the get-go. We got precious little sleep. Daylight hours were spent washing and feeding and changing and bathing and, for me, working my ass off. Lu resented me. Chloe, I was convinced, knew I wasn't cut out to be a father.

Then, it fell into place.

I was exhausted after finishing an eight-hour shift and got home to a screaming baby and a frazzled Luisa. She shoved the child in my arms and announced she was taking a bath and there was nothing I could do except learn how to deal with my daughter.

It took a good hour, maybe more until she settled and I curled up in an armchair with her in my arms, damned if I was going to put her down in case she started screaming again. I must have fallen asleep like that because months later when we were getting the rolls of film from those first few weeks of her life developed, there was the picture.

Me, fast asleep in a dark brown leather armchair; Chloe, her face peaceful but wide awake, staring up at me. Lu had framed it and given it to me as a Christmas gift, and I cherished it as evidence that I was not a terrible father after all.

"Does she look like you?" Chris asked as he set the frame back in its place on my dresser.

"Chloe? No. Not at all. She takes after her mother."

When he kissed me again, there was a new kind of low, constant heat that smoldered in my belly and jumped in my throat. His breath was warm and sweet; at some point in the evening, he'd clearly switched from beer to some kind of liquor.

My fingers went to the hem of his T-shirt, drawing it up over his head in a swift movement. If he was surprised at my forwardness he didn't let it show, letting me remove my own shirt, then slowly slide leather through metal and metal through denim.

I was almost sure his breathing was faster than it should be, and it was clear that he was aroused. I wanted to know everything about him, though, all his secrets and his desires and what made him tick.

"Sorry about the bed," I said, wondering if he'd noticed that it was a three-quarter size and not a full double. "The last owner left it here. Apparently he spent a fortune trying to get a double mattress up the stairs, and even then it wouldn't fit around the door."

"I'm sure we'll manage," Chris said as he inelegantly toed off his shoes and socks, leaving them where they fell.

He was naked and I nearly so when we finally made it to my soft, soft new sheets, and Chris looked so right there, lying on my bed where I'd imagined him so many times before that I had to take a moment to commit the sight to memory.

There were other tattoos, ones that I'd known the existence of but not the location. I wanted to touch them, so I did; the swallows that dove over his hips, following the natural contours of his body.

And he was naked, of course, so the birds were really pointing the way toward what was an inevitable conclusion. He was erect. Painfully so, if I had correctly interpreted the shiny skin, swollen head, and taut, drawn-up testicles.

I realized I was staring and looked guiltily back up at his face. Chris hitched an eyebrow and dropped his knees open in clear invitation. Stretched out beside him, I placed my hand carefully on his stomach and leaned in for a kiss. He responded with a slow, slick, wet slide of tongues that pooled heat in my groin and made me want him even more, if that was even possible.

Kissing down his neck, I took time to find the spots that made him shudder and squirm. I hoped and had a feeling that this wouldn't be the last exploration of his body that I took. It was still worth making these mental notes for future reference.

As I shifted down the bed, I risked another glance up at his face. Chris was smiling serenely, an arm thrown casually above his head and the other resting gently on my back. I kept my eyes trained on his as my tongue circled his nipple, flicked it, then sucked the pink, puckered flesh into my mouth.

It was like I'd flipped a switch.

Gone was the calm, composed man of half a moment ago. Chris arched his back from the bed, thrusting his body up toward me and muttering a string of curses and expletives. Delighted at his reaction, I continued to tease and torture him, drawing the most delicious sounds from his mouth.

"Fuck," he said, laughing now as I pulled away. "You found my weakness."

I nodded and replaced my tongue with the pad of my thumb, still circling his nipple slowly.

"Can you come from just this?" I asked.

"No. But I can get really fucking close."

Wanting his lips, I leaned in for another kiss, this one tasting of the spike of heat between us. I reached for my admittedly small stash of condoms and lube. While I was reaching over, I turned on the single lamp, which emitted a soft glow. I wanted to be able to see him.

Chris took them from me and maybe realized that it was my turn to get some attention, but in the form of gentle reassurance. Then he got a look at my chosen brand of lubricant and huffed.

"Really, Rob?"

"What?"

He smirked. "This is jerk-off lube, not fucking lube."

"What would you prefer?" I asked, stung.

"Don't worry," he said, pouring some of it onto his fingers. "I'll bring better stuff next time."

Next time. We hadn't even gotten there yet and he was already talking about a next time. I watched, entranced, as he spread the lubricant between his legs, over his cock, down to his hole, which he painted liberally with the viscous liquid, but he didn't attempt to push inside himself.

Before I could formulate a response to his actions, he rolled over onto his stomach and up onto his hands and knees, pushing his ass back toward me.

"No," I said, giving him a sharp, stinging slap on the rump. "Flip over."

He frowned but followed my instruction, resuming his previous position. On his back, he brought his knees up to his chest, knowing now what I wanted. The sound of his breathing was loud in my ears as I fumbled with the foil encasing the condom and rolled it down over my cock with shaking fingers.

My efforts to stretch him were met with a frustrated "Fuck it, now, Rob. Now," so I abandoned that task and moved between his legs. When I positioned myself, one hand braced on the bed next to Chris's shoulder, the other guiding my cock, he looked up at me with the same lazy, indulgent expression that he'd worn earlier. Only now I knew how to change it, how to turn him into a writhing, desperate thing. I lined the head of my cock up but watched his face as I pushed forward, knowing that without much preparation, this could hurt him.

Achingly slow, I pushed into him, waiting for a moment for him to adjust before sinking the rest of the way into him.

"Wow," he murmured. "Oh, wow."

It didn't seem to hurt; his mouth stretched wide in an "Oh!" of pleasure, and he arched back off the bed so only his shoulders and feet and bunched-up fists kept the contact. I wanted to give him time, I really did, but he was pushing back onto me, and I had little choice but to go with it.

"How do you like it?" I asked, my voice sounding lower, rougher, and inexplicably more Scottish as I bottomed out inside him. His legs locked around my waist, and I found his mouth with mine, kissing him desperately as we rocked together, carefully at first, learning each other's limits one step at a time.

"Hard," he whispered. "Hard and fast. And rough."

I smiled. "Only if you look at me."

Blue eyes flickered with something raw and uninhibited as they met mine, and I kissed his lips once before rocking back and slamming deep inside him. His cry was enough to send a harsh shiver down my spine.

"Fuck!"

Despite my being years out of practice, it was like riding a bike, sort of, inasmuch as I hadn't forgotten how to do it even if I wasn't doing it particularly well. Chris didn't seem to mind as I varied my thrusts, changing up the angle until his fingers dug into my arms tight enough to leave tiny crescents from his nails and one thumbprint-sized bruise.

"There…," he said, his eyes still wide but unfocused. "Right there."

Now that I had something to focus on, I pulled back up onto my arms, locking my elbows in tight and letting go, finding a rhythm that seemed to suck us both in. My eyes would flick to where we were joined, the incredibly erotic sight of part of me disappearing into part of him, to his cock, locked tightly in his fist, but always back to blue eyes wide with lust.

His ass clamped down hard on me, and I knew he was going to come moments before he actually did. A red flush spread across his chest and up his neck as he screwed his eyes tightly shut and arched his neck, baring his throat to me as his own hand took him over the edge.

I still watched as he continued to pump himself and thick ropes of white come painted his chest and stomach.

"Shit," I muttered and actually tried to get deeper inside him as I came too, feeling the aftershocks ripple through his body and set off my own.

My muscles had turned to pudding, and my elbows gave out, causing me to slump forward onto him with an inelegant "Oomph."

Chris groaned, and I rolled off him enough to pull off the condom and dispose of it, then roll right back to him.

Chris was wearing what one could only call a shit-eating grin.

"I knew it," he said emphatically, although the inflection was lost somewhere in the deep, panting breaths he was still taking.

"Knew what?" I asked and realized my own breathing wasn't a lot better.

"I fucking knew you'd be great in bed," he said, and slapped his hand down on the bed next to him as he cursed, although it caught a spring and bounced back up again comically.

I laughed and found enough energy to roll over to him for a sloppy kiss. My feet kicked at the edge of the blanket that hung over the end of the bed, drawing it up over my calves until it was close enough to my hand for me to reach down and drag it up over us both.

His breathing evened out over the next few minutes, and I found my own matching his. It was soothing, this breathing in synch business. Then he leaned over, kissed me on the cheek, and rolled off the edge of the bed and started looking for his clothes amongst the mess on my bedroom floor.

"What are you doing?"

"Can't find my underwear," he grunted.

"Were you wearing any?" I couldn't remember. I didn't think so. "And why? You can borrow some of mine if you don't like sleeping naked."

Chris stopped dressing and looked at me. His appearance—one sock, his open shirt, and nothing else—was verging on ridiculous. When he didn't say anything, I shuffled over on the bed.

"Come back here, you silly bugger."

"You... fuck. You want me to stay?"

"Yeah. 'Course I do."

He looked baffled, but stripped again and sat tentatively down on the bed. I took his arm and pulled him back down onto his bed and sort of found a way to snuggle into him.

"Are you sure about this?" Chris asked as his fingers tentatively combed through my hair.

"Yeah. Shut up and go to sleep."

"Okay. Night, Rob."

"Good night, Chris."

CHAPTER
FIVE

THE next morning brought grey sunlight washed out by the rain and a warm body in my arms for the first time in years. Chris was snoring softly, facing away from the window, probably not yet woken by the fact that my body was shielding his from the light. I hadn't bothered to draw the curtains before we'd fallen into bed last night.

My movement seemed to disturb him, though, and as I listened to his deep breathing lighten, he turned to rest his face against my chest. I kissed his forehead.

There were plenty of things I should have been doing on a Saturday morning. My routine was to wake early, as I did during the week, and start to go through my lecture plans and check through papers that needed to be marked. I needed to return a book to the library and find a suitable birthday gift for my mother. I really should have called her and accepted or declined her invitation to lunch the following day; I hadn't responded yet. By midafternoon I'd usually be working on marking essays or planning lectures, freeing up my Sunday for whatever it was that I wanted to do.

Chris sighed heavily in his sleep and rolled over, pressing his chest full-length against my back, slinging a leg over my hips and an arm around my waist, effectively trapping me in bed. I took his hand and held it tight to my chest.

It can wait, I thought vaguely before drifting back to sleep.

SETTING up the meeting between Chloe and Chris proved slightly more difficult than I had initially anticipated. My access to Chloe was limited; Lu and I were still on good terms, but Chloe had a whole host of extracurricular activities that filled her weekends and evenings, and she lived nearly an hour away. Not that Chris understood this. He asked me nearly every time we spoke if I'd called Luisa yet, what the progress was, when I'd see Chloe again.

Finally, a few weeks after the first (disastrous) conversation, the opportunity arose for me to spend a Sunday with my daughter. Not that it was a perfect arrangement for any of us. Far from it. Chris often had a gig on a Saturday night, working well into the early hours of the morning. And I had work to prepare for the week ahead. And Chloe would have a cheerleading competition the day before, meaning she'd likely be tired too.

I knocked on the front door of Luisa's house and was greeted by her husband.

"Hi," I said to Mike.

"Hey, Robert," he said, shaking my hand and welcoming me in. "Lu is in bed. The pregnancy is taking its toll on her now."

"How much longer does she have left?" I asked. Dates had never stuck in my head.

"Two weeks," he said, thumping the door twice. "Knock on wood."

"She'll be fine. She's a trooper," I opined. He tilted his head to one side and gave me a bland smile.

"Chloe?" I called up the stairs.

"Coming!" she yelled back.

Mike and I made small talk as she banged about in her room for a few more minutes, then appeared at the top of the stairs wearing the tightest pair of jeans I had ever seen—they looked like she'd painted them on her skinny legs—and a loose, torn tank top. Her hair was scraped into a ponytail; the curls bounced down her back as she bounced down the stairs.

I gave Mike a look that clearly said, *Do you let her out of the house looking like that?*

He replied with an equally silent *It's not worth the argument.*

"You'll need a jumper or something, honey," I told her. "It's chilly out."

"Dad," she whined. "No one says 'jumper'."

"Sweater. Cardigan. Hoodie. Coat, jacket, fleece. Bloody poncho, Chlo, just put something on."

She rolled her eyes and stomped back up the stairs.

"Good luck," Mike murmured, slapping me on the shoulder and wandering back off into the house.

She appeared with a hoodie with the logo for her cheerleading squad on it and, at my raised eyebrow, threw it on over her head.

Chloe had taken after her mother in the looks department for the most part; like her mother, she was petite, her eyes too big for her face, giving her a permanently startled, deer-in-headlights sort of look which had always amused me when she was a baby. As she'd grown, so had the lashes framing her rich brown eyes (the color, at least, she'd inherited from me), making her more of a doe-eyed Bambi now.

"Not that cold," she said as we headed to the car.

"Cold enough," I told her.

As we pulled off down the street, I looked over at my daughter. "How did the competition go yesterday?" I asked.

"You remembered," she said, looking at me like I was an alien. I felt like one.

"Of course," I told her. It was a little white lie. Lu had reminded me.

"We got second place," she said. "Out of fourteen teams, it was pretty good."

"Congratulations," I enthused.

"Yeah. Thanks."

We went through our normal script of questions: how was school (boring), homework (done), boys (Dad, *please*), her mother (fat). I laughed at the last one, and she cracked a smile.

"She was huge when she was carrying you," I said. "For such a little woman, it was funny. She was like a weeble."

"What the hell is a weeble?"

"Weebles wobble but they don't fall down?" I said. "No? Oh. They were toys your Aunty Jilly and I had when we were kids."

She shrugged and gave me that blank teenager look that said, *You're old.*

"So, Dad," she said, her eyes fixed on the road. "Why aren't you married and having kids?"

I choked on nothing. "I don't know," I said after clearing my throat. "I'm just not."

"Don't bullshit me, Father."

"Language."

"Tell me."

I sighed. "Who have you overheard? I'm not mad, Chloe. I'm just curious."

"Mom was on the phone to Aunty Jilly and said something about a boyfriend," she muttered.

"Ah. Um. Yeah. Well."

"Concise," she said sarcastically.

"I've been seeing him for a few months."

"Oh." Silence. "How come you never told me before?"

"It was never an issue. You were too young to understand, and I didn't want to upset you by trying to explain."

"I don't care," she said, screwing up her nose and frowning.

"That I'm… gay?" I asked.

"No. It's cool."

I nearly swerved off the road. "Are you kidding me?" I asked.

Chloe rolled her eyes. "Liza at school has two gay dads. They buy her whatever she wants." She looked at me hopefully.

"Well, Liza—" The name caught in my throat. "—is lucky. Your gay dad is still just a poor professor."

She sighed dramatically. "Well, I think you should marry a rich guy. Then I can be a bridesmaid at your wedding. Blake's parents got married the other week and they had a huge wedding at the country club and loads of gifts. And cake."

"Is Blake a boy or a girl?" I asked, teasing.

"A girl," she said, clearly scandalized at my ignorance.

"I don't get this name androgyny," I said. "How are you supposed to know if it's a boy or a girl?"

"Not everyone is called John or Jane these days," she said. "It's cool. Mom is going to call the baby Columbus or Carter if it's a boy or Kennedy or McKenzie if it's a girl."

"God help us all."

"Dad! Be nice. You chose my name, right?"

"And you should be glad I did," I told her. "Otherwise you might be stuck with a monstrosity of a name like McKenzie McKinnon."

"You could have been a bit more imaginative, though. Like Khloe Kardashian. She spells her name with a K," Chloe informed me.

"Who's Khloe Cardigan?" I asked her. I was being a dad on purpose, and it prompted the right kind of reaction from her. My daughter sighed heavily, and I could almost hear her eyes rolling in her head.

"Dad."

"Well," I said. "There's no precedent for how the letters K H should sound next to each other in the English language. It could be like 'knife' with a silent K."

She muttered something about having a teacher for a parent, which I chose to ignore.

"So her name could be pronounced like…." I considered it. "Hulooo. Hulooo Cardigan."

The snort of laughter was inelegant and sounded so much like her mother it made my heart ache. "You're such a geek," Chloe informed me.

"Thanks," I said. "Tell your mom that for me, would you? It's the risk she's taking with all of those creative spellings."

She smiled and tried to hide it by looking out the window.

"So, what's his name?" she asked.

"Chris," I told her.

"Do I get to meet him?"

"I think he'd like that," I told her.

Chloe kicked her heels up onto the dash. I decided not to argue with her and let her do it.

"You look different," she said suddenly, sitting up straighter.

"I do?"

"Yeah. You've had your hair cut. And you're growing a beard."

"I'm not growing a beard," I said, laughing. "I just didn't shave this morning."

"And… and… you look… different," she finished lamely.

"Better?" I teased.

"Anything is an improvement."

"I'll call Joan Rivers, see if she can get you a job. Your critical eye is clearly an untapped talent."

"Ha ha," she deadpanned. "He's changed you," she accused.

"Maybe," I said lightly. "I don't mind if he has. Like you said, it's an improvement."

She turned the radio on then, effectively ending the conversation with Lady Gaga. I considered calling Chris and picking him up on the way back to the flat but decided against it, thinking Chloe would probably be more comfortable meeting him in a more public, nonthreatening environment. Neutral territory. Switzerland. She would probably rejoice at a trip to Europe, actually. Although my first choice of location would be taking her back to my homeland.

But I digress.

I needed to stop back at the flat to pick up my wallet, which I'd forgotten in my haste to leave the house that morning, and Chloe wanted to see the cat. We ended up crashing in front of the TV with two mugs of coffee, leaving me wondering when my teenage daughter had started drinking the stuff. I blamed her mother.

We were tuned in to Oprah when my phone buzzed. I smiled as I answered it to Chris.

"Hi," I said, trying not to let the goofy smile escape from my face.

"Hey. Did you pick her up okay?" he asked.

"Yeah, we're just chilling before we go do something."

"'Kay," he said, and I heard him shifting about.

"Are you still in bed?" I asked incredulously. It was closing in on 11:00 a.m.

"Dad, please," Chloe muttered.

"I didn't get in till three," Chris protested.

I told him to hang on and turned to Chloe. "Is it okay if we pick him up in an hour? I'll take you out for lunch."

"Sure," she said, shrugging it off.

"Get your ass out of bed," I said to Chris. "We'll be there in an hour."

"Fine, fine," he muttered and rang off.

Chloe was silent, staring determinedly at the TV. I wasn't too concerned. I was aware of the soporific, trancelike effects of television, especially on young minds.

"Where did you meet him?" she demanded after a few minutes.

"Hmm? Oh. At a pub," I said.

"A gay bar?"

"No, Chloe," I said gently. "Just a pub. We just got to talking."

"Then how did he know you're gay? You don't look gay."

This was the part of the coming-out-to-my-daughter process I was dreading. Explaining things. Maybe it would have been easier to tell her when she was younger.

"I was out with Alex. He sort of orchestrated our meeting."

"Oh."

More silence.

"Chloe," I said, attracting her attention. "I know this is a lot to take in all at once. But I hope you'll give Chris a chance. He's a very nice person."

She nodded and stood, taking both our mugs back to the kitchen. "We should go," she called.

If possible, the drive over to Chris's place was even more awkward. I could tell she was nervous, on edge, and strangely defiant in her own way. I couldn't figure out why.

I beeped the horn rather than getting out of the car, and he was halfway out the door already, shouting obscenities at his housemates.

"Motherfuckers," he yelled, laughing as he jogged down the path. He was smiling.

"Hi," I said as he hopped into the back of the car.

"Hey, baby," he said, leaning through the divide to plant a quick kiss on my cheek.

"Chris, this is my daughter, Chloe," I said.

"Oh," she squeaked.

"Nice to meet you," he said, awkwardly angling his arm through to shake her hand. And he gave her one of those cheeky, sexy, winning smiles. She was a goner.

Chris smelled nice, not too strongly of anything but enough that his presence was announced to our olfactory senses. His hair was a mess, and he was wearing jeans and a soft, gray knitted sweater that covered his arms to the wrists. It covered nearly all of his tattoos, but not the skull on his hand.

Chloe was staring.

"I thought we could go to Bennie's," I said, suggesting Chloe's favorite Italian restaurant, one that I hadn't had a chance to take Chris to yet.

"Oh, I love that place," Chris interjected quickly. "They make the best NY cheesecake I've ever had."

"Their cheesecake is the best," she said breathily, physically twisted in her seat now, trying to get a better look at him.

"She likes me already," Chris stage whispered to me.

I smiled and kept my eyes on the road.

Chloe excused herself to the bathroom once we'd been seated, and I turned to Chris, leaning forward so my forehead touched his. He kissed me quickly and sat back.

"Okay?" I asked him.

"Of course. She's great."

"I think she likes you," I teased him. He rolled his eyes.

"Everyone likes me."

The waitress came over, and I ordered Chloe a Coke, not sure if she was still on her iced-tea obsession or not. When she came back from the bathroom, Chloe had taken her sweatshirt off, and I would have sworn the tank top was dipping lower over her chest than it had when we'd left her mother's.

She nodded her thanks at the Coke and looked up at Chris.

"How old are you?" she said frankly.

Chris nodded, as if he'd been expecting her question. "Twenty-three."

"Bit young for you, isn't he, Dad?" she said as she concentrated on her drink.

"Chloe," I said, my tone issuing my warning.

"What?" she said. "He's only nine years older than me."

"And nine years younger than your dad," Chris said reasonably.

"If it's not such a big age gap between you two, then it's not such a big age gap between your boyfriend and your daughter," she said.

I went to speak, to chastise her, but Chris gave me a look. A look that clearly said, *Shut up and let me handle this*. I decided to trust him. Besides, I couldn't figure out how best to argue with her.

"Chloe, I'm younger than your dad. There's no use in trying to pretend that I'm not," he said. "But it's because of this that we get on so well. With my career, I've spent a long time bouncing around from place to place and partying. Since we've been together, I've brought that sweet, fun nature out of him, and he's given me something to ground myself to."

"I don't see where you get the benefit from this," she said bluntly.

Chris laughed. "I get someone who is willing to take the time to get to know me rather than having rather… brief relationships."

"So you fuck around," she said.

"Chloe!" I exclaimed. "That's out of order. Apologize."

She did, reluctantly. "But you're safe, right? I mean, I don't want my dad to die of AIDS."

"Jesus Christ," I muttered.

"Rob," Chris said sharply. "She has questions. This is a lot to handle. Give her a break." He turned back to the daughter he knew how to handle a lot better than I did. "I don't have AIDS, Chloe. I don't have HIV. I don't fuck around, no, but I'm not exactly famous for having long-term, committed relationships."

She nodded. "I'm sorry."

"Don't be," he said quickly, before I could get a word in. "I don't have a problem with answering your questions."

She seemed to soften after that, and I was happy to let Chris orchestrate the conversation about their shared interest in music and Chloe's favorite bands. I heard the word "Bieber" and tuned out. Besides, watching them interact was far more interesting to me than actually taking part in their conversation.

For all I knew, these could well be the two most important people in my whole life.

We ordered another round of drinks and a few baskets of chips to share as awkward conversation softened into something slightly more natural. It was clear, to me at least, that Chloe's guard was still up and she didn't trust Chris just yet. That was okay, though. If there was one way that Chloe took after me that I was actually happy about, it was in her natural reluctance to trust people.

By the time we were ready to leave the restaurant, I was getting a bit tired of Chloe's attempts to flirt. Apparently she didn't need to trust the guy to flirt with him. Any confidence in her that I'd gained slowly slipped through my fingers.

Every day she got a little older, a little bit more like her mother, and suddenly the sheer loathing Lu's parents still had for me got a little bit more understandable.

When Chloe climbed into the car after saying goodbye to Chris, I led us away a few steps for a more private conversation.

"Okay?" I asked him.

"I'm fine. Stop worrying."

I kissed him softly.

"Why don't you come over later?"

I considered the work I needed to do for my upcoming lectures. Dismissed it. "Yeah. I'll let you know when I'm back."

He shook his head. "Don't bother. Just turn up. I'll be there."

"Okay." I kissed him again. "See you later."

Chris waved to Chloe as we pulled out of the lot. She had turned the radio on as she waited for me. I considered turning it down to talk to her. However much I wanted to ignore the repercussions of our afternoon, it wouldn't be responsible of me to turn my back on her.

"Can we talk?" I said, raising my voice over the music.

"I'm sure we can," she muttered. I turned the radio down.

"I'm not upset with you, Chloe," I said, sighing. "In fact, that went a lot better than I was anticipating."

She looked at me in shock.

I refrained from rolling my eyes.

"I promise," I continued. "I don't blame you for having questions. I think you could do a little bit of work on respecting your elders—"

"Chris isn't my elder," she interjected. "He's practically my peer."

"He's my boyfriend, so I'd be grateful if you treated him with the same respect you show to your stepdad."

"Mike has been living with me and Mom since I was five. I only just met Chris," she said.

When had my daughter gotten to be so reasonable? That certainly wasn't something she'd inherited from her mother.

"That's a fair comment," I conceded.

"He's young, Dad," she said, fiddling with the hem of her shirt. "And hot."

"And gay," I said gently.

She scowled.

I parked up and escorted my daughter back into the house, determined to speak to her mother. At that point Luisa could have been in labor with her third spawn and I still would have wanted to talk to her. Probably.

Fortunately for me, she was not in labor and was out of bed.

"Come in, Robert," she called from the living room. I kissed Chloe on the cheek, and she stomped back up to her bedroom without saying goodbye. Luisa was perched on an armchair looking like a shrine to some goddess of fertility; with her legs folded up underneath her and her large belly swelling over her knees, she once again resembled one the weebles that our daughter had never heard of.

"I thought I'd give you some advance warning," I said, sitting when she directed me to the sofa.

"Oh?"

"Our daughter met my boyfriend today."

"Oh."

"Pregnancy seems to have rendered you incapable of normal speech."

She threw a cushion at me.

"What happened?" Lu asked.

"I think she has a little crush," I admitted sheepishly.

"On your boyfriend?" she asked, incredulous.

"Yes."

"Oh."

"Luisa! If she hadn't overheard you and Jilly discussing it in the first place, this never would have happened."

"Ah. Sorry."

"Bloody hell. Women," I muttered.

"Tell me all about him," she said while rubbing her hands together with glee.

"He's a twenty-three-year-old rock star with tattoos and a Mohawk haircut."

She squealed with laughter and rubbed her belly with both hands, gasping for breath. "I like that one."

"I'm serious," I said. "He plays drums in a band. And he hasn't shaved his head, but his hair spikes up in the middle."

"You are serious," she said, frowning. "He's twenty-three?"

"And this is where I think Chloe's problem comes from," I said. "She was quite happy to tell us that Chris is only nine years older than she."

"Oh dear. And he has tattoos?"

"Yes. Quite a few."

Luisa sighed. "Teenagers."

"She asked Chris if he had AIDS."

"Oh lord."

"Yeah, that was my response too."

"Robert? I'll talk to her."

I stood. "Thanks. I thought I'd just give you a heads-up."

"Thanks," she echoed, struggling to stand. I pushed her back down into her chair.

"Sit. Stay," I commanded. "I'll see myself out. Call me when you have that baby."

"I will. Thanks, Robert."

I kissed the top of her head before I left. She was still a friend, more so since big decisions about Chloe's life needed to be made. Luisa never made me feel left out, even when I never felt like I had a valid opinion or even a right to make the decisions between us. She was the one who had to deal with the consequences, anyway.

THE period of coming out of the closet, for me, took several years. I'd laid out the bones of the story for Chris, but the details were mine, and I kept them locked in a fairly dark part of myself. My first, tentative "Mum, Dad, I think I like boys too," had happened aged seventeen when my whole world barely made sense to me. My parents initially blamed the stress of the move and my trouble fitting into this new environment. America was so, so different from Scotland, and I ached for the familiar feel of home.

Despite my inability—or unwillingness—to adjust, the rest of my family seemed to think the U.S. was the dream that they had all been waiting to live, and I was alone in feeling so utterly lost. In that environment it sort of made sense that these new questions about sex and my own sexuality would get buried under the aching need to fit in.

I lost myself in my schoolwork and found much of it was targeted for an intelligence below my own. With my parents' reaction to my painful coming-out being to refer me to a psychiatrist and school counselor, I decided to take a more scientific approach to my situation and explore my other options.

Thus, Luisa.

She was a friend already and a good one, at that. I was pretty sure she latched onto me at the beginning because of my accent, but that was quickly forgiven as she proved herself a useful aide and good friend while showing me my awkward way around my new environment.

She chose Boston for college even though it was clear to me, at least, that her heart wasn't in academia. Being a little social butterfly, though, well, she would undoubtedly outshine me in that respect.

I bungled through the first semester, throwing myself into my studies with an energy and enthusiasm that I'd not felt in nearly two years. Here I was challenged and my opinions probed, not just "What do you think?" but "Why do you think that?"

I wasn't living the out-and-proud lifestyle that I'd been dreaming of but something close to it. I didn't date females, I cautiously frequented the occasional gay bar, and I started taking the first steps to discovering myself.

That Christmas, when I returned home, I had decided not to flaunt anything in front of the two people who were funding my education. They were thrilled with the grades I was pulling in, and their utter refusal to discuss my sexuality seemed to cement my opinion that they considered it little more than a passing fancy, something that had undoubtedly been counseled out of me.

Two nights before Christmas, there was something of a high school reunion for those of us who had been away for the past three months. Lu wore a dark red dress made of some floaty material; it skimmed over her collarbones and flared at the knee, showing plenty of the pale golden skin that graced her body. Her hair, dark, shiny curls of it, bounced at her shoulders, and diamonds (or their false counterparts) glittered at her ears.

I was confused. After spending so many weeks trying to find my identity as a homosexual person, these strange, unfamiliar heterosexual longings made me feel something of a phony. A phony and a failure, since I clearly couldn't even make a decision about something as natural and intrinsic as my sexual orientation.

I had never been much of a drinker, not like my father, who considered whiskey and water to be equally as important to his personal survival. Please don't mistake me; he wasn't a drunk or abusive with his liquor, although some of his behaviors could certainly be considered those of an alcoholic.

The respect I had for my father was the type that came with love and a healthy dose of fear. He never beat me, not once, not even when I deserved it, but as I grew, I started to understand his own personal brand of emotional blackmail that he used on Jilly more than me. She was the princess to his king of the castle.

And I became the disappointment, the only son who managed to drunkenly impregnate a girl who was a friend, a good friend, and a nice person. The last thing Luisa Robinson ever deserved was me. At least, that was the message that was repeatedly imposed on me over the following year.

The act of conception itself took place in the basement of my parents' home. My mother claimed the reason she'd chosen our house was because it reminded her of Scotland in its architecture, and I could see why; it was one of the oldest houses in the town and built at least partially from stone rather than the more modern wooden erections that surrounded it. The stone and a buffer of a whole story of house between us and my sleeping family meant neither Lu nor I had any concerns about being heard or caught.

Clearly contraception was not at the forefront of either of our minds as we fumbled our way toward a mutually unsatisfactory conclusion.

Then there was her panicked voice on a telephone call about six weeks later—"No, Robert, I'm *late.*"—and the dawning realization of the possibility of fatherhood, at that time something I was not cut out for. I could barely take care of myself and clearly could not take care of my sexual partners on any level.

And from that one night, my singular, awkward, sexuality-confirming experience of making love to a woman, Chloe was created.

There was a lot of "We're very disappointed in you, Robert"s and "We taught you better than this, Robert"s even though that wasn't strictly true. The facts of life, the birds and the bees, if you will, was all information I'd gleaned from books, and mostly scientific books at that. My high school's abstinence-only sex education course had reached its natural conclusion because even though I knew what contraception was and what it did, the message to use it had not been strong. The message had been not to do it at all, but a fat lot of good that had been for Luisa and me.

The only light in the entire knocking-up fiasco was that Lu was due in the last weeks of August, only a short time before she was due to start her second year of college, but those few weeks proved enough for the college admissions to allow her to enroll.

Since it was all naturally my fault, I was the one who moved to a new college and worked in a coffee shop by day, bar by night establishment that paid me peanuts but showed my parents that I was serious about taking care of my responsibilities and consequentially kept us secure under the roof they put over our heads.

The moment my daughter slipped her way into the world, ten days early, bloody and screaming but blessedly healthy, was one that defined my short life to that point. Lu changed in my eyes from amazing woman to goddess. I read, after, that the pain a woman experiences while giving birth is comparable to fracturing twenty bones in your body in one go. When I delivered this information to Luisa, she merely raised an eyebrow in what was a clear threat to my testicles.

She was placed in my arms first at Lu's insistence with the words "Congratulations, Mr. McKinnon, it's a girl," and my world tilted on its axis. I'd spent the previous nine months going to every doctor's appointment, every ultrasound scan and birthing class and parenting class, but nothing could prepare me for the moment when I became a man and a father.

Our little family was naturally dysfunctional, but even as Chloe grew up with a stepfather and weekends-only dad, she never stopped being perfect to me.

As for my parents, they continued to ignore their gay son and only heap praise and love on their straight son, despite all the work Jilly and I did to try to make them understand the latter did not exist. After they were frankly abysmally rude to one of my exes, I stopped taking him to any family functions and swallowed the bitter realization that I would never be good enough for them and as long as I continued to follow my wicked and sinful path through the world, they would never accept me.

That was okay, though. My contact with them grew less and less, their interest in my bastard child waned, and our relationship became, although cool, still cordial.

Sometimes I resented them, and at others, when the news of another gay teen suicide came through the news, I felt blessedly relieved that they didn't care enough to make my life that difficult. Things could have been so much worse, and I was well aware of it.

I'd learned a long time ago how differently my body responded when it was smooth, hard muscles under my hands rather than soft, squidgy curves and the unyielding hardness of another man's sex rather than slick, wet heat. Chris reinforced my desires on every level, but the chances of me introducing him to my parents, even if we stayed together forever, were slim to none. They wouldn't understand him, and to be fair, it would probably only upset them or convince them that I was suffering from a midlife crisis.

I'd stopped being sad at their reactions years ago. I had finally found someone special. And nothing they could say or do could spoil that.

CHAPTER
SIX

IT TOOK me a while to get used to the fact that Chris communicated almost exclusively in text messages. Not that I was complaining. It was nice to pick up my phone and find three messages from him. It fell under the category of "yet more things Robert needs to adjust to."

I would normally keep my phone locked in my office during the day. This was partly so I knew where it was and partly so it wouldn't go off during my lectures and annoy me. The only people who would regularly call or text me were Luisa and Chloe, anyway. And they knew to call the college if there was an emergency, not my phone.

My life was so sad.

Chris, however, sent me a text when he woke up in the morning. And sometime midmorning, asking me how I was. And again at lunchtime. If I sent a reply to one of his messages, I had a reply almost instantly. Although this was disconcerting at first, I began to anticipate his choice of breakfast cereal update, which was usually formatted in the style of *The Fast Show*: *Today, I will mostly be eating Cheerios.* It made me feel warm and fuzzy inside that he even knew what *The Fast Show* was.

Almost all communication regarding the place and time of our reuniting took place via text message.

Do you want to go to a bar tonight?

It was Friday. So: *Sure. The Ship?*

A pause.

No. I was thinking of checking out one of the more exclusive establishments catering to our sinful homosexual desires.

I laughed, out loud, in the quietness of my office.

A gay bar?

While he composed his reply, I couldn't help but think of how much quicker and easier this conversation would be if we used the mobile telephones for their intended purpose and called each other. For heaven's sake.

Yeah. I was trying out talking like you. I'll come over about 8ish. We can get a cab.

For reasons that seemed obvious to me, I rarely frequented gay bars. There were plenty in Boston to choose from, ones that catered to the leather crowd, or the techno, flashy-lights-and-drugged-up-twinks crowd, or the drag queen crowd. I'd never really found my niche in the gay community. My earlier attempts at trying to fit in had failed dismally. When other men found out I had a daughter, I was met with one of two reactions—they either ran for the hills or wanted me to raise pretty babies with them.

Neither of these things were particularly conducive to a relationship.

I knew that if Chris didn't get on well with Chloe, it would put a serious damper on things between us. I wouldn't necessarily split us up—she was a teenager and appropriately stroppy due to the fact—but if things went terribly wrong, I would have to seriously consider which way forward things would go. At least he didn't mind the fact that she existed. And that she had a part of my life that I wasn't going to be able to give to him.

So, in practice, the activity of dressing for a night in a gay bar was not one I was especially good at.

When Chris knocked on my door at twenty past eight (I wasn't surprised at his lateness), I was wearing my pair of dark jeans and nothing else. Not even socks.

"Oh, hello," Chris drawled and wrapped a hand around the back of my neck, drawing me down into a kiss. "Very nice, Professor. Very nice."

I returned his kiss with a smile on my lips and drew the smell of his cologne into my lungs. He was spicy sweet tonight, delicious in jeans and a blood red T-shirt that he would undoubtedly remove at the first opportunity. I knew his type. And, to be fair, I couldn't resent the fact that his type like to strip off. If my chest and stomach had looked like his, I would undoubtedly have stripped my shirt off too.

"I don't know what to wear," I admitted, feeling like a teenage girl.

"Nothing," he said emphatically. "Just this. You look *hot*."

I shrugged awkwardly, probably blushing as well. "You don't have to flatter me, Chris." I caught his wrist and tugged him to my room and my dull-as-dishwater wardrobe.

"I'm not flattering you," he protested as he followed obediently. "If you left your shirt off all night, they'd be beating off the men with a stick. A really, really big stick," he added because it was Chris, and he couldn't help but take advantage of any rude innuendo situation.

I found socks and sat on the edge of the bed to pull them on. Chris hummed tunelessly as he flicked through the contents of my wardrobe, wincing at most of it but occasionally making a sound of something like approval.

I reached for my shiny black shoes and found that they'd been put back in the shoe rack and replaced with a pair of shit kickers, as we used to call them back home. Sand-colored desert boots. Chris was clearly the fashion expert in our relationship (and just when had I started thinking of it as a relationship?), so I pulled them on and laced them tight without comment.

"This is hard," Chris muttered.

"Really, really hard?"

"Shut up," he said, but smirked. I could play the innuendo game too. "I don't want you to feel not like you, but I don't want you to wear what you usually wear to work or whatever."

After a few moments, he threw a shirt at me. It was a white one, washed so many times that it was now thin and incredibly soft to touch. I could never bear to throw it away, even though really, it was only an inexpensive white cotton shirt. It was what I had been wearing the day Chloe was born.

It was slightly tighter now than it had been fourteen years ago but still fitting. I buttoned it, feeling smug with myself. Not all was yet lost.

"Aha," he muttered and pulled one of my suit bags out, hanging it from the door and extracting a pinstriped, dark grey waistcoat. "This too."

"Are you sure?" I asked dubiously. He nodded.

I pulled it on and let Chris do the buttons. His fingers then went to my throat and slipped the first three buttons on the shirt back through so it hung open at my throat. Then he leaned in and pressed his lips to the little hollow there.

My hair was yet to be styled, and he did that for me too, locating the gel that I so rarely used and playing with it until he was satisfied that it looked right. I was sat back down on the edge of the bed, Chris standing between my knees, when I smiled and told him, "Thank you."

"You don't see yourself in the same way other people see you," Chris said. He was gently running his hand through the soft hair at the nape of my neck.

I frowned and shook my head silently.

"It's true," he insisted.

"There's no need to flatter me," I said, smiling. "I like you already."

He huffed and pulled himself to his feet, taking my hand and hauling me up too. "Come here."

We moved out to the hall, where I kept a mirror I never looked in. Chris took my chin, stood behind me, and forced me to look up. Unsurprisingly, I was blushing.

"You're adorable," he started. I went to interrupt him, and he pressed his fingers to my lips. "Shh. You have gorgeous eyes. And a very masculine jaw, for a queer." He winked at me in the mirror. "It looks nice like this… all stubbled."

I rarely looked at myself. Really looked, you understand. I saw my face every day, shaving, dressing, but I never took stock of myself the way Chris was doing.

"I think," he continued, "that you are perfect. And I should know. I have great taste in men."

"In which case," I said, turning to him, "I definitely should not argue with you."

"Come on," he said. "We should get going."

I surprised myself by not being nervous when we got to the club. There was a line, but not a particularly long one due to the early hour, and I didn't mind waiting outside in the cold because Chris snuggled up close to me to share our body heat.

The doorman looked from Chris to me, then demanded, "ID."

Even as a little warm ball of delight lodged itself beneath my ribs, I worried that I wouldn't have any identification on me. I didn't carry it routinely. Chris found his easily, but I fumbled for my wallet before thankfully locating my driver's license. I handed it over to the rather burly bearded gentleman, who scrutinized it for a moment too long before handing both back.

"Mr. Ford," he said. "Mr. McKinnon. Have a good evening."

Chris wore a cheeky smirk as we checked our jackets at the door before finding our way to the almost half-full bar.

"You're trouble," I said without malice. "Beer and a whiskey, please."

The music wasn't too loud yet, and we stayed at the bar for a while, drinking and generally enjoying being in each other's presence. As the night crept on and the room filled to bursting point, Chris stripped off his T-shirt (as I'd known he would) and tucked it into his back pocket, kissed me deeply, and bounced off to join the throbbing pulse of people—*men*—on the dance floor. He'd asked me if I wanted to join him, but I was decidedly not drunk enough to dance, and I liked watching him. And I had no issues with staying at the bar and drinking.

When I was offered, "Can I get you a drink?" my initial response was a polite but distanced "No, thank you."

Then I turned and was faced with an old friend.

"Elias!" I laughed, accepting his hug. "How are you?"

Elias and I had met at college. He was a languages student while I obviously took Literature. I hadn't known that he was gay at the time, and even if I had, I would have considered him so far out of my league it wasn't worth mentioning.

We were assigned to the same dorm building in our first year and bonded over being outsiders, immigrants in America, as it was. Elias had both the body and the looks of a privileged European upbringing. He was from Switzerland, a small town not far outside Zurich. We'd made promises that one summer I'd take him back to Edinburgh and act as his tour guide around the city and he'd do the same for me in his hometown. The trip had never happened. Chloe had arrived instead.

Now, close to six or seven years since I'd seen him last, time had treated my old friend well. He still wore his dark blond hair long, to his shoulders in impossibly shiny, thick waves. His eyes, piercing blue, now had a few laughter lines around them. He wore a grey shirt with plenty of buttons undone and dark leather pants, which cleared up my last few questions regarding his sexuality.

Maybe Chris had helped me refine my "gaydar", or at least have some confidence in it.

"I thought you went back to Switzerland," I said after accepting his offer of a drink, now I knew who he was.

"I did," he said, "for a couple of years. My mama was sick for a while. She passed back in the spring."

"I'm sorry," I said. He nodded.

"Thank you. My sisters are still there, but I decided to come back for a while. I was going to look you up, but then I run into you here, of all places."

I laughed. "Yes. It's not one of my usual haunts, I'll admit."

"You're looking good, Robert," he said, unashamedly looking at me. "Time has treated you well."

Through the crowds of men (hot, sweaty, some nearly naked men), I could see Chris bopping around on the dance floor looking happy as anything, so I led Elias over to one of the booths at the other end of the bar and sat opposite him.

He asked about Chloe, remembering her by name, which pleased me endlessly. He was theatrically dismayed to learn that she was a teenager now.

"A little lady?" he asked.

"A little madam is more like it," I said. "She takes after her mother rather than me, which is an endless relief to all three of us."

"Are you wanting more?"

His halting English served to remind me that he had been out of the country for a long time.

"Children?" I asked. "No."

Elias nodded knowingly. "She was a blessing, no, but an unexpected one."

"Exactly." I laughed. "I wouldn't change her for the world. But I'm done with raising children. Luisa has another daughter now, though, and she's pregnant with her third."

He pouted and tilted his head to the side. "Lucky Luisa."

When our conversation found a natural dip, I offered to buy the next round of drinks. Accepting, he offered to keep the table for us while I went back to the bar via the men's room.

Chris was in there, washing his hands as I passed him.

"Are you having a good night?" I asked, placing my hand on his sweaty lower back and kissing his shoulder.

"Yeah," he said, smiling broadly. "Come dance with me."

"Later, maybe," I said. "I've just found an old college friend, and we're catching up. You can come join us if you like."

He made a face. "Nah. I'm gonna keep dancing. Burn some calories. Do you mind that I've ditched you?"

"Not at all," I said. "I'm glad you're having a good night. I'll see you later."

When he kissed me again, it lingered long enough to elicit several wolf whistles from the room's other occupants.

"Later," he said and patted my cheek as he left.

I ordered our drinks and was offered table service from an alarmingly hairless young man wearing naught but a pair of silver shorts (very tight silver shorts) and a lot of glitter. All I could think was that I hoped he didn't get any in my whiskey.

My conversation with Elias turned to our careers. He was somewhat surprised to learn that I was still in Boston after all this time. I'd had a dream, a long time ago, to return to the U.K. to teach there. As much as I'd wanted to—and the opportunity had been there had I wanted to take it—I found plenty of excuses to stay. They were obvious ones, and things that I could have easily worked around should I have so wished.

But the university in Bath had remained without a Professor McKinnon while I continued to grace the halls of the college with my presence.

Elias, I learned, had taken his five languages and taught them all over the world. I knew that there was a strong need for intelligent, committed people to teach English as a foreign language, and he'd done it in places from Jakarta in Indonesia to Shanghai in China and Hanoi in Vietnam, and back again. Of course I was jealous. This man had taken all the ideals and plans we'd made at eighteen and fulfilled them.

Despite his upbringing, I learned that he'd spent the better part of a decade helping raise the fortunes and futures of children around the world. But then again, I'd always gotten the impression that Elias wasn't going to follow in his family's footsteps.

"Romance?" I asked him, emboldened by the liquor.

He smirked and raised an eyebrow at me. "I've never been one to be without a man around the house, Robert," he said with a lazy grin. "Or several men. The Thai are surprisingly open-minded about these things."

I couldn't help but roll my eyes at him. In college, I'd always thought of him as a terrible flirt and something of a lady's man. At least I'd been half-right.

Before he could return the question, Chris bounced over to us and I realized that we were both leaning across the table. Chris had a little frown on his face. My proximity to Elias was only because of the noise in the club but there was no way of explaining this to Chris without sounding guilty.

I immediately shuffled up on the bench to let him in next to me. For some reason, when he threw his arm around my shoulder and kissed me loudly on the cheek, I was embarrassed and somewhat annoyed with him "branding" me.

"Chris, this is Elias," I said. "We were at college together. Elias, this is my partner, Chris."

I felt guilty springing this on him at such a late point in the evening. There had just been other things to talk about, other things to catch up on that seemed more important. And with that thought, the hot embarrassment turned to shame.

Elias raised a sculpted eyebrow and smiled pleasantly, offering his hand to Chris over the table.

"Nice to meet you, Chris," he said.

Chris's responding smile was saccharine sweet. "Likewise."

I took his hand and linked our fingers under the table, squeezing gently. The tension mounted for a moment as I tried desperately to engage both men in conversation and failed dismally. When Chris slid back out of the booth, he didn't let go of my hand, tugging me with him.

"Will you come dance with me now?" he asked.

Lingering, residual bad feelings made me agree.

"Excuse us?" I said to Elias, who nodded warmly.

"I will see you again, Robert, I'm sure."

I heard Chris mutter something, but it was too loud to discern his words. I got the idea, though, loud and clear. When he dragged me off and the dance floor really was our final destination, I was somewhat confused.

He gripped my hips and drew me forward against his chest, then ran his hands up my arms to wrap them around my neck.

I wasn't a terrible dancer, but I certainly wasn't the best out there. I knew enough to keep my hands on his sides, ribs, waist, hips… and

Chris seemed more than happy to just grind up against me. I had no objections.

Despite the erotic sway of our bodies, when I caught Chris's eye, he was distant, somehow. I lowered my head, leaning in for another kiss, but he turned away at the last moment so I caught his cheek instead.

Fine.

I followed his eye line and couldn't see anything of discernible interest. Then Elias walked past, right at the edge of the dance floor, and suddenly my mouth was invaded with pliant lips and a hot tongue.

Subtle, Chris, I thought to myself.

I made sure to pull away gently. "However much I appreciate your affections," I said, louder than I would have liked, but it was a necessity over the sound of the music, "there is little need to scent mark me as your property, Chris."

"Oh, fuck off," he said and stomped away.

Well. I wasn't expecting that.

For a moment I stood dumb in the middle of a throng of sweaty, thrusting men and wondered why the hell I allowed myself to get into these situations. Then I decided it was because it made my life interesting, and followed the direction Chris had taken out toward a smoking area.

Sure enough, he was leaning against the brickwork, only his T-shirt, which he'd pulled back on, and portable patio heaters protecting him from the night air. One foot was propped up against the wall, and he smoked in short, jerky movements.

"Do you want to talk?" I asked, deciding to be the one to offer an opening.

"Not to you," he said petulantly.

I sighed and rubbed my face. "Don't be such a child," I said, scolding him.

"Why not?" he said. "You treat me like a child, you think of me like a child, so I'll fucking well act like one."

He threw his cigarette on the ground and stomped on it, then went about rolling another one with nimble fingers.

"Is this about Elias?"

"Duh," he muttered. For Christ's sake....

"Elias is a friend, Chris. A *friend*. One I haven't seen or spoken to in a long time. I didn't even know he was gay until tonight."

"Yeah, right."

My tolerance level for childish muttering was being sorely tested.

"Is this really about him? Or about your own insecurities?"

"How fucking dare you," he spat. Inhaled another lungful of toxic smoke. "You're so fucking superior sometimes, you know that?"

"Not intentionally," I said. "But you do seem to evoke that reaction when you act like a total brat."

Chris pushed off from the wall and paced to the other side of the small smoking area and back again. It was enclosed on three sides, opening on the fourth to the parking lot behind. Invisible from the road and the sidewalk, more than one couple had decided to brave the elements and use the courtyard—for want of a better word—as a dark space to grope in. Although I got the impression the groping was giving way to some voyeuristic car-crash argument watching instead now.

"He's much better for you than I am."

"What makes you say that?" I demanded.

"He's all... fuck. Pretty. And European. And educated and shit."

"You're pretty. His nationality has nothing to do with it. And you're a very intelligent man, Chris, although you're not displaying that side of you to your best right now."

"You're not getting it!" he exploded, throwing his hands in the air, and yes, the other men in the courtyard were definitely watching us now, and not even bothering to hide the fact. "Even if it's not Elias, stupid fucking name—"

"It's *Swiss*," I said, wanting to rile him up now, doing it on purpose.

"Even if it's not Swiss Elias, then it'll be someone like him, don't you get that? One day you'll decide you've had enough of playing with the younger man, ooh, he's dark and mysterious, he has tattoos and is nearly a decade younger than me. And you'll decide you're done with your Professor Higgins act and push me back to the gutter, and you'll go and find a man like Swiss Elias."

"You're not a 'phase', Chris," I started, but he interrupted me now.

"Yes I am! I'm exactly that. I'm the type of guy who finds these unintentionally sexy men and brings them out of their shell and makes them see just how wonderful they are… and then they realize, oh yeah, I'm actually too good for this little piece of shit, and they waltz off into the sunset with a guy called fucking *Elias*."

I reached for him then and drew him into my body. It was fucking cold outside, and I was still absorbing what he'd unintentionally told me. His breath stuttered for a moment, and then he pushed back against me, palms flat against my chest.

"No. No. I'm still mad at you."

"I didn't do anything," I said softly.

"Were you not listening to me at all?" he said, desperate now. "It's not what you did, it's what you're going to do. That's what hurts."

"Will you come inside? We're going to freeze out here."

He accepted, reluctantly, but he let me lead him inside, then upstairs, to a balcony where it was marginally quieter than the dance floor beneath us but had the added inconvenience of having another varied group of men midcoitus around the place.

Fucking gay bars.

I ordered more whiskey from the bar because it seemed to be a night for hard liquor rather than piss-weak Yankee "beer." At least the Scottish know how to make a fucking man's drink. There wasn't a sofa free—they were all full of people having a far better time than I was—but we managed to snag a table with two rickety chairs overlooking the rest of the bar.

For a long time, longer than what was probably advisable, I just stared at him.

To catalogue his features seemed like something of a fruitless task, seeing as how I'd already done it, more than once. But there was something of a touch of sadness in his blue-grey eyes that I'd not seen there before… sadness, and desperation.

"Can we talk like reasonable adults now?" I asked him.

"Dunno. Can we?"

"Clearly not," I muttered, and tipped my head back to swallow my whiskey in one. It was cheap crap, anyway. "If you want to play the wounded little boy, Chris, then go ahead. But don't think that you'll be playing on my sympathies, because to be honest, you're grating on my last nerve."

I could see the "Fuck you" on his lips, ready to spring free as he stormed away dramatically, and I caught his wrist before he could manage it. He whirled back around, and for a moment I wondered if he'd smack me—I wouldn't put it past him—but for some reason he stopped.

His hand twisted and his fingers caught hold of mine, and silently, he led me back down to the dance floor.

I had no idea what this silent communication meant, only that when he wrapped himself back up in my arms, I could almost feel the discontent rolling off him. He needed reassurance. This was one of those few times where the nine years that separated us were really highlighted. Sweetness and gentle touches and *it's you, I promise, only you*; well, that I could give him.

"Not going to leave you," I told him, my words strangely juxtaposed with the electronic thump of the music in the room. "I want you, Chris. No one else."

He nodded against my chest but made no other indication that he'd heard me. When he did speak, it wasn't in apology, not that I wanted one.

"Should I go speak to Elias?"

"I don't think so," I said. "He'll already have found someone else to entertain him for the evening. He probably won't appreciate the interruption."

"Can I come home with you?"

It was getting late, and I had just about had my fill of gay bar for the night too. Maybe had enough of gay bars for the next six months. Or a year.

"Of course. I'll get our coats."

He followed me and asked the doorman to hail a cab for us but seemed subdued when I passed him his jacket. We waited on the street, and I wanted to hold him close to me. This quiet, introverted Chris wasn't one I was used to—or liked.

I leaned over and only lowered my voice slightly. "Can I fuck you tonight?"

The corner of his lips twitched. "I don't know. Can you?"

"Yeah." I smirked. "I can. Do you think you'd like that? Hard and deep until you scream for me?"

"I know what you're doing, Rob," he said, but took hold of my hips and leaned against my chest. I kissed the top of his head.

"I don't like you being upset with me," I told him quietly.

"Me either."

I sighed and let my arms wrap around him. When the taxi pulled up, he kissed me quietly on the cheek.

"Come on. I want to scream for you."

CHAPTER
SEVEN

ONE might have thought that having the head of my cock poking at the back of Chris's throat would distract me from certain uncomfortable truths. But when he reached to cup my scrotum in the palm of his hand, I jerked back instinctively.

"Sorry," I muttered. "Sorry."

Chris coughed a little bit and sat back on his heels, rubbing his arm, then sighed.

"So what's the deal with you not wanting me to touch you there?"

I knew this was going to be a difficult conversation, but I had to give it to him for going with honesty. My wrist caught his, and I drew him down to lie next to me. I decided to give him the same honesty back.

"When I was twenty-three," I started, "I had testicular cancer."

"Oh."

"It's okay, they caught it in time and removed it. I had to have chemotherapy, but I've had the all-clear at five years, and I have to go back next year again for another ten-year check."

"But you're okay."

"Yes," I said. "There were a couple of complications…. Usually they put a prosthetic one in to replace the one they take out. But my body reacted badly to it so I had to go for another operation to remove that as well. So I only have one."

He played with my fingers for a moment, silently thinking to himself. "Did it hurt?" he asked eventually.

"Yeah. At the time it was pretty uncomfortable. And I was still working towards my degree as well. I graduated on time despite all of the operations and everything."

"That's pretty amazing. I barely graduated high school." Chris chewed the inside of his cheek as he looked at me again. "Does it still hurt?"

I shrugged. "Sometimes. Not very often, though. Because they went in through the same scar on my abdomen twice, and sometimes that itches. But it's mostly okay."

"Are you messed up about it?"

I laughed and pulled him closer to me. "Probably," I said. "There was one guy, oh, years ago now who was quite cruel. Refused to touch me there in case he caught the cancer too. Which is ridiculous, but he wasn't the sharpest tool in the box."

"Tool is about right," Chris muttered. His response pleased and lifted me to keep explaining.

"I was so young when I had to deal with it that I was lucky my parents had such good health insurance. People talk all the time about, you know, 'having balls', and I don't. I have ball. Singular."

"This was after Chloe was born, right?"

"Yes. And just after I'd moved out from the apartment that Lu and I were sharing, trying to raise her together. But I'm still fertile. It still works."

"It's okay, you know," he said suddenly, interrupting my flow of thoughts. "I don't mind. I just don't want to hurt you."

"You won't," I said gently. "I suppose I'm just self-conscious about it."

"I think you can be as self-conscious as you like if you survive cancer before you even hit twenty-five."

"I don't think of myself like that," I said.

"Like what?"

"A… cancer survivor. It was just there, you know, so they took it out, and then it was okay. I only had to have radiotherapy, you know." I shrugged.

"You're talking shit, Rob," Chris said dismissively, shaking his head.

Maybe I was. I hardly ever thought about the cancer or my absent testicle anymore, except when I met a new partner or had to go for a checkup with my doctor. Being so young when I contracted the disease was something of a blessing as well as a curse; I was one of the most generally fit and healthy men my surgeon had ever treated, and I recovered very quickly. In so many ways, I was lucky to have noticed it so quickly and to have a doctor that took me seriously, especially since testicular cancer in younger men is much rarer.

It had been a difficult couple of months when I first noticed that I was getting tired and rundown a lot easier than before, but I'd chalked it up to stress from the decision to leave Lu and Chloe and move into my own place. I still had plenty of contact with them both after I moved out. It wasn't like I never got to see my little girl, and Lu never tried to restrict my access to her. From a situation that could have turned out to be a complete and utter nightmare, we found a way to stay such close friends even as our lives were turned upside down.

To be told I had cancer when my daughter wasn't even in school yet was fairly terrifying. Lu had just met Mike so I knew she'd be taken care of, but those few months taught me that I didn't want my daughter to only know and have a relationship with her stepfather. It was a wakeup call, for sure.

I didn't even tell Luisa that before the operation I went and banked my sperm so that just in case the worst happened, I'd maybe be able to father another child, a brother or sister for Chloe one day. Well, she already had those from Lu, but I never wanted that opportunity to be taken away from me.

As it was, they only had to remove the one testicle in the end, and the other one seemed to pick up the slack without any obvious trouble. I wanted, more than anything else, to be able to put the entire episode behind me and move on. Just… fucking move on from it all and the pain and the tiredness and the stress of it all, to graduate from my degree with honors and to start my career and leave all of that in my past.

And then there was Chris, a man who was the epitome of youthful excess—beautiful and fun and creative and such a free spirit. It didn't seem fair to drag him down with my history, full as it was of dark tales about unwanted pregnancy and the awkward discovery of my own sexuality and the one illness that makes mice out of men and doesn't discriminate against any of us. Gay or straight, black, white, blue, rich or poor… there's no way of avoiding the paralyzing fear of the grip of cancer.

I wanted to keep him away from all of that and at the same time was desperate for him to know every part of me so that he might better understand where I came from. In my occasional odd, dark moments, I went back to that place where I was sure I wasn't going to make it through, to see my daughter grow up or ever really, truly be in love.

"Well, I definitely killed that particular experience," I said with a touch of weariness.

"Don't worry," he said. "I'm glad you told me."

There wasn't any energy left in me to return his affections so he turned out the light and let me hold him as we inched toward sleep.

He, at least, found peace quickly while I lay awake for a long, long time. Too many memories that I'd worked hard to keep locked away had been stirred back up to the surface by our conversation.

In the darkness his face was so calm and peaceful, a stark difference from the stress of the day we'd had. I knew I should probably let him sleep, but I couldn't stop myself from reaching out and gently stroking his face.

"Sorry," I murmured as he stirred and woke.

He moaned a little and rubbed his face. "'S okay. You all right?"

"Yeah." I wasn't sure what I wanted of him until it was staring me in the face. Or rather, straining to escape from my boxers. "Can I have you?"

His dry lips stretched into a smile. "Course."

"Are you sure?" I had to check. "I didn't mean to wake you up, but you just look so beautiful sometimes and I couldn't sleep—"

"Rob," he said, pressing a finger to my lips to shut me up. "Come be inside me."

Of course, it was the most perfect thing he could possibly have said. Even though I was completely incapable of expressing what I wanted from him, he seemed to understand. I wanted—no, I needed to be as close to him as physically possible.

Claiming him was easy; I could do that with kisses. Still, I felt somewhat awkward as I pushed my boxers down off my thighs and played with the waistband of his, partly to tease the soft hairs that made a line from his belly button down, and partly because I was still nervous about pushing my fingers underneath the slightly worn elastic.

Sighs and smiles against my lips were encouragement to search out his cock; warm, not fully hard yet, the skin silky-smooth against my enquiring fingertips. There was something almost heartbreaking about his whispered pleas for more, the way his fingers wrapped around my arm as I smoothed his hair back from his face.

It was Chris who pushed his underwear off his hips, lifting his bum from the bed and managing to get them down as far as his thighs before my mouth was on his cock and he stopped trying to move them.

I knew from the moment my mouth wrapped around him that I'd left him in a state of frustration earlier in the evening. He tasted of salt and desperation, and with my cheek on his stomach, I could feel the rush of blood through his body.

When my body separated from his, I chanced a look up at him. My gaze was met with wide, blown pupils so large that there was only the tiniest rim of bluey grey left. This clearly wasn't the time for a slow buildup. Already we were both on the edge of something, and I didn't want to wait, I just wanted him.

With slick fingers I twisted and pushed inside him, the careful movement still drawing some inhuman sound from his throat as he arched his back from the bed and leaked steadily against his own stomach. A moment, just a moment of wishing I didn't have to suit up for the occasion and be closer to him than we ever had before.

But that kind of attitude had not borne good results for me in the past, and I slipped the condom on with practiced ease as he rid himself of his boxers and spread his feet wide, offering himself to me. In some ways, in these moments he seemed so innocent to me. Or maybe innocent was the wrong word. Vulnerable. He offered me everything: his body, his heart. And he trusted me to take care of them.

As I pushed into him, I kissed him hard, distracting him with two points of pleasure at opposite ends of his body. I wasn't really prepared for him to cross both his legs behind my lower back and his arms under my arms and around my shoulders, clinging to me while he pressed his face to my chest.

Again. So vulnerable.

So it was easy to treat him as precious cargo, moving with him like a delicate thing that I had the power to break. My own desire bubbled below the surface, only being set free in the noises I made in response to his.

"Tell me," he demanded.

"I love you," I said, forcing my voice to be strong. It wasn't just the words; it was the act of it, too. I wanted him to feel it right down to his bones.

I slowed down the movement of our bodies even further, now just a deep grind rather than the powerful thrusts that usually sent him over the edge. The soft sound he made could have been a sob or his voice catching as I found his prostate and stayed there, rocking against it over and over.

"Tell me again."

"I love you. Love you, Chris."

The second time it was definitely a sob, then a cry set free from a throat thick with emotion. I hadn't known that I had the power to do that to him, to strip him bare and, with just my words, make him orgasm.

I buried my face in the stretch where his neck met his shoulder and let go. There was no use in hiding anymore, not now that I'd given him pretty much everything that I was capable of giving to another person. There was no way I could let him go anymore.

"Love you too, Rob," he whispered as the last of the shudders wracked through my body, and even though I knew it, hearing it set something different off inside me.

It didn't feel right to pull away after what had just happened, and even though we'd both want nothing more than to fall asleep with me still inside him, neither physics nor biology were on our side.

Still, clothes were out of the question as we realigned our still-sticky bodies and I pulled his head to my chest. This wasn't the time to talk about it but to try and cling to the last wispy moments of what had passed between us as they disappeared through our fingers like smoke.

I slept then.

I RECEIVED a text from Chloe with the news.

It's a boy. Carter Michael Draco Robinson-Doyle xoxo Chlo

"Draco?" Chris asked. "As in Harry Potter's Draco?"

"I wouldn't put it past her," I muttered darkly. "Then again, her other daughter is Cassiopeia, so maybe she's going with the astrological bent."

"At least it's not Columbus," he said soothingly, patting my hand. "Cassiopeia?"

"Cassie, for short," I corrected. "She's three. And a little terror."

"What's her middle name?"

"I can't remember," I said honestly. "I'll ask Chloe, she'll know."

I sent off a text message, offering congratulations from us both and making the necessary enquiries.

"Cassiopeia Ariana," I said after a few minutes.

Chris shrugged. "I don't get it."

"Me either. Chloe was just Chloe Ellen. I have no idea what happened to Lu since Chlo was born, but something has clearly messed with her head."

"Did Lu not fight you on Chloe's name?" he asked.

"No," I said, thinking back. "We discussed it, and we both liked Chloe, but I think she understood that I wouldn't have any other kids, so she let me go with what I liked best."

"That was nice of her."

"Yeah. She's a good person."

We arranged to go and visit the new mother and baby a few days later, once they were home from the hospital. Chris said he hated hospitals, even if it was only a maternity ward. I had a suspicion it was precisely because it was a maternity ward.

"Do you want to come and meet Luisa?" I asked Chris.

"Why would I want to meet your ex?"

"Because she's one of my best friends," I said reasonably. "And she's Chloe's mother. And I need to go and see her new baby and I'm scared."

He laughed. "Really? But you've got a kid!"

"Newborns terrify me. They're so… breakable."

"Was it different with Chloe?"

"Mm. A little bit. I was terrified but in a completely different way. She forced me to be there when she gave birth, you know."

"What a bitch."

"Yeah. If I didn't know I was gay, I did after that experience." The memory still haunted me.

"So when will you be going to visit?" he asked, playing with a rip across the knee of his jeans.

"Hopefully on the weekend. She'll be out of hospital by then."

He was silent for a few more minutes, during which the cat stopped prowling and decided he was going to settle on Chris's lap. Flea had turned into my first line of defense for when Chris decided it was time to leave. Despite all his powers of resistance, a grey ball of fluff on his lap seemed to be all it took to get him to stay.

"Okay," he said eventually, once Flea had stopped pawing and turning circles and settled down. "I'll come with you."

Clearly I had an ulterior motive inasmuch as getting him to visit Lu would stop her from nagging me that she wanted to meet him. Apart from that, I really did need him as backup when it came to the baby.

I'd called ahead so she knew to expect me, and Mike had taken their now middle child out for the afternoon, leaving my daughter as the responsible adult in the house. She answered the door, scowled at me, smiled brightly at Chris, and skipped back up to her room.

"Lu!" I called out.

"In here!"

She was sitting in some kind of rocking and reclining chair with a bundle of blankets on her lap.

"Hi," I said, and she beamed at me. "Lu, this is Chris. Chris, this is… my once ex-girlfriend, current good friend, and mother of my daughter. Luisa."

"Hi, Chris," Lu gushed. "I've heard so much about you. Not from Robert, of course, but Chloe has plenty to say about you. Have a seat."

"I'm sure she does," I said darkly, taking the sofa next to Chris and hopefully providing a buffer between him and my over-inquisitive friend.

"Nice to meet you," he said, turning on the Southern charm and making my tummy flutter in response. "How's the baby?"

"Oh, he's good," she said, bouncing the bundle in her lap. "All seven pounds, ten ounces of him."

"That sounds like a lot," he said.

"Oh, Chloe was nearly nine pounds," she said breezily. "He was fine. Want to hold him?"

"Nope," I said quickly.

"Thanks," Chris said. "But I'll pass, if it's all the same to you."

Lu laughed and hoisted the baby up onto her shoulder, rubbing his back slowly and murmuring to him. I could remember having that connection to Chloe when she was still a baby. Comparing my memories of the tiny little person who'd commanded all of my time and love and attention to the grown-up person who commanded all of my money hurt, just a little bit.

I heard a shriek from the direction of the front door and Mike calling out that they were home. Then Cassie, white dress, blue tights, blonde ringlets Cassie, who looked like an angel but I knew better, came skidding around the corner into the living room.

"Mommy—" she started but stopped short when she caught sight of Chris.

Suddenly she turned on the coy, sweet charm and dug her toe into the floor, twisting the hem of her dress between dirty fingers. Luisa winced. I had to wonder why she'd thought putting Cassie in a white dress in the first place was a good idea.

"Cassie, did you want me?" Lu said gently.

"Who's he?" she asked in a stage whisper.

"Hi," Chris said, smiling at her widely. "My name is Chris. I'm Rob's friend."

"My friend," I clarified. Then, to Chris, "She knows me as Uncle Robert."

"Hello. My name is Cassie, and I'm three years old." She held up four fingers. Chris gently folded down the fourth, and Cassie blinked at him. "Do you want to come play with me?"

"Sure," Chris agreed. He winked at me as he took Cassie's hand, and she led him out to her playroom.

"How is she handling having the baby around?" I asked Lu, relaxing a bit more now.

"Not so good." Chloe had been eleven when her younger sister was born, so there wasn't much sibling rivalry. She had the good grace to be completely bored and disaffected by Cassie's arrival. Cassie, however, was used to being the little princess of the family.

"I guessed maybe as much."

"She'll get used to him soon enough. I'm not worried," Lu said, hoisting Carter up further onto her shoulder. "Tell me more about Chris."

"What do you want to know?" I said. "Talk to him yourself. He's actually very nice."

"I don't doubt it." She frowned. "He doesn't have a Mohawk, though. I'm disappointed."

"I made him brush his hair before we came out."

Lu smirked and tilted her cheek down onto Carter's head. "Are you happy, Robert?"

"With Chris? Yes, of course."

"He's much younger than you."

"I know that."

And I knew she was only being protective of me. There wasn't anyone *other* than her to be protective of me, and although that thought stung just a little bit, at least I had her. We made a very odd little family.

Carter started to fuss, and I took that as my cue to leave.

"Let me… go round up the troops," I said to her. Luisa was barely listening to me. That was okay, though.

I knew where Cassie's room was, but only in relation to Chloe's. Fortunately for me her bedroom door was open, and I stood slightly back from it as I watched her with Chris. They seemed to be conducting high tea around an impossibly tiny table and chair set, several stuffed animals making up the numbers.

"I'm sorry to interrupt," I said, approaching them at last. "But we need to go."

"No! I want Uncle Chris to stay!" Cassie cried.

"She started calling me Uncle Chris," Chris said. "It seems to have stuck."

I offered him a hand to pull him up from the little chair, and he smiled as he took it. Cassie looked at me as if I was the root of all evil for stealing her playmate.

"I'll bring him back to play again," I promised her.

Passing Chloe's door, I knocked on it lightly. "Going now, Chlo," I called out.

"Bye, Dad."

"That's what I've been reduced to," I said to Chris as we took the stairs back down to leave. "Hi Dad, Bye Dad."

He squeezed my hand. "Cassie is adorable."

"Oh no," I groaned dramatically. "She's snared you."

In the car on the way home, I held his hand and wondered if this was equal to me introducing him to my parents. Since he was unlikely to ever meet my mother or father, I decided it was, and that the afternoon had been an unparalleled success.

Clearly, we needed to celebrate with sex.

tied a towel around his neck to serve as a cape, and with the steam from the shower swirling behind him, I couldn't help but laugh. Christopher Jacob Ford the first and only certainly knew how to make an entrance.

"You're trouble," I said. "Thank you for the shirt."

He pressed his lips together to hide his grin. And gestured to his erection. "Actions speak louder than words, Rob."

He really did have an answer for everything.

Still, I didn't mind spending a few minutes on my knees, especially when it meant taking his warm, soft, blessedly clean cock down my throat. His skin was still warm and damp from the shower, and his knees gave way when he came.

"Your turn to get dressed," I said as he helped pull me to my feet.

"Ugh," he groaned. "No sleepy time?"

"No time for sleepy time," I said. "Gig, remember?"

"Don't want a gig," he said and wrapped his arms around my neck. "I want to stay here and let you fuck me."

"Later." I laughed.

"Promise?"

"If you're a good boy."

"Oh, Professor," he sighed. "That happens so rarely."

I FIELDED no less than six calls from Lexi as Chris took his time getting dressed and styling his hair. He was, according to the only female and official timekeeper of the group, the last person to turn up to the venue. But he looked hot, really hot, so as far as I was concerned, it was worth it. Lexi didn't seem to agree.

He wore what I'd first assumed were a pair of his biker's leather pants, but closer inspection (much closer inspection, particularly of his ass) revealed that they were far too tight to give him any protection on his motorbike.

Made of soft, worn leather, these were—in his words—the holy grail of leather pants. He didn't wear underwear with them.

"Why distract from the goods?"

And a black tank top.

"You're going to freeze."

"Then you better keep me warm, Professor."

Over the weeks my bathroom counter had amassed a rather impressive collection of Chris's personal grooming products, from three different types of hair stuff to shaving paraphernalia and cologne. I was somewhat surprised to find a black eyeliner pencil in amongst his things and dismissed it, assuming it had been stuffed into his bag by mistake when he was collecting things to bring over. It was probably Lexi's.

My assumption was incorrect.

While I was taking another of Lexi's calls, I found him leaning over the counter, peering into my mirror and smudging the black pencil along his lower lashes.

"Makeup?" I asked when I finished the call with a solemn promise that we were practically in the car. "Really?"

He shrugged. "It makes me look hot."

When he finally left the bathroom, I couldn't help but agree with his assessment. His now lined eyes made him look moody and edgy and, yes, hot. When added to his outfit, it put him over the line from hot into fucking gorgeous.

"Kiss me," he demanded. "It makes my lips all swollen too."

"I want them all to know you're mine," I said as I gripped his hips and attacked his mouth with tongue and teeth. "Mine."

It was childish, but I placed a little hickey behind his ear for good measure. Mine.

While the band warmed up with the sound tech, I was left alone at the bar. Not that I really minded. There were a few other people around, and I found an old paperback in the car, and a pair of reading glasses so I could see in the dim light, and ordered a bottle of beer.

As the evening slipped on, I became more engrossed in one of my favorite stories and didn't notice when Chris crept up behind me and slid his arms around my waist.

"Do you have any idea how hot you look?"

"Hmm? Do you want a drink?"

"I want you to fuck me. Right now. Over the bar. Don't take the glasses off."

I laughed and twisted in his arms, kissing him swiftly on the nose. "Is that behaving yourself, Christopher?"

"No," he said petulantly. "Vodka?"

"Straight?"

"Never."

I rolled my eyes.

"On the rocks," he clarified.

He threw the drink back, shuddered, and kissed me with liquor lips. When I finally drew my eyes away from his throat as he swallowed, I noticed that the bar had filled up considerably.

"Our set starts at ten," Chris said. "Do you want to hang out here or backstage with us?"

"I'm okay here," I said. "I expect I'll only be a distraction if I come back with you."

"The best kind," he said, but didn't push. "I'll come find you when we finish."

The atmosphere was electric as the first two bands played. I got the impression they were local and certainly got the crowd on their side. I started to think that maybe I should have accepted Chris's offer to go backstage with him. My naturally self-conscious nature kicked into gear, and I couldn't help but scan the crowd for signs of my students or worse—my colleagues.

But I seemed to be safe.

And then Chris came onto the stage, and I tuned out everyone around me. I'd wanted to stay in the same spot so he could easily find me, if he wanted to, and sure enough he scanned the crowd and smiled when he found me.

No one else would have noticed it. But I did.

They launched straight into a roaring number that caught the attention of the last few doubters and their applause, and mine, when it finished.

John angled his microphone and pushed his hair back from his face.

"Hi," he said with a smile. "We're Ice on the Tracks."

Chris thumped out the rhythm, and they started again.

Their strategy of playing a mixture of their own stuff and covers, from the inevitable Pink Floyd to Kings of Leon, Lady Gaga, and David Bowie, kept the crowd on its toes and willing to listen to their own music, which was good.

My boyfriend, though hidden at the back, drew attention to himself like bees to honey. After the first few numbers, he pulled his tank off and used it to wipe the sweat from his face, much to the approval of the female portion of the audience. He sang, too, which was a surprise to me. They had positioned his microphone up and away from the drums, so he tilted his head up and back slightly to sing into it. From that angle the hickey I'd left on his neck was visible to anyone wanting to look for it.

Good.

They caught a quick break, and the band grabbed bottles of water as John breathlessly introduced everyone.

"This is Lexi." Sparkling in gold sequins, cut so high on her thigh her black shorts underneath peeped out. Thigh-high leather boots. Red lips. Stunningly beautiful. If you were into that kind of thing, of course.

"Danny." Screams for the dark, brooding, attractive man who lifted a hand from his guitar in greeting.

"Chris...." Louder, more desperate screaming for the man in black leather, who played them right back by crashing his cymbals.

"And I'm John. Thanks for coming tonight."

Chris yelled something at him from around the mic. John nodded and lifted his guitar again.

"This one's for Rob," Chris said into the mic, grinning in my direction.

They played a rocked-out version of "Mrs. Robinson" by Simon and Garfunkel. The little shit.

For a climactic moment, if they even needed one, Lexi, John, and Danny put down their instruments mid-song. leaving Chris alone on the drums. Not that he stopped drumming....

The others left the stage, Danny jumping right into the crowd, John hopping off more gracefully and lifting his arms for Lexi to drop into a dizzying spin to the floor. Chris added his voice to the rhythms, slow, sexy phrases designed to elicit exactly the kind of reaction he got, and the others walked to the bar, toward me.

This was clearly a well-rehearsed part of their set as the barman immediately pushed three short glasses of clear liquor toward them, which they toasted and slammed back before taking to a run through the crowd to get back to the stage.

Seamlessly, they picked up the beat and finished the song.

I felt like I'd had an experience. And I was hard. Not halfway there, the state of semi-arousal that Chris's mere presence seemed to cause, but real, button-fly-straining erection that pointed right to what it wanted. Which would be Chris's naked, sweaty, hard-muscled chest.

I had no idea what would happen when we got home. Bad things. Very bad things.

They finished the set, and after an encore, a DJ took over and tried to keep the party atmosphere going.

True to his promise, as soon as they were done on stage, Chris pocketed his drumsticks and made his way through the packed club toward me. He was stopped every few minutes to exchange a few words of conversation or an offered hand to shake, kiss a girl on the cheek, and flirt outrageously with everyone he came in contact with. He still hadn't put his shirt back on; it had been tucked into another pocket and trailed behind him limply.

He clearly had a reputation to uphold as something of a rebel and a terrible flirt, and I didn't mind that part so much. It was more like… he was flaunting it in front of me, this carefree troublemaker persona that he wore with such ease.

"You were great," I said as he finally sidled up to the bar.

"Thanks," he said with an easy grin. The bartender let him skip the line and poured him two shots of vodka. The first he threw back, the second he held on to.

I curled my hand around his hip possessively, and he gave me a look that clearly said he knew what I was doing. I didn't care. Mine.

A breathy, busty, blonde girl flitted over to us and gave Chris a pouty smile.

"Could I get your autograph?" she asked, batting her false eyelashes. She looked ridiculous.

"Sure."

She presented him with a red marker.

"Oh…." False fingernails flew to her painted mouth. "I don't have any paper."

Chris raised his eyebrow, tucked his tongue into his cheek, and obligingly signed her breasts with a flourish.

"Do you want another drink?" I asked him as he handed back the marker.

"Nah, I'm good for a minute."

The groupies were still lingering.

"Introduce us, Chris," the girl with his name on her breasts said, clutching at his arm. "Is this your dad?"

He pulled a variety of faces as he tried to hold in his laughter, ending with his lips pressed tightly together. In my head I repeated one mantra: *I must not hit girls, I must not hit girls, I must not hit girls.*

"No," Chris said eventually. "This is my… friend, Rob."

"Nice to meet you," she simpered and gave me a look that clearly said, *Fuck off.*

"Excuse us," he said, grabbed my arm, and dragged me into the crowd of people. When we were a safe distance away, he caught my eye and burst into laughter.

"Don't," I said in my scariest teacher voice. "Don't you fucking dare."

"I wouldn't dream of it. *Daddy*."

"I thought you were being good tonight," I said, pulling him close. "Are you being a good boy, Christopher?"

"I'm trying so very, very hard."

"Not hard enough," I said, playing the game now. "Do you know what happens to boys who can't behave themselves?"

"Oh, I hope I do," he said, his voice right next to my ear now so I could hear his husky tone.

"Want to stay awhile?"

"Fuck no."

"Then let's get out of here."

Our escape was somewhat hampered by Chris's insistence that we stop in the parking lot to make out. He made what I decided was a very valid point—that since he didn't have a jacket, or even a shirt on, he should share my coat. It made walking slightly difficult. Hence all the kissing.

When we arrived home, there was a moment when we silently discussed with a look whether the game would continue. The look on his face begged for it.

"You acted like an outrageous flirt tonight," I started, giving him an opening if he wanted it.

"Yes," he said. Averted his eyes to the floor.

"I don't like you touching girls," I continued. None of this was part of the game. It was all completely true—and he knew it.

"I'm sorry." His words were barely more than a whisper.

"And making me feel like an old man did not help your case."

"I don't think you're an old man."

"Good. But that's not enough. I warned you what would happen if you couldn't behave yourself."

The quickening of his breath was all the indication I needed that he was desperately aroused. Chris's eyes were locked with mine as he unbuttoned, then slowly drew his pants down, stepping out of them and casting them aside. Standing in front of me, gloriously naked, he cast his eyes down submissively.

The sight of him like that was all I needed—if any confirmation was required—that I was not interested in having a passive, submissive man as my lover. I grabbed his chin and dragged it to my kiss.

"Over my knee," I instructed.

I was still clothed and he naked; this only added to that delicious spike of naughtiness.

I rubbed a cool palm over his ass, warming the area slightly before letting a stinging slap grace one cheek.

"Fuck," Chris hissed.

"Now, now," I admonished. "I don't expect such language from you, young man."

I slapped Chris's ass again, letting the heat spread and rubbing the area before spanking again. And again. Chris's moans intensified as I turned up the pressure and delivered three hard slaps in quick succession, appreciating the way a pink tinge spread across his pretty, round ass.

"Please," Chris begged incoherently.

"Please what?" I asked, punctuating my question with another thump. "Please spank me harder, Daddy?"

"Please spank me harder, Daddy," he begged, and I had to fight back my orgasm, which was threatening to break free from those words combined with the friction of my cock rubbing against Chris's hot body.

"Stand up and turn around, Chris. Hands on the bed. Spread your legs a little bit. I want a nice view for what I'm about to do to you."

Chris quickly followed my instructions. It was incredible how turned on he was just by being punished. I, too, wasn't quite sure if it had more to do with my being in complete control over the situation or if it was simply the sexual tension in the room, which almost seemed to coat every surface with our desires. Either way, I knew Chris would do anything I asked of him.

Once Chris was in place, I took a few moments to appreciate the manly work of art presented before me. No one had ever turned me on as effortlessly as Chris was able to do just by standing there in submission.

"Close your eyes, baby," I said in a breathy whisper directly into Chris's ear. Quietly, I undid my pants and let them pool around my ankles, making my cock spring free without the confines of underwear to hold it in place. I grabbed myself and slowly stroked from base to tip, twisting my wrist just slightly near the end to get the friction I so badly wanted, but I knew I couldn't finish yet. After a couple of minutes of pleasuring myself, I gently started to rub my dick on the backsides of Chris's thighs and ass cheeks. Chris moaned in appreciation and muttered a quiet "Fuck."

"No talking, boy. I'm not done punishing you yet."

So slowly that it was torture for the both of us, I moved my cock up from his right thigh toward where he wanted to be buried deep enough to make us both cry out in ecstasy. I pushed forward just enough that Chris could feel the pressure but never close enough to penetrate like I so desired to do.

Chris was going wild with want. He couldn't help but scream out a strangled "God, Rob, just put it in already." It was exactly the reaction I'd been hoping for. Smirking, I quickly pulled my cock back and came down hard with my hand to the left side of his backside. Pleased by the loud whimper that came forth from his mouth, I started rubbing the tender flesh as I had only a few minutes earlier.

"Tell me what you want, Chris, and I might give it to you," I stated with a calm voice that belied the pent-up tension my body was feeling without the release I desperately wanted.

"You, Rob, I want you in me… now!" Chris was almost pleading by this point.

"Need to be more specific than that, baby. Turn around and get on your knees. You know what to do."

With a frustrated groan, Chris fell to his knees before me.

Chris dipped his head slightly and peeked up at me through the hair that fell in his eyes. Giving a wink, he let his tongue come out to taste the precome that had gathered at the tip of my dick. He swirled his tongue around the head before slowly engulfing the entire thing as far as his mouth would allow. He was quite proud of his ability to deep-throat me like no other had ever been able to do before. Just as the tip reached the back of this throat, he swallowed, allowing it to go that much deeper.

Pulling back just a little bit, he lightly scraped his teeth close to the base, making me fist my hand in his hair to pull him back only to thrust myself into his eager mouth once again. It was a tango we both knew well by now—a give and take we were well practiced in.

Reaching up, Chris cupped my ass and started massaging it to the rhythm he set with the back-and-forth sucking motion he'd adopted on my cock. He could tell when his man was close: I would start to lightly chew the corner of my lip. He ran his left hand up the back of my thigh and gently caressed just behind my scrotum while his right hand was busy furiously pumping his own dick.

"Chris…," I warned, and he hummed, in pleasure or agreement, neither of us was sure.

I came first, shooting hard into Chris's mouth and moaning in a deep, gravelly tone the entire time. True to form, the hand flying over his cock caused him to follow only moments later, swallowing my come as his own sprayed over the pale skin of his stomach.

Firstly making sure he'd licked off any remaining spunk, Chris sat back on his heels to look up at me from under sex-heady eyes, basking in the glow of being able to turn me on in that way. I leaned down and gently ran my fingers through his blond hair affectionately, my heart still pounding from the ferocity of my release.

He grabbed his shirt and wiped off his stomach, then climbed wearily up onto the bed, still naked, but he probably guessed I wouldn't mind. I pulled on a pair of boxers, then slid into the other side of the bed and pulled my boy in close.

"Jesus, Chris, I can feel how hot your ass is."

"Yeah, it is," Chris mumbled sleepily.

"No." I laughed softly. "I meant your skin is hot. Did I hurt you, baby?"

"I'm okay," he said. "It feels nice. All zingy. Gimme a kiss."

I obliged by laying my lips down on my lover's shoulder. "You know I love you, right?"

"Love you too. Sleep with me."

CHAPTER
NINE

SATURDAY afternoons had become "our" time, a natural extension of Friday nights, which Chris had claimed as well. My routine, once such a well-worn thing that I barely had to think about it, or even acknowledge its existence, warmed and flexed around him until he was completely incorporated into it. I taught him the pleasures of breakfast tea. One week he made me a "proper" American breakfast with eggs and bacon and blueberry pancakes. The next week it was my turn, and I made him a traditional Scottish fry-up.

The following week, we argued over whose was the best. Then agreed to disagree, and made toast. Toast was one of the few things we could readily agree on—he still grouched about the tea.

Saturday afternoons held less structure. We never showered until after breakfast, usually together, which most often led to some rather intimate groping-type activities. Since Chris tried to work as much as possible on the weekends, whether that was a gig with his band or freelancing, our Saturday nights together were slightly more limited.

Sundays, however, meant different things to the both of us. I had to go over my lectures for the week and make sure all of my notes were together so I could maintain my reputation as one of the best lecturers the university had to offer. Things like that were important to me.

Sometimes, though, I managed to get all of my shit together so that we had time to spend together on a Sunday afternoon as well. When the stars aligned like that, I'd text him, since he never seemed to want to answer his phone when I called, and figure out a time to pick him up.

Chris was waiting on the front steps of the house when I pulled up and beeped at him. Unsurprisingly, he was texting someone on his phone.

"Everything okay?" I asked him as he bounced over to the car and leaned in for a kiss.

"Yeah. Mm. You taste good. Do we have plans?"

"I don't think so," I said. "Why, do you have something you need to do?"

"Well, I've just been talking to Chloe. Apparently she's finished all her homework for the weekend and is bored out of her fucking mind."

"There are too many things wrong with that statement for me for to even begin to process," I muttered, pulling away from the curb but heading out toward Luisa's anyway. "How do you have Chloe's phone number? Why are you texting her? Why on earth does she voluntarily want to spend the afternoon with me when she doesn't have to?"

"She gave me her number the last time we saw her," Chris said reasonably, winding down the window and turning up the stereo. I could never understand why he seemed to want to both freeze and deafen himself while he traveled. And me in the process. "She asks me sometimes how you are, what we're doing, that kind of stuff. She wanted to come to a gig, but I said you probably wouldn't be down with that."

I cast my mind back to the breast-signing incident.

"I am certainly not."

His tongue was lodged firmly in his cheek as he responded. "But I guessed going out for ice cream was probably okay."

"The only ice cream place around here is in the mall."

"Well, fancy that," he said, mocking me, his voice dripping with pure innocence.

"Fine." I sighed. "What time is she expecting us?"

"Whenever," he said with a casual shrug.

I managed to catch up with him about what had happened during both our weeks, the time alone something that was surprisingly welcome, even if it was in a cold, noisy car. When we got to the house, I parked on Lu's drive and blocked her in, because I could, and just caught sight of my daughter in her upstairs bedroom before she disappeared out of sight. The thought that maybe she was waiting for us, looking forward to spending time with Chris and I, was fairly alien to me. I'd spent too long thinking she hated me. Or resented me for leaving her and her mother alone at such a young age.

I knocked on the door but didn't bother waiting for an answer, just letting myself in since I wasn't sure if Lu and the baby were napping or if Chloe would bother answering the door. The house was full of activity, the TV blaring and a baby screaming from somewhere out the back. As I called out, a small purple ball of sparkly material threw itself down the hallway, screaming, "Uncle Chris!" and threw herself at my partner's legs.

"Hey, Pumpkin Pie," he said, catching her deftly and swinging her up onto his hip. "Don't you look like the prettiest little thing I've ever seen?"

Cassie beamed at him. Simply beamed.

"Do you intend to charm any and all females and children in my life?" I asked him as Lu stuck her head out of the kitchen door.

"Come in, come in," she called. "Cassie, leave Chris alone and go play nicely."

Pouting, Cassie turned to Chris for confirmation that she had to go. He shook his head at her and winked. Of course, since Chris spoiled her, she naturally loved him, and when I turned back to the pair, Cassie had a red lollypop in her mouth and an innocent expression on her face set to rival Chris's.

"It's sugar-free," he whispered to me, as if that mattered or I cared.

I rolled my eyes at him.

"Chloe!" I yelled up the stairs.

"Coming, Dad, chillax," she told me in a bored voice as she sauntered down the stairs. "Mom's breastfeeding. I wouldn't go back there if I were you."

Both Chris and I cringed, and she smirked before pushing through the swinging door into the kitchen. When Lu came out—both breasts covered, thank God—she looked more than slightly harassed.

"Thanks for coming by," she said. "You wouldn't mind stopping by the grocery store for me on your way back, would you?"

"Not at all," I told her. "What do you need?"

She dug a folded piece of paper out of the pocket of her jeans and handed it to me. "Thank you, darling, you're a star. Couldn't do it without you."

"Yeah, yeah," I said. "You ready, Chlo?"

"Yup."

"I wanna go with Uncle Chris," Cassie whined, her big eyes filling with tears as she wound a lock of hair around her finger.

"Not today, sweetie," Lu said, reaching to take her daughter from Chris's arms.

"No!" Cassie shrieked.

I sensed both a storm and a tantrum brewing and looked to Chris for guidance.

He beat me to it. "Do you mind if we bring Cassie, Chlo?" he asked.

She shrugged. "If you've got a suicide wish, it's not my place to stop you tying the rope."

"Be nice to your sister," I said, although the words came out just as bored as hers.

"Come on Cassie-Bean," Chris said, bouncing the toddler. "Find some shoes and you can come with us."

As Cassie ran up the stairs (the kid only seemed to have one speed), Lu leaned up on her tiptoes and took my face in her hands.

"You're more than a star," she said, overdoing the gratitude just a little bit. "You're an angel. You're a god. You're a god of gods."

"Don't thank me. Chris is the one who gets to look after her."

We managed to bungle Cassie's car seat into the back of my car and expressed very, very strong opposition to taking Carter with us as well, then escaped before Lu could pawn off any other children on us.

"Are we going for ice cream?" Chloe asked as she helped Cassie tie the laces of her bright pink Converse sneakers.

There was a sick sort of gratification in knowing that I was going to load two thirds of Lu's kids with sugar before I returned them to her.

"That was the plan," Chris said brightly.

"The only ice cream place around here is at the mall," Chloe said.

Chris snorted with laughter. "So I'd heard," he said, taking my hand over the gear stick and lacing our fingers together.

Fortunately, there was a parking space right next to the main entrance to the mall, so I didn't have to drive around in circles for ages looking for one. As soon as she was released from her car seat, Cassie attached herself to Chris and started talking a mile a minute about school and ballet and something from the TV.

I hung back a little bit and let them lead the way, and Chloe fell into step next to me.

"I didn't know you and Chris had exchanged numbers," I said lightly.

She shrugged. "Do you have a problem with it?"

"No."

"Then why mention it?"

I sighed, feeling like I was almost at the point where attempting conversation with my teenage daughter was something best avoided until she turned twenty-one. Then she flicked her eyes at me and looked so bloody vulnerable in that moment that I forgave her.

It also made me realize that maybe she needed someone like Chris in her life. He wasn't a parent or a parental figure, and he was old enough to have experienced the big wide world and young enough to know what a fucking horrible experience growing up could be. He was gay, so he knew about going through difficult shit, and had tattoos, which made him cool and relatable.

"I don't mind," I said as we passed what I was sure was the second Gap since we'd entered the building.

It was completely out of character for me to reach for her hand and take it in mine. I hadn't held her hand while we were out since she was about eight. But she let me, and didn't complain when I brushed my thumb reassuringly across the soft skin between knuckles and wrist.

Of course, the moment was quickly broken when Cassie spotted the bright pink sign for the ice cream parlor, escaped Chris's control, and sprinted off toward it, forcing the rest of us to chase after her before she fell over or got abducted.

I got the impression that Luisa wanted her back.

Chris snagged the last booth for us, and Chloe made her sister sit on the inside to reduce her escape routes. I sat opposite the girls and risked leaning my arm along the back of the booth so that if Chris leaned back, it would be around his shoulders.

When a waitress came over, Chris immediately asked for crayons for Cassie, and my heart stuttered in my chest for him. He didn't want children, and thank God, because neither did I, but if he could have this sort of relationship with Cassie and Chloe, and maybe his brother's children as well it wouldn't be such a huge waste.

"Shh," Chris said, squeezing my knee. "I can practically hear you thinking."

"I'll tell you later," I said.

He nodded and turned back to his menu card. "What are you having, Cassie-Bean?"

"Strawberry," she said with authority, selecting a blue crayon to color a gnome's hair.

"Chloe? Before you say anything, I'll tell you right now that if you try and order frozen yoghurt because you're 'watching your weight', I'm going to get them to pour so much chocolate syrup on it that you'll actually be sick."

She smirked before answering him. "Mint choc chip sundae, please."

"Good girl," he said with enthusiasm. "Rob?"

"Chocolate and caramel sounds good."

"It is," Chloe said, surprising me by offering something to the conversation unprompted.

"That's settled, then," I said happily. "What about you?"

"Oh, I don't know," Chris said airily. "I don't think I'm in the mood for ice cream today."

"What?" Cassie cried and slapped both her hands down on the table. "You have to have ice cream, Uncle Chris, it's the law!"

He laughed and leaned into my side. "Okay. If it's the law, then I'll just eat your strawberry sundae, then, yes?"

"No," she countered, sounding scandalized.

"But strawberry sounds so good."

"Then have one of your own." For a three-year-old, she was a surprisingly bossy, eloquent little madam.

"That sounds like a fantastic idea," Chris said. Then, to the waitress who had just appeared, "Two strawberry sundaes, one mint choc chip, and one chocolate and caramel." His voice dropped to a stage whisper. "Extra sprinkles on the strawberry ones, please."

The waitress, an older lady with chin-length grey hair and a red hairband threaded through it, nodded and winked, joining the conspiracy, and collected our menu cards before leaving. I was quite happy to let Chris take charge of this particular excursion; he seemed to be able to easily juggle the attentions of all three people at the table with his limitless enthusiasm and energy, the sweet, childlike side of him shining through.

When our orders were delivered, I couldn't help but laugh at the huge swirl of whipped cream on top of Chris's dessert, covered in brightly colored sprinkles and a shiny red cherry. Cassie's eyes looked just about ready to pop out of her head.

"Looks good," Chloe said with a little smile in my direction. "Thanks."

After the ice cream, we walked off some of the calories, letting the girls drag us from one store to another but buying very little. Chloe needed new sneakers for the cheerleading squad tryouts and let me buy them for her as a good luck charm. Cassie got a new tiara to match her dress.

"We have spent far too long doing girly things today," Chris said as we loaded up the car to drop the girls back home.

"I've probably got a couple of ideas for some boys-only activities later on, if you like?" I returned, keeping my voice low. It served the dual purpose of making sure the girls didn't hear me and being something akin to my bedroom voice.

Chris smirked.

"I'm sure we can think of something, Professor," he said with his tongue lodged firmly in his cheek.

"You," I said, opening his door and giving him a light smack on the ass as he climbed in, "are trouble."

CHAPTER TEN

I WAS mid-lecture when a phone beeped; I scowled and let it disrupt the flow of what I was saying to make a point, but didn't comment at the time. It was only when it beeped with a reminder that I realized that the noise was coming from my own briefcase and not from my rather un-enraptured audience.

Since ignoring these things and pretending they didn't happen is always the best policy, I continued on until the end of my lecture and physically crossed my fingers that it wouldn't go off again.

It seemed to work, although I still didn't dare to check the message until after the last of my students had filed out.

What are you doing on the weekend?

Despite the embarrassment, I smiled and sent him a quick message back. It wasn't my weekend with Chloe so I was pretty much free. We made tentative plans for Saturday afternoon, which would undoubtedly spill over into Saturday night if I knew Chris well enough, so I ended up staying until nearly midnight on Friday to get all my work completed.

The arrival of my weekend was bright but bitterly cold, and I wished that there was a warm body next to me to wake up with. I thought about giving him a call and offering to take him out to breakfast, then thought better of it, then caved and sent him a text. I was trying so hard not to appear needy and/or desperate, but the man evoked both emotions so frequently I was afraid I was nothing but.

When he arrived to pick me up with a spare motorcycle helmet, I knew that this was the moment I had been dreading.

"Do you feel like being naughty?" he asked with a gleam in his eye.

"No," I told him firmly. He only laughed.

"Come on, Rob. Live a little."

I changed into jeans and a beat-up leather jacket to give me the minimum amount of protection if Chris managed to crash the bike. He wasn't too impressed when I expressed my concerns.

"I've been riding since I was fifteen," he said. "I've only ever crashed once, and then it wasn't my fault."

I gave him a dubious look.

"Honestly," he said. "I'll tell you later, after you've survived."

"Thanks," I told him. "You know how to just fill me with confidence."

Still, I got a peck on the lips before he showed me how to adjust the helmet to fit me. It belonged to John, who had either a larger head than me or a lot more hair. I suspected the latter.

There was no point in asking him where he was taking me—he wouldn't tell me, even if I begged. But it would be an understatement to say I was surprised at pulling up outside a tattoo parlor. Tattoo studio. Whatever they call them now.

"Really?" I asked him.

Chris nodded. "I just want someone to hold my hand," he said innocently, blinking his big blue eyes at me.

And how was I supposed to resist that?

The studio had a peculiar smell of ink and antiseptic that assaulted my olfactory senses the moment we stepped through the door. That and the buzzing of what sounded like a swarm of angry bumblebees and the presence of a pink-haired, highly pierced young lady made me feel like an old, old man.

"Chris Ford," Chris said to the young lady, who I took to be a receptionist. Of sorts. "I'm booked in with Payne."

"Pain?" I said faintly.

He laughed and spelled it to me. The receptionist snapped her gum at us. It was the same color as her hair.

"Take a seat. She'll be out in a minute."

"Payne is a woman?" I whispered as we took a seat on a wide black leather couch.

"She's the best in the area," he said. "I'm going to get my chest piece started."

My opinions toward tattoos were changing the more I got to know Chris; his told a story, that of his life, his family and friends, the experiences that had shaped him. That wasn't to say I wouldn't hit the roof if my own daughter came to me with one, because I'd absolutely never forgive her if she did. But on Chris, they were nice.

Payne seemed, at first, to be a thoroughly sensible young lady, unlike her gum-snapping receptionist. Her rich dark hair was braided down her back, and she wore soft makeup, long socks, brogues, and a blue and white dress. It was only when she removed her thick knitted cardigan that I realized both arms were covered in ink from shoulder to wrist.

I tried not to stare as she led us back to her station, a long, black leather-covered table and a tiny, fingertip-sized pot of black ink.

"Is that all you need?" I asked, imagining pots of the stuff would be needed to cover Chris's chest.

"Yeah," she said with a small smile. "I'll only do the outline today. The color will come later."

It took a while for her to finish setting up, to get the stencil aligned over the curves of muscle and bone that shaped Chris's skin. I allowed myself to be pleased with the fact that she opened a new needle in front of us and threaded it through her machine and snapped on a pair of black latex gloves before asking Chris if he was ready.

"No," I answered for him.

Chris just laughed. "Go ahead," he said.

There was a black plastic chair next to the table, and I took my seat there and reached for his hand as the buzzing started.

"Does it hurt?" I blurted after a few minutes.

"It's not so bad," he said. "Not the worst. Not yet, anyway."

"My chest piece was pretty rough," Payne said. "But I'm a girl. And our anatomy in that particular area is obviously different."

"Why do you have them?" I asked. "You're so pretty."

She glanced at me with a small frown. "I get that a lot," she said carefully. "People think that girls can't be attractive if they have tattoos. Or that they'd be more attractive if they didn't. Do you think Chris would look better without his?"

"No," I said. "I like them."

"But it's different on a girl?"

I was forced to reassess my views on modern femininity pretty damn quickly. "I have a teenage daughter," I said after a moment's hesitation. "I'm using that as an excuse right now."

Payne smiled then, just a little bit. "I don't blame you," she said. "It's a standard view that women with tattoos are still on the fringes of our society. It's almost like we're still in the 1930s, with the tattooed lady being the freak show at the circus."

"I don't think you're a freak show," I said quickly.

"Good."

"Is your name really Payne?"

She laughed then, lifting her needle from Chris's skin and throwing her head back. "Yes. Elizabeth Payne."

"You don't look like an Elizabeth."

"I know. For this job, going by my surname works rather well for me."

Our conversation drifted to other areas as Payne worked on the heart and crown and wings and fire that would eventually make up the bold design that stretched outward from his sternum to the tips of his shoulders.

"How long have you two been together?" she asked after a while. I looked at Chris and smiled.

"About a month."

"Is that all? You act like you've been together forever."

"We're pretty tight," Chris said. I liked that. I knew the modern connotations of the phrase, but to me, it always brought to mind keeping him close. Holding him tightly.

"Would you ever get a tattoo, Rob?" Payne asked. "One for your daughter, maybe."

"No," I said quickly. "My mother would kill me."

"How old are you?"

"Too old," I said, at the same time Chris answered, "Thirty-two."

"Ancient," I added. "And far too old to worry about what she thinks. But the fact remains that she would kill me."

"Just a little one," Payne said slyly. "What's your daughter's name?"

"Chloe," I said. "And still no."

"Rob was telling me once about living in Edinburgh when he was a kid," Chris said and winced when Payne hit a sore spot. "His house was next to a church that was covered in gargoyles. I thought that would make a great upper arm piece."

"Black and grey," Payne said immediately. "Something that wraps around the bicep a little bit. Sort of coming out of the skin."

"Exactly," Chris agreed.

"It sounds wonderful," I added. "But you're not doing it."

Chris squeezed my hand. "I thought you said you weren't going to be a grumpy old man anymore?"

"When did I say that?" I demanded. "I like being a grumpy old man. It suits me."

"You need to be young and cool to keep hold of your young and cool boyfriend," Payne said, teasing me. She yelled out into the shop for someone called Chad. Another highly pierced young person appeared, dressed head to toe in black.

"What's my next appointment?" she asked.

"You don't have one," he said with a grunt. "You wanted to finish early today."

"Can't think why," she said breezily. "Would you mind doing some research for me? Gargoyles on churches. Scottish, if you can find them, but that doesn't matter too much. Don't bother with anything that looks too much like, you know, 'fantasy'."

"Look," I started in my most reasonable voice. "I really appreciate you taking the time to think about this, but I really don't want a tattoo."

"Of course you don't," she said in the same reasonable tone. "I'm nearly done with Chris."

After a few more minutes, she wiped over his chest with more antiseptic wipe. It looked red and angry, the black lines raised on sore, swollen skin, little dots of blood still welling from the needle. He took a look at it in the mirror and smiled, then let her wrap the skin with plastic wrap and tape.

"Have a seat," Payne said to me. "And take your shirt off."

Chris was re-dressing in his plaid shirt and smirking at me. I shot him a panicked look, and he took long strides over, catching my chin in his fingers and kissing me hard.

I took my shirt off.

Chad arrived with several printed pictures of the external stonework of churches, and Payne handed them to me silently to look through as she packed up and cleared away from her session with Chris.

"This one," I said, handing him a picture.

"Looks like the painting in your apartment," he agreed.

When she was done, Payne studied the image for a few minutes and nodded. "I can work with this."

I was terrified to the point of raised heartbeat and sweaty palms but fortunately still had control over the most base of bodily functions. She rooted around in a drawer for a moment, then produced a bunch of Sharpies on a key ring.

"Marker pen," she said, selecting an orange one. "All I'm gonna do is draw it on you."

"You're going to freehand it?" Chris asked, sounding impressed.

"Yeah. It's easier than trying to make a stencil work."

I hated her for putting me through the entire ordeal, but let the girl manipulate my arm this way and that as she sketched the orange ink onto my skin.

Chris held my hand, same way I did for him when it was the needle on his skin. I startled when she reached for a red marker, and Chris assured me she was just adding the detail.

When she was done—it took about twenty minutes—she nodded to herself and then to me.

"Go take a look."

I felt silly, going to look at a drawing on my skin while others around me were making it permanent.

And it was fairly perfect.

Despite the fact that it was drawn in orange and red ink, the gargoyle snarled and sneered out from my skin, its neck arching and jaws wide. I could see the marks she'd done to guide the shading, and my head filled in the details, making it look like stone.

"Can you do it?" I asked. "I wouldn't want to disturb your afternoon."

"It would be my pleasure," she said with a disturbing Cheshire Cat grin. "I always love to pop an ink cherry."

The feelings of nausea only increased as I watched her unwrap a fresh needle and set up the station again. This time it was for me. Chris had replaced his shirt but left it unbuttoned over his chest; he grabbed my hand and ran his thumb back and forth over it reassuringly.

"Just relax," he said.

"It's going to hurt," I said grimly.

"Probably."

"That's not so reassuring. Why am I doing this?"

"Peer pressure," Payne offered. "To fight your fear. Rebellion." She paused and tilted her head to the side. "Delayed rebellion in your case, maybe. Because it's cool. To impress your young, cool boyfriend."

"All of the above?" I offered.

"Excellent," she said. "Let's get started."

To be fair, it didn't hurt as much as I had expected. Chris and Payne kept up a seemingly unending stream of chatter, asking about my job, my daughter, Scotland and my heritage…. There were points when I winced, or the low, constant pain turned into more of a burn, but I couldn't quite face looking at the needle, and after a while my arm ached more from holding the uncomfortable position than from the actual tattoo itself.

"If you ever tell Chloe about this…," I said to Chris.

"Won't," he promised.

"Or Luisa. Or my mother."

"Are you going to introduce me to your mother?"

"No," I told him. "She's the most conservative, uptight, WI woman you will ever meet."

"What's WI?"

"The Women's Institute. Google it, you heathen."

Laughing, he leaned over and kissed me lightly. "It's nearly done," he whispered.

"Yeah?"

"Yeah."

"Thank fuck for that," I whispered.

Payne heard me and laughed, pulling her machine away from my skin for a moment.

"I'm just going to do a few more highlights, then we're good," she said. "Thanks for letting me do this. It's been fun."

"For you, maybe," I said darkly.

The pain was starting to set in now, feeling like the worst sunburn of my life with sharp edges around the throb. Each time I dared to glance down at my arm, it was smeared with a combination of ink and red, red blood.

"It looks a funny color at the moment," she was saying, and I forced myself to concentrate. "And it will until the swelling goes down. Chris knows how to take care of it properly, but I'm going to tell you as well."

She proceeded to give me a list of instructions on how to best care for my tattoo, to not wear anything too close to my skin for the next couple of days to let it heal and to keep applying lotion. And most importantly—to not pick at the scabs.

"Scabs?" I repeated faintly.

"Yeah, Rob, scabs," Chris said, sounding amused. "They won't last long, but if you pick them off, you'll be left with holes in the tat."

"That's disgusting," I muttered.

"Right," Payne said, interrupting our bickering. "Done. Do you want to take a look?"

"No," I said. "Frankly, I'm terrified."

Payne smirked as she wiped the last of the blood away with a cloth soaked in alcohol; it stung but soothed my abused skin at the same time.

Chris took my good arm and tugged me to my feet, lacing his fingers with mine as he led me over to a large mirror mounted on the wall.

I didn't have time to feel self-conscious about my semi-naked state. It was beautiful. Behind the welling drops of blood, the gargoyle clearly looked like it was carved from stone, crouching, its face following the lines of my arm so much so that it looked like it was designed to go there. Which, of course, it was.

"It's amazing," I said as Chris ran a comforting hand down my back.

"It really is," he agreed. "I almost feel jealous that it's not on me."

I tore my eyes away from the mirror long enough to look at him. "It wouldn't fit on you," I said, my throat somehow making my words sound hoarse.

Chris shook his head. "No. But it's beautiful on you."

He tried to pay for it as Chad wrapped dressing around my arm, claiming it was a gift, but I wouldn't let him. Still, Payne charged me what I was sure was a lot less than her standard rate for the work she'd done on the condition that I'd go back to her when it was healed so she could take a photo and pin it to her wall.

That night the sting had gone out of it, but the ache remained, and I was convinced this had more to do with the awkward angles I had been forced to hold than with the tattoo itself. It was a little thrill to think I had a tattoo. It was so, so far beyond anything that I had ever considered myself doing. Prior to this my greatest act of rebellion had been Chloe, and even that hadn't been calculated.

I let Chris order pizza for dinner even though it was far from my favorite thing to eat. He seemed to live off the stuff, and I preferred to cook for myself. Even so, it was Saturday night and we were both coming down from an adrenaline high, and I wanted to snuggle with him on the sofa.

Not that I'd use the word snuggle in his presence. He'd never forgive me for it.

But Chris was probably the snuggliest person I'd ever met.

He probably appeased me by ordering a pizza that was loaded with vegetables rather than meat and cheese. I was trying to educate him on the value of wine over beer, and he accepted the compromise of a nice bottle of red since I'd let him choose the content of our meal.

We ate sitting on the floor leaning back against the sofa, the pizza box on the coffee table between us. There was an old James Bond movie showing on the TV, which seemed like the perfect thing to not really watch while I spent as much time surreptitiously watching the man my world was slowly starting to revolve around.

After my two slices to Chris's six, we curled up on the sofa. It never failed to surprise and secretly thrill me how neatly this man seemed to fit to the contours of my body. He wasn't shorter than me by much, a couple of inches at the most, and his body was more slender because he went to the gym and kept fit and I didn't. We were almost equals, yet he was the one who liked to be held.

Around two thirds of the way through the film, we gave up on discussing our favorite Bond and put an equal amount of enthusiasm and energy into kissing the living daylights out of each other. I liked the way he never submitted quietly to me. If I wanted him on his back, I had to put him there. If I wanted his hands to slow down, I had to pin them to the armrest. If I wanted him to stop bloody squirming, I had to press my hips into his—although that didn't work as well as I'd hoped it would.

When I rocked my hardness against his, he grabbed my arm, a natural move but one that made me hiss in pain.

"Shit, shit, sorry," he said as he pulled back. "Sorry. Are you okay?"

"Yeah, I'm fine," I told him. "Honestly, baby. I'm okay."

He smiled at me with a slow, easy smile that liquefied my spine. "Good," he whispered.

Climbing off the sofa, I extended a hand to him and helped to pull him to his feet. Flea immediately relocated himself to the warm spot we'd just vacated, and I rolled my eyes at him while I locked up the front door, then hesitated.

"You're staying tonight, right?" I asked.

Chris nodded. I held his hand as we wandered back through to my bedroom.

He didn't stay every night of the week but often enough that I felt almost confident that he'd want to sleep next to me. Mostly because him staying the night meant we'd have sex, and Chris liked sex. A lot. But also because I got the feeling he was starting to actually like sleeping in my arms.

"We should take a shower," he said. "Clean off the ink before we go to bed. I'll put some lotion on for you as well."

"Do you want to share?" I asked as my fingers started unbuttoning his shirt, revealing his new ink.

The slight tilt of his head was one that I recognized. It meant *Kiss me, now*. He was such a little slut.

"You're such a little slut," I whispered.

"Mm. Your little slut."

My eyes were transfixed by his, a connection between us that didn't want to be broken. It had taken such a short amount of time for him to become so much more than just my boyfriend. He leaned in and pressed a soft, soft kiss against my lips and reached for my hand, bringing it up so my fingertips pressed against his body, over his heart.

I was sure I was hurting him as he pushed my hand further into the red skin with black lines. I pulled away harshly, from both his kiss and his touch.

"Hey," I said softly. "That has to hurt."

His eyes flickered down to where my fingers had left little round marks, and back up to my face. He shrugged. I stripped the last of my clothes, careful not to snag my new tattoo, and, with his hands in mine, walked backward to my bathroom.

It was imperative that the water wasn't too hot, but when it was just right, I dragged him in under the gently falling spray. Even so, I winced when the water washed over my newly sensitive skin.

Chris let the water pool in his hands and used soft touches to clean my arm of the dried blood and ink that Payne hadn't caught in her cleanup earlier in the afternoon. Following his example, I splayed my fingers over his chest.

"It's really perfect for you, you know," I said, looking at the finer details in the thin black lines.

"You think so?"

"Yes," I said, smiling. "Because it has passion and fire and freedom and energy."

"And love. Don't forget the love."

"You're incredible," I said.

Chris leaned back into my touch as I pushed shampoo through his hair, roughly, as he liked it. As I expected, my actions caused his cock to stir and grow against my thigh, lengthening and filling until he was hard. Despite his reaction, we were both too tired to do much more than lazy kissing as we finished showering and dried off.

I let Chris slick the cool lotion over my tattoo, irrationally pleased at how much it helped ease the residual sting. After he'd done the same to his own tattoo, we both dressed in T-shirts to protect the ink and climbed into bed.

Weeks of sleeping naked next to each other made the layers of cotton between us more of a barrier than I was used to. Still, I curled up around him and carefully laid my arm across his stomach.

"I can't believe I got a tattoo today," I said against his shoulder.

Chris laughed. "Me either. It's hot, Rob. You're badass."

"I'm far from that."

"Rob?"

"Yeah?"

"All of this… being with you… sometimes I think it all comes down to those three scary little words," he said softly.

"Dad, I'm pregnant?"

He laughed and dropped his head back against my shoulder. "I love you."

It wasn't the first time he'd said it. Or the last. But I felt it, right down to my bones, I felt it.

"I love you too."

CHAPTER
ELEVEN

WEDNESDAY was my day of back-to-back lectures in the morning, thankfully all in the same room because with barely half an hour between each one, moving from one side of the campus to another would be practically impossible.

After my last class had filed out, I allowed myself just a moment of putting my head in my hands and groaning before starting to load up my bag with all my papers.

"Professor McKinnon?"

"I'm sorry, my office hours are printed on my door," I said with a touch of irritation. "I don't have time…."

Since my interrupter hadn't re-interrupted me, I looked up.

Chris was leaning against the doorframe with his arms crossed over his chest. He was wearing a dark blue cashmere sweater and jeans, his leather jacket layered over the top and a striped scarf I recognized from my own closet around his neck.

"Git," I muttered under my breath, shaking my head as I finished putting my things away and swung my bag over my shoulder. "What are you doing here?"

"I missed you," he said simply. "So I thought I'd come and find you and let you buy me lunch."

"I meant, what are you doing here," I said, taking his hand as I reached him and pulling his body to mine. "The campus is huge. How did you find me?"

"Bribed a girl at the office," he said, raising his eyebrow as he wrapped his arms around my neck. "You're a popular man, Professor McKinnon."

"And you're a persuasive one, Mr. Ford."

"Are you going to kiss me now?" he asked, his blue eyes wide and blinking.

"I might," I said softly and leaned in to brush my mouth across his.

The campus was fairly busy as we made our way toward the cafeteria, and Chris stayed close to me although refrained from holding my hand. I couldn't quite decide if I was relieved or disappointed by that.

We both chose hot soup to take away in little covered cartons and a sandwich to share. And coffee and chips and cake because I was dining with Chris, after all, and he could eat an incredible amount and never seemed to put on any weight.

"Do you want to stay here or go back to my office?" I asked him. "It's not far from here."

"I want to see your office," he said.

"It's not that impressive," I warned him as we walked back.

"I know, but you won't let me poke around in your office in your apartment, which has provoked my natural curiosity."

"Natural curiosity my arse," I said with a snort. "You want to look at porn on my computer."

"That too," he conceded.

Unlocking my office, I took a moment to be grateful that the usual piles of paperwork that covered my space had diminished in recent weeks. It was a nice feeling, smug, almost, to be on top of my game.

"Nice," Chris said with a low whistle as he turned a full circle in my office. "Posh."

I rolled my eyes and shut the door behind us.

"I usually go for 'sophisticated' or 'charming'," I corrected him.

"It's that too. Can I have the big chair?" He meant my office chair, the one that spun around in circles. "I've always wanted to have a go on one of these."

"Knock yourself out," I said and set the paper bags of food out on my desk. "Don't make yourself sick, though."

"I won't. Daddy."

"Don't start," I warned him, but his sunny smile made my chastisement fizzle out to nothing.

I opened all the containers of food and took the chair traditionally offered to guests and students. It felt odd, sitting in the wrong seat.

"Tell me about your ex," he said with a delicious sort of glee as he pulled a pot of soup toward himself.

In a fit of what could only be described as post-coital lack of memory function, the previous weekend we'd confessed to each other the number of lovers we'd both had. Chris called it his "magic number." It was significantly higher than my own, but I'd prepared myself for that possibility.

"Oh, don't," I groaned and dropped my face to my hands. This only made him laugh around his spoonful of soup and reach for his half of the sandwich.

"Go on."

"You would have hated him," I said. "He was just so—and this is coming from me, mind you—he was just so dull."

"I don't think you're dull," Chris said.

"I do. Brett was very conservative and an upstanding citizen. He was a teacher too—we met at a conference one year."

"And?"

"And after six months of serious, intellectual, culturally enlightening dates, we decided to cohabit. Which lasted for about two years. Shit." The memory of the man just made me angry now, for some unfathomable reason. "We hardly ever had sex."

"Hold up," Chris interrupted. "That's one of the top perks of being gay. All the dirty, horny man sex."

"I know," I said. And I did know. "It just never happened between us. We'd give each other hand jobs or blow jobs sometimes, but I suppose he bottomed once every couple of months."

"And he never topped you?"

"No," I said. "Never. I didn't want that, so I told him I was saving myself for my wedding night." Chris snorted in appreciation of that. "You have to understand, Brett was the sort of man who aspired to being part of the only gay couple in the suburban neighborhood. He wanted to be the token minority, where he and his—and I quote—life partner would be invited to dinner parties with the Joneses and exchange tips on how to make the perfect soufflé."

"You're right," Chris said, deadpan. "I hate him."

I laughed. "Good."

"So why did you break up?"

"I never loved him," I said with a small shrug. "He was convenient, a warm body to sleep next to, I suppose. We both made good incomes and had a nice life together. There was just no spark. Barely any intimacy. And I didn't want more children and he did."

"Ah," Chris said knowingly.

"Ah?" I repeated.

"I know you think you don't have a good relationship with Chloe, but she clearly means the world to you."

"She's my daughter," I said, feeling slightly awkward. "Do you want kids?"

"I don't think so," he said. "To be honest I haven't given the idea a whole lot of thought. I like children. My brother has a couple, and they're great. But to have kids means you give up on the whole young and free lifestyle, and I like that. I like my independence, and I'm so totally not ready for that yet."

"How do you feel about Chloe?" I said. It was a question that had been burning in the back of my mind for weeks now, but I'd yet to pluck up the courage to ask.

"She's cool," he said in the most offhand, nonchalant voice I'd ever heard. And I worked with college students.

"She's my teenage daughter," I told him, exasperated. "She's anything but cool."

He smiled. "I think Chloe is more like you than either of you realize. She's clearly a smart kid but sassy with it, and I know you don't think you're a great dad, but she clearly worships you."

"I didn't ask that," I mumbled.

"Like hell you didn't. If I'm going to be a total bastard, and I might as well since we're on the topic, I think you could make more of an effort with her. You're closer to her age than most of her friend's parents, and I know you don't like to think of yourself as a father figure, but you're actually quite young and cool. For a dad. Plus, you have a super-hot boyfriend, and what with the number of actually cool people who are out and proud at the moment, I think the gay angle is one you should work."

It was one of the longest monologues I'd ever heard from him, and I wanted to figure out a way of both slapping him and kissing him at the same time. In the end I laughed and shook my head.

"Bloody hell."

"And fuck me if your accent isn't the sexiest thing in the world. Wanna fuck?"

"In my office?" I asked.

His eyes darkened. "Oh, hell yeah. I'm up for that."

"You're always up," I said, pleased to be able to turn his words back around on him. I finished the last mouthful of my soup and pushed the carton away. "And however much I'd love to bend you over and fuck you senseless on my desk, I have seminars this afternoon."

"Oh, really?" he whined. "Come on, Robbie, where's your sense of adventure?"

"Rob I put up with because it's you," I said. "But Robbie is out of the question."

He stood and walked around the desk to sit across my lap, purposefully wiggling his ass as he did so but wrapping himself up in my arms in a manner that could only be described as sweet. I rubbed my nose against his, teasing for as long as I could before pressing our lips together.

His mouth still tasted of spicy tomato soup as I flicked my tongue against his, searching for the taste of him underneath. My hands edged up under the hem of his sweater to gently stroke at his hot skin, knowing how he was so sensitive there on his sides.

It wasn't a surprise to discover that I liked kissing him. What did surprise me, however, was the sheer amount of time I seemed to spend doing it. Whereas with the ill-fated ex-boyfriend there were casual pecks on the cheek in greeting or goodbye, and the longer, slower kisses that defined our dull lovemaking, Chris wanted to kiss me all the time. Proper, deep kisses, and he didn't give a damn who saw us.

But I laughed when a knock at my door had him springing up from my lap as if he'd been burned.

"Come in," I called, standing too to start clearing away the remains of our lunch.

A colleague, Annette, stuck her head around the door.

"Oh, sorry, Robert. I didn't know you had company."

"Don't worry," I said. "What can I do for you?"

She launched into an exasperated complaint about the photocopier in the History department being broken and her card not authorizing copies on any other machines, not even in the library because of some official mess-up in the authorities department, and just as I started to figure out her point, she asked to borrow my photocopy card.

"I promise I'll let you use mine when everything's up and working again," she finished in a rush.

"Sure, no problem," I said. "Chris, would you pass me my bag?"

"I didn't realize you were with a student," she said guiltily. Then her eyes narrowed at the lunch bag on my desk.

"Chris isn't a student," I said calmly. "He's my partner."

"Oh," she squeaked. "Nice to meet you."

"Likewise," he said drily, and I had to press my lips together to hide my smile.

Annette scuttled off, my precious card clutched tightly in her hands and the air of someone who knew something gossipy hanging around her like a mystic fog.

"Are you out here?" Chris demanded as I shut the door behind her.

"Sort of," I said. His expression was fairly murderous. "Some people know, others don't. I'm not too bothered, really."

"You introduced me to her as your partner," he said, stepping closer to me again.

"Well, you are," I said and took hold of his hips. "I'm far too old for a boyfriend. And the word sounds too… flighty for my liking."

"I'm not flighty?" He wrapped his arms around my neck.

"No," I said emphatically. "In fact you're the exact opposite of flighty."

"What's that?"

"Permanent," I said as I touched my lips to his. "Absolutely permanent."

As much as I might have liked staying in my office all afternoon, firmly locking the door and having sex with my partner, my partner over and over again, I had a seminar to host. Chris was due in rehearsals for the orchestra later in the day, which explained why he was dressed more conservatively than normal.

I walked him back to where he'd parked the bike and just about refrained from kissing him, instead letting him go with the promise that I'd text him before I went to bed. He was likely to go out to a bar for a drink when he was done with rehearsal, and I was okay with that. When I was with Brett, we kept tabs on one another's every movement, almost without thinking about it. It was something that we'd developed over time, and after a while it struck me as faintly ridiculous that I couldn't even meet up with my friends without telling him beforehand where I was going and what time he could expect me home.

There was certainly a freedom with Chris that I hadn't had in previous relationships, and it struck me that experience would dictate that I was more cautious because of it. But despite all the facts that, on paper, suggested that I shouldn't trust him, I did.

THE flat was a mess.

There was no use in denying it any longer. In my moments of being wrapped up in my new boyfriend and all of the distractions that came with him, I'd completely ignored any kind of housekeeping. Dirty dishes piled up in the sink. I hadn't vacuumed in days… maybe a week. Or more. My supply of clean clothes had dwindled down to almost nothing.

I had to clean.

Years of living on my own had made me self-sufficient enough to be able to do all the basic household chores needed to keep me alive. I could cook and wash and clean, although they were far from my favorite activities on a bright but cold Saturday morning in November.

It was different from organizing things, which was one of the few things that could calm me once I had riled myself up into a foul mood, usually over my job. Organizing things meant finding an order where there was disorder and making it aesthetically pleasing at the same. Whether it was the Dewey decimal system or alphabetizing my CD collection, order was good.

Mess, however, had no effect whatsoever on order.

I started with laundry, since I could get that going while I tackled things like scrubbing the bathroom, which definitely had not been done in weeks. There was a fair amount in the laundry basket and plenty more scattered around my bedroom. It was only when I was separating colors and whites and darks that I noticed that there was considerably more underwear around than there should be.

And I definitely did not own a bright red jockstrap.

As I worked through the pile that I'd amassed, I became more and more amused, partially because I was doing Chris's laundry for him, and by the fact that by my finding it all on the floor, Chris must have been leaving the flat either wearing my underwear or none at all.

It wasn't much of a task to separate out what was his from what was mine. A pair of tiger-striped boxers with RAWR printed across the back? Definitely his. Black Calvins? Mine. Animal from the Muppets? His. Bright yellow with the words "It Isn't Gonna Suck Itself" on the side? Oh yes. His.

I considered clearing out drawer space for him, but I wasn't sure if we were at that stage in our relationship yet. Instead I neatly folded a considerable pile of clean clothes that inexplicably contained T-shirts and a pair of sweatpants too and left them on the chair in my bedroom.

When cleaning the bathroom, I found a bright pink toothbrush living next to my blue one. It shouldn't have come as a surprise since I'd watched Chris brush his teeth many a morning. And I joined him most nights as we brushed side by side, taking it in turns to spit into the white porcelain.

His phone charger was plugged in next to the bed. On the nightstand was a nearly empty bottle of Boy Butter H2O and one sad, lonely little condom in the bottom of a 24 Jumbo pack.

A closer survey of the contents of my fridge revealed two different types of beer that I didn't drink, strawberry-flavored milk, a jar of face cream, and *Out* magazine. In the cupboard over the fridge, there was a tub of marshmallow fluff, half a box of Pop-Tarts, and a jar of beef jerky. None of these things had been purchased by me.

I spent about three seconds freaking out, then laughed.

Chris was probably the most unsubtle person I had ever encountered, so it was fairly understandable that it would come as a surprise that he'd practically moved in with me without my noticing. Pink toothbrush and all.

IT HAD been a long, rainy, grey day, which was bad enough, but I'd left my umbrella at home, which meant every time I walked from one part of the campus to another, I got soaking wet. Another downpour had started just as I left my office, and I drove home with condensation fogging up the inside of my car.

The presence of Chris's motorbike outside the flat was surprising, and I wondered where the hell he was, since the rain was still hammering down and the bike didn't exactly provide much protection from the elements.

"Honey, I'm home," I called as I let myself in.

He had clearly found a way in somehow, and I questioned my home's security as he called out from the kitchen.

"I'd think you'd broken in," I said as I shrugged off my wet jacket, "if it weren't for the smell in here."

"I cooked," Chris said, appearing in the doorway wearing an apron with an image of a naked man on it and brandishing a spatula.

I gave him a light kiss on the lips. "I guessed that. Why? How did you get in?"

"Because I wanted to. And with your spare key."

"How did you know I had a spare key?"

"Rob. Seriously. It was in a drawer with a tag on it that says 'spare key'."

I laughed and gave him another kiss. "Okay. You're clearly a stealthy super-spy with hidden and untapped talents."

"I am," he said and preened at the compliment.

"So what did you cook for me?"

He led me through to the kitchen, where the steam and smells converged into a wonderful mess. "Moroccan lamb casserole and couscous and grilled vegetables with halloumi cheese."

"Wow," I said. "It sounds fantastic. I didn't know you had such skills in the kitchen."

"I like cooking," he said as he stirred a large pot of what I assumed was the stew. "I don't get to do it very often because it's rare that we live somewhere with a decent kitchen. But your place is pretty stacked, so…."

"I appreciate it," I said honestly. "I had one hell of a shitty day."

Chris reached up and tucked a strand of still-damp hair behind my ear. "Do you want to go and get changed? This will be ready soon."

I nodded and caught him by the hips, drawing his warmth close to me and tilting my face against his temple.

"Or we could just fuck in your kitchen?" he whispered. "I don't think we've done it in here yet."

For some reason this just made me hold him tighter.

"Hey. Rob. Are you all right?" My nod seemed to appease him, and he gave me a squeeze. I brushed my lips over his cheek once more and headed for my bathroom to get a decent hot shower before I got too cold from my still-wet clothing. I wasn't sure why his little act of defiance, breaking into my home to make me dinner, had affected me so much. No one had really ever done it for me before, not the stealth, not the doing something purely to make me happy.

I dried my hair absently with a towel and dressed in sweatpants and a T-shirt. With the heat on and the added warmth from the oven, it was warm enough for me not to have to worry about socks; I liked the feel of bare floorboards under my feet, even in the winter.

The apron was gone when I rejoined him in the kitchen, and I spent a moment mourning its loss.

"We should probably have wine with this, right?" he said.

"If you want," I said. "I've got a few bottles. Or there's beer and soda in the fridge."

"It's a school night," he said, smirking.

"Cheeky." I grabbed his belt loops and used them to pull him close to me again. He took the opportunity to sneak a kiss.

"Mm. You smell all lovely and clean."

I kissed his nose. "Wine?"

"Yeah. White with this, I think."

I checked the wine rack in the fridge and found a good New Zealand chardonnay. "Will this work?"

He glanced over and nodded at the label. "Looks good."

While he served up the food, I found a corkscrew and poured the wine into the large bowled glasses I preferred. Chris had set the table too, something he never seemed to do of his own volition.

"Is this in honor of some anniversary that I've forgotten?" I asked as he passed me a plate.

"No," he said. "Would you just sit down and enjoy your dinner? I am capable of doing things for you too, you know."

"I know," I said, wounded at his wounded tone. "I really do appreciate it. Thank you."

"It's okay," he said. "You do a lot for me, you know that? Letting me stay here all the time and everything."

I took a forkful of couscous and hummed in pleasure. "This is really good. And you can stay here whenever you want. I like having you here."

"I'm used to having lots of people around all the time and a serious lack of personal space. Your place is like a little sanctuary, you know? I don't have to listen to John and Lex bickering or Danny playing music full blast. Even when I was at home, there's always my sisters running around and my mom yelling."

"Sounds like a lot of activity."

"Yeah. It was. Is. Plus, you always have food here."

I laughed. "Yeah. That's true."

The meal was good. Better than I had expected and teaching me the lesson that underestimating Chris in any capacity was only something that would make me look foolish. He was younger than me, yes, but he wasn't young.

"The stew should traditionally be made with goat," Chris explained after I asked him to tell me more about where he learned to cook. "But they didn't sell goat at Walmart."

"No," I said seriously. "Goat is certainly difficult to come by at the larger supermarket chains."

"But lamb works fine," he conceded. "I saw it being made on TV one day so I went online and stole their recipe."

"I'm glad you did. It's delicious."

Since he'd managed to use nearly every single one of my kitchen utensils while creating the delicious meal, and a fair few pots, pans, and baking sheets too, we split washing-up duty. I hated leaving a kitchen dirty; it only meant scrubbing everything harder in the morning.

"Are you staying?" I asked when we were done.

He nodded. "If that's okay."

"It's always okay."

I had work to do. Not a lot, just marking some short assignments, but there wasn't a rush for me to get it done so I conceded to a night on the sofa. Chris sat with his back in a corner and his feet in my lap, letting me massage his arches and appreciate how nice his feet really were. I hadn't had a good look at them before. His toes weren't too long, and they were only a little bit hairy. Good feet.

"Is everything okay at the house?" I asked. From his tone earlier, I'd guessed that maybe there were tensions between his housemates.

"Yeah," he sighed. "Just, usual shit, you know?"

"Not really," I admitted. "The only people I've ever lived with other than my family were Lu and Chloe."

"Oh." He fiddled with the remote for a few minutes. "We've been on the road together for ages now. When we left, John and Lex could barely admit that they were attracted to each other, and now they're fucking like rabbits. And Danny is cool, you know. But he's really, really into the music and the art of it. He was bugging me about being here all the time because when I'm here, I'm not immediately available to the rest of them for impromptu band practice."

"Does that happen a lot?"

"I don't know. I suppose so. We jam a lot. I never thought of it as official band practice before; we were just having fun and making music. But now he's making out that it's something that we should all be committed to doing, and he's... fuck. He's leaching all the fun out of it."

"Are you saying you want to quit?" I asked. This sort of dramatic suggestion often worked with my students who really only wanted to have a bit of a whine and a moan. If they wanted out, I was opening the door for them. If they wanted to stay, it was enough of a shock to the system to make them realize that.

"No," he said slowly. "I don't want to quit. But… Rob, you know we're touring, right?" He was still refusing to look at me. "There was never any intention for us to stay here forever."

"I know," I said. "Are you leaving?"

"Not yet. But soon. Probably soon."

"Was that why you were arguing with Danny?"

"We weren't arguing. He's just getting restless here. He wants to go on to Chicago where the gigs will be bigger."

I nodded. "Let's not worry about it until the time comes," I said. It was clearly hurting him, this conflict of interests. "Come to bed?"

My cat was perched on my pillow and was wearing an air of *I'm not moving.* Chris snorted.

"Let him stay there." He blinked and yawned.

"Tired?" I asked.

"No."

I ignored him and undressed him like a child, having him lift his arms for me to take his T-shirt off and sliding his jeans to the floor. They practically hung off his ass anyway. I was yet to be let in on the secret of where gravity-defying denim was being manufactured and sold. Chris's jeans seemed to perch precariously on the edge of his ass.

When he flopped facedown on the bed, Flea gave him a look of utter loathing, then relocated himself onto the dip at the bottom of Chris's back. I joined them, lying on my side so I could better stroke the spot between Flea's eyes that made him go all squidgy for me and the spot under the swell of Chris's ass that elicited a similar reaction.

"Night, baby."

"Night."

CHAPTER
TWELVE

I WOKE to the undeniably lovely feeling of Chris snuggling into my side.

"What are you doing today?" he asked, his fingertips tangling and tugging the hairs below my belly button.

"Mm. Office hours this morning," I said, forcing my sleepy brain into action. "It's Wednesday, right?"

"Yeah. What does office hours actually mean?"

I ran my hand down his back and sighed. "It's when annoying students who have spent all semester out drinking come and beg for extra time on their assignments. Sometimes I get a genuine one looking for help or guidance, but that's pretty rare."

"What happens if you're not there?"

"I'm not bunking off," I said firmly.

"Not doing what? Is bunking off like getting off?"

"No." I laughed. "Although the two are sometimes related. Bunking off is like playing truant. It's slang from my youth, I'm sorry."

"Robert," he said, equally as seriously. "When was the last time you took a sick day?"

I thought back. "I can't remember," I admitted.

"Mhmm. Just as I thought."

Chris rolled over to his side of the bed and leaned off the edge, no doubt looking for the pile of clothes he'd left down there the night before. I considered slapping the bare ass that was wiggling in my face. Then gave in to temptation.

When he pulled himself back to sitting, he had his phone in hand, and with the other braced on my chest, he swung his leg over my waist to straddle my thighs.

"What's the number for reception at the college?"

"I'm not telling you," I said petulantly. He took my one good testicle in his hand and squeezed threateningly. I gave him the number.

"Good morning," he said pleasantly, smiling down at my naked and struggling form. "My name is Christopher Ford, and I'm Robert McKinnon's partner. His partner," he repeated. "His husband, for all intents and purposes? Yes. I'm afraid Professor McKinnon is unwell this morning. I think it must be some kind of bug. He has office hours today, so could you post some sort of note on his door?"

I opened my mouth to protest, and his hand squeezed my scrotum. I shut it again.

"I should imagine he'll be back tomorrow, yes. Thank you for your help."

He tossed his phone back on the floor and adopted a rather smug expression.

"Proud of yourself, are you?" I asked. "I have an excellent attendance record, and you've just—"

"Blah blah," he interrupted. I wasn't really mad, anyway. "Blah."

He reached over once more, pulled his lube from the nightstand, and helped himself to a generous amount. I watched, slack-jawed, as he reached behind and prepared himself, his eyes fluttering closed with the touch and a soft sigh escaping from his lips.

For all the fuzzy thinking I was capable of, I couldn't think of one good reason not to take advantage of the situation that had presented itself. So when Chris tossed a condom on my chest, I opened it carefully and rolled the thin latex over my cock. When had it gotten hard? I thought back and decided it had probably been around the time Chris had used the word "husband."

He took a good grip of the base of my cock and angled it just right so he could sink down on my length. I'd lost count of how many times we'd had sex to this point; to my utter delight, the last number I'd forced myself to remember was fifty. And that was a good few weeks ago. The look on his face when he took me inside him would never become routine, though. It was beautiful.

I took hold of his hips as he wriggled, trying to find the best angle and his deepest spot. I knew the moment he found it because he threw his head back and gasped, then braced one hand on my chest and began to rock.

Chris generally didn't ride me like this, although neither of us had a problem with the position. I had a feeling it was something to do with him being a lazy bugger and preferring for me to take control while he lay back, spread his legs, and let me get him off.

After a few minutes, he started to bounce, the sticky head of his cock making contact with my stomach with a soft *thunk* before the momentum took it back up to repeat the action against Chris's stomach. The head of his cock always looked swollen during sex, red and angry and sore. So pretty.

He must have been horny before we even started because it didn't take long for a telltale red flush to start creeping over his neck and chest, a redness that echoed the color at the tip of his cock. My grip on his hips tightened, and I started lifting my own to meet each generous downward thrust that took me deep inside him.

"Gonna come," he said, and I barely had time to tell him "I know" before he took his cock in hand and spurted a generous amount of sticky white come all over my chest.

A combination of three things triggered my own release: his shiny pink lips open in a little, silent "oh"; his eyes screwed shut with the force of it, then opening, unfocused, to find my own; and the incredible clenching of the muscles in his ass as he orgasmed.

He leaned forward and brushed his sour morning-breath lips over mine, smiled, then squirmed with his belly pressed against mine to spread his rapidly cooling come between us.

"Eughh," I groaned. But held him close when he tried to pull away and I attempted to catch my breath. "What's the plan for the rest of the day? I suspect I'm going to need your guidance on how to do this properly."

"Well, there are rules," Chris said, propping himself up on my chest. He winced and disposed of the condom, then came back to me. His come was now nearly gluing us together by the short and curlies.

"Shower," I said firmly. "Tell me the rules in the shower."

"Number one," Chris said once we had relocated under the hot spray. "You're not allowed to get dressed all day. You have to wear pajamas."

"What if I get cold?" I complained.

"That brings me nicely to rule two," he said. He took another handful of soap and applied it to my ass in an overly enthusiastic manner.

"You're just groping it now."

"I know. Rule number two: we drag your duvet out onto the sofa so we don't get cold."

"Can't we just wear sweatshirts?"

A very slippery finger insinuated its way between my bum cheeks and pressed lightly against my hole.

"Behave," Chris warned. "Rule number three. We are not going to leave the house all day. There will be lots of tea because you make the best tea in the world. And there will be takeout for at least one meal."

"Is that all?"

"No. We shall have sex. Lots and lots of sex."

I smiled and leaned down to capture his lips with mine. "I think, with a lot of guidance from the expert, I might be able to manage it."

"Good," Chris said. "Want a blow job?"

I DECLINED that first offer, and Chris conceded that rule number one could be bent just a little bit because it was, in his words, "bloody freezing." Not surprising, really, since we were edging further into

November, but the outcome was long-sleeved T-shirts and a pair each of my fluffier socks.

After making tea in my only, beautiful teapot and finding proper teacups and saucers to drink it from, I loaded up a tray with the tea-making paraphernalia and some proper Scottish shortbread and joined Chris under the duvet that he'd brought through to the sofa.

"I'm going to feel guilty about this all day, you know that, don't you?" I said.

"Don't worry," Chris said, accepting a cup of tea. "I'm an expert at this. By the end of the day, you'll be so orgasmed out that your hard-working little testicle will be begging for mercy."

"Watch it on the 'little'," I said.

"Your absolutely mammoth, goose-egg-sized testicle," he amended. And slurped his tea.

"Better."

Moment by moment, the guilt eased as I spent the morning curled up with a warm, happy, tea-slurping man in my arms. Chris hogged the remote and the cat and demanded kisses with startling regularity.

"Oprah?" I asked as he flipped the channel once again. "Must we?"

"We must," he said, mocking my accent. "Chat shows are definitely part of the sick-day rules."

"I have a feeling you're making this up as you go along," I said, poking my finger into his ribs to make him squirm.

"Never," he protested. "What are you making me for my lunch?"

By midafternoon I was bored to the point my eyes were starting to lose focus. Surely the television programming had not been so bloody terrible when I was a kid? Still, Chris seemed disproportionately happy with my small act of rebellion, and I'd managed to mentally atone for my absence by reasoning that I'd not missed a lecture or seminar, that it was only office hours, and that spending nearly an entire day wrapped up with Chris was something possibly heaven-sent, and who was I to argue with the powers that be?

Our conversation, unsurprisingly, moved to sex.

"Do you have any kinks?" Chris asked. He was lying between my legs with his back to my chest, running his fingers up and down my arms.

"I thought you did when I first met you," I said, neatly deflecting the question away from myself. Chris took the bait just like I knew he would.

"Really? What sort of kink?"

"An older man kink."

"That's not a kink," he protested. "Kinks are… you know. Kinky."

"You don't say," I said drily.

"They have to be naughty or it doesn't count. So what is it? Leather and bondage and whips?"

"No, thank you."

"Or… PVC? Lace panties? Corsets and fishnet stockings?"

I shook my head. "I'm not into cross-dressing."

"Hmm. Spanking?" He smirked at me, a wicked gleam in his eye.

I wriggled my hips. "I'm not opposed to doing it again, if I think you deserve it."

"Really?" he repeated, sounding delighted. "I think I'd like that."

"I'll keep it in mind. What about you?"

"You can spank me anytime you like." I rolled my eyes, not that he could see me, and poked him in the side. "Okay. Promise you won't think bad of me?"

"I promise," I said.

"I haven't done this before, before you start getting all upset," he started. "But I want someone to come inside me. Bareback."

"Without a condom."

"Yeah. Then I can… fuck. Feel it sliding out again." The last few words were whispered.

"Deviant," I said and kissed the shell of his ear.

"Yeah. You're not disgusted with me?"

"No," I said, realizing as I did that it was the truth. "It's not whips and chains, so I reckon I can just about handle it."

"Thanks."

"You know you have to be careful, though, right? That sort of thing is dangerous in a whole new way."

"I know," he said, somewhat defensively. "I'm not likely to go up to a random guy in a club and ask him to fuck me bare. It would be with someone I love."

"Maybe one day I could do that for you."

"I was hoping you'd say that," he said, tilting his head back and grinning.

I looked over at the clock, surprised to note how late in the day it had gotten without me paying attention to the time passing. He really was such a distraction.

"Am I allowed to check my e-mails?" I asked him. I was starting to feel a little more edgy about the fact that I hadn't logged on to a computer once yet today.

Chris sighed dramatically. "I suppose so. Can I come and poke around your office when you do?"

"Are you keeping tabs on me?"

"Nah. Just being nosy."

I had an old, large-screened Apple computer that sat on an antique Edwardian desk that was something of my pride and joy. Considering the amount of time I spent in my office working, which was a lot, I felt the purchase of nice equipment to go in it was justified. Even if that equipment—like its owner—was now a little out of date.

I kept half an eye on the screen and the other on Chris as he wandered around the small room, his fingertips trailing lightly over the spines of hardback books.

"You've just got so many," he said in a hushed voice.

"Books? Hmm. I'm an English teacher, Chris. It kind of comes with the territory."

There wasn't a guest chair in this office since no one ever came in here except me. Not one to stand on ceremony, Chris sat on the floor and leaned back against the wall, his restless hands now flitting over the wallpaper.

"What's your favorite?"

"Book?" I asked. "That's a tough question. What's your favorite piece of music?"

"Gershwin," he replied immediately. "To play, anyway. Or the score for *West Side Story* has a pretty cool rhythm section. To listen to… at the moment is a chick called Laura Marling, although I change my mind fairly regularly."

I logged on to my e-mail account and frowned as I waited for it to load.

"I suppose I have different books for different moods," I said as I scrolled through announcements, looking for any genuine correspondence. "I used to read Kipling to soothe me, but I haven't done that in a while now. I suppose that's the danger of studying and teaching it."

"I wish I had the patience to read," Chris said. "When I was a kid, I had that attention deficit thing."

"ADHD?" I could believe that.

"Yeah. I grew out of it. Mostly." He smirked. "They got me playing the drums when they realized I'm not dumb, I just learn in different ways."

"A good teacher can do that," I said. Concluded I had nothing to worry about, or at least no pressing issues, and began the laborious task of logging off and shutting down. "Do you absorb things well by listening?"

"Like in your lecture? Yeah, I suppose so. I remember quite a lot of it."

I was irrationally pleased at his confession. Standing, I crossed to him and offered a hand to pull him up, then kept hold of it while I searched for and quickly found an old volume of poetry.

"I learned swathes of Kipling by heart," I said to him as I led him back to the sofa. "It's really easy to do because of the rhythm. But it's always nice to hear something new."

We resumed our previous position with Chris sitting between my outstretched legs, and I unfolded the book on his chest. And started to read.

The last time he'd heard me recite anything was when he'd come to my lecture, and even though it was only a matter of weeks ago, we'd become so much more comfortable in each other's presence, to the point where I could read to him in my pajamas. Due to the lateness of both the season and the hour, the sun was starting to set, meaning I had to strain a little to see the words but was loath to turn on the lamp lest it interrupt the soft orange glow of the sunset through the window.

I stopped when it got so dark I couldn't see anymore and carefully set the book down on the sofa next to me. I was convinced by his steady, deep breathing that Chris had fallen asleep somewhere around *Gentlemen Rankers*. But he gave a sigh of content and dropped his head back to my shoulder when I finished and angled it to press a warm, wet kiss to the side of my jaw, just underneath my ear.

"You have the sexiest voice in the history of ever," he said in an emphatic whisper.

Those sorts of compliments no longer made me uncomfortable but sometimes still made me blush. I glanced over at the clock on the mantel once again, and the hot feeling changed to embarrassment as I noticed the late hour.

"Sorry," I murmured. "I didn't know how late it was."

"Don't apologize. I loved it. Can we have Chinese for dinner?"

I laughed softly and brought his lips back to mine. "Anything for you, my love."

I LET Chris call and put in the order since I didn't really have any preferences as to what we ate and he clearly did. While he was engrossed in a menu and choosing various dishes, I wandered around my little flat and threw a load of laundry in my washing machine. Then made black tea with lemon, which would go nicely with the Chinese food.

For some reason I felt the need to keep active. I had done almost completely nothing all day, and the lack of activity was making me lethargic.

"We haven't had nearly enough sex yet today," Chris complained.

As the day had worn on, I'd gotten used to the fact that he was wandering around half-naked. Sensing an opportunity to kill two birds with one stone, I let my eyes linger lasciviously on his bare chest. The sight of his chest was usually enough to turn me on, and as my gaze lingered, I found the spark that would turn everything up to just the right notch to be able to act on.

"Take your pants off," I said in a low, commanding voice. "Put your hands on the back of the sofa. And spread your legs."

He hastened to respond.

This position was clearly comfortable and probably fairly familiar to him as he dropped his head between his outstretched arms and arched his back, which thrust his ass up into the air. If there was one thing I'd learned about Chris, it was that he was incredibly aroused by anything stimulating his ass. This kind of play was what really turned him on.

I knelt down behind him, kicking off my own pants as I went. My thumbs skimmed over the soft, pale swell of his ass, and I leaned in to press a wet kiss, lick, and bite to the fleshiest part. He whimpered, which was just the reaction I'd been hoping for.

With one hand on each of his cheeks, I spread them wide to reveal his pink, puckered hole. His hips were rocking slightly, a clear invite for me to do more, go further, but I wanted it to be on my terms so I gently slapped his ass.

"No."

My tongue flickered lightly over his hole, so lightly I knew it would drive him insane. With the contact he groaned deeply and arched his back, thrusting his ass toward my face. I lapped at him, slowly at first but building a regular rhythm of long licks and soft flicks that caused a litany of curses and prayers to fall from his lips.

The beautiful, foul-mouthed little angel that he was.

"Bedroom," I said emphatically.

He didn't argue.

I stripped off with my usual abandon, now that I was so comfortable in his presence. Still, as usual Chris was more comfortable with his own nudity than I was. That was understandable, really; he was young and perfect and beautiful. The sort of man who goes to the gym three times a week. I would be surprised if I'd been in a gym three times in my entire life.

I pulled the curtains closed just in case any of my neighbors decided to investigate the goings-on of my bedroom. I wouldn't be surprised if they did—most of them were nosy buggers.

There was no way of disguising our obvious desire for each other, evident in straining, bobbing erections as Chris flopped dramatically onto the bed.

"Come on."

I went to him and attempted the same belly flop onto the bed. My effort didn't have quite the same level of disdain. Then Chris rolled on top of me, pinning me to the bed with hips and knees and the look in his eye that made me want to surrender to whatever he wanted from me.

"You want to bottom tonight?"

I balked at that. "Not really."

"Yeah, I know. See, the thing is, Rob, we can talk about this for weeks and give you plenty of time to work up a full head of steam worrying about it. Because I know you will. Or we can just do it now and get it over with."

"I'm not convinced those are our only two options," I said drily.

"I want you," he murmured and brushed his fingertips over my forehead. "I'll take care of you, I promise."

"I know you will."

"Will you let me?"

I had a choice in the matter, of course I did, but I also knew that Chris wouldn't push me too hard. He'd push for a while, but if I kept saying no, he would respect my decision and back off. I didn't want to be a hopeless case, and I did want—one day—to lose my virginity, so to speak. To bottom for someone. For someone who mattered.

There was just the matter of gaining the courage to do it.

And on consideration, if I was going to do it with anyone, I wanted it to be with him. I trusted my strange, impetuous man to take care of me, and that didn't make sense at all, but neither did most of my relationship with him so I was willing to just go with it.

"Um, Rob?" Chris said, playing with the tips of my hair. "You haven't said anything in quite a while."

"Sorry," I said and shook my head. "Yeah. Okay. Do it."

"It's not quite as simple as that," he said. His lips quirked up at the corners. "Are you sure?"

In response, I drew him down into one of the long, slow kisses that I was starting to feel defined our relationship. He made my spine feel weak. And like I was a dizzy, crazy teenager again, swept up with the wanting of someone that never seemed to abate.

"Please," I asked him.

"Okay. Rob. It's gonna be alright."

I believed him.

To start, he moved sensuously down my body, laying soft, loving kisses over my sensitive spots, searching out the places where I needed his reassurance. Then swallowed my cock into his throat in one ridiculously smooth, practiced move.

As he sucked me deep, his fingers brushed up and down the outsides of my thighs, giving me sweetness that fit so perfectly against the raw sexuality that seemed to flow from him. And when his fingers brushed over my hole, they were whisper soft and barely pushing at all.

"Chris, I have had things up my bum before," I told him with a smile tugging at the edges of my mouth.

"All right," he muttered and reached for the lube. "Thought you were a virgin, but fine…."

"I am," I said. "But I've touched myself there before."

His mouth fell open in a little "Oh." And he groaned. "That's hot."

I spread my legs for him, hoping that this might distract from my masturbatory experience, and his slick fingers soon appeared at my hole. Although I'd admitted to touching myself there before, I'd actually never really penetrated myself beyond one searching finger. It took a lot of faith for me to relax enough to accept his gentle stretching, even though I knew that he was doing it so I wouldn't get hurt.

One slick hand loosely worked my cock to keep me on the edge of pleasure, and he seemed to know just when to push me and when to ease back so I could find my comfort zone again. Every now and then, his fingers brushed against my prostate, and I'd never, ever had that kind of stimulation before. It was a little overwhelming and a lot pleasurable.

Even though I'd always flinched when someone touched my testicle, when Chris did it, it felt like he was doing it for all the right reasons. And I didn't mind his curiosity. After having not been touched there in that way for over a decade, it took a moment to adjust to.

I was taking big strides in learning to trust him with my body.

When I was ready, Chris curled up behind me in the position we often slept in, although I was usually the one holding him. With sure hands he gently rearranged my body, bringing my top leg up closer to my chest and making sure I was comfortable.

I wasn't scared, I was apprehensive. And barely aroused.

His warm, dry hand held my hip in place, his lips pressed against my shoulder, and he pushed inside me. My body arched back, and some sound was ripped from my throat; it wasn't pain, he'd spent too long preparing me for this to now cause me pain. Chris stopped moving long enough for my body to adjust, then pushed forward again.

Slowly. So, so slowly.

When he stopped, I wasn't sure if he was giving me a moment again or if this was it.

"You're inside me," I gasped.

"Yes," his voice said, warm breath tickling my shoulder.

"All the way?"

"All the way."

I could feel the tension radiating from his body, but he still kept his movements careful and gentle, little rocks of his hips until I was actively pushing back into his body. When I searched for his lips, they were right there, waiting to give me the reassurance I needed that I was doing okay.

I craved his body, and it came as a shock to me that this was no different. Even though it was him inside me instead of me inside him, those same feelings of *mine, now, I love you* were still right there on the surface.

That first time I came in more of a desperate sort of release than the sorts of orgasms I had when I was topping. Chris assured me that it would take a while for my body to relearn how this was a source of pleasure for me, so I trusted him.

The next time he fucked me, I was facedown on the bed and didn't get off at all. Being the sweet little thing he was, Chris sucked me afterward and decided that "from behind" was not going to be the best way for me to enjoy bottoming.

The third time, I lay on my back and looked up at him. He'd wanted me to ride him, as if the physical act of being on top might ease some of the issues he thought I was developing. I argued that I just wanted to be able to see him, to see his face and the person who was being so intimately close to me.

He wasn't quite as slow and slightly more assertive than he'd been before, demanding my kisses and delivering them back with bruising passion. I wrapped my fingers around his arms and hooked my ankles under the curve of his ass, waiting for the moment when I'd feel what he seemed to feel every time we were together.

He made sure my pleasure was at the forefront of this experience, whether it was his fingers in my hair or our kisses, or his hand stroking my cock in time with his deep, even thrusts. The sweet little whispers of his love, the question "Okay?" asked over and over, the concern and unrestrained love in his blue-grey eyes as he made love to me.

Then it happened. Not in the physical sense that I was expecting, though. Instead, what he'd been telling me about letting someone else have access to my body, letting someone I loved be inside me, suddenly made sense. I got it.

And with that thought, along with the amazing things his body was doing as it played mine, I had an orgasm so intense my come hit my chin. Chris laughed softly as he licked it off.

Then, after that, I didn't bottom again and our sex life returned to the normality that we'd created for ourselves:

"There?"

"Fuck."

"Tell me, Chris. There?"

"Yes! Fuck you, you beautiful bastard. Harder."

"Shit. God, you're tight."

"Yes. And you're huge."

"I prefer 'generously proportioned'."

"How can you—" *Gasp.* "—even think—" *Gasp.* "—of words that long—" *Gasp.* "—when you're fucking me?"

"That's why I went to college. To learn to multitask."

"Now? Please now…."

"Wait—I'm nearly there."

"Fuck, Rob, fuck fuck…."

"Yes."

"Yes!"

I was starting to get annoyed with come stains on my nice sheets, so I got used to the feel of various different fabrics wiping it off my body. Then finding my place in his arms again, long, slow, searching kisses, the kissing marathons we liked to take part in as we curled up together in bed or on the sofa or in the bathroom… or anywhere, really.

Or that one time in the kitchen. It felt like coming full circle, from the first, jerky hand job he'd given me with my back to the fridge, to me bending him over the kitchen table and damaging one of the legs beyond repair.

And the kisses after, when we were both sticky and the window was fogged up with condensation, the heat in the room now at odds with the freezing wind outside.

He broke away, laughing breathlessly. "I'm half-hard again."

"I'm going to need longer than that to recover," I said as my hand skimmed down his side. He grabbed a bottle of chocolate milk from the fridge and wandered, bare-ass naked, back toward the bedroom.

"Coming?" he asked over his shoulder with a hint of sass. I liked it.

Back in bed, it felt just right for our sweaty bodies to tangle together as we rode out the endorphin high. When Flea wandered in, I couldn't help but wonder if he'd been inside for the entire performance, and if he'd watched.

"Do you want to get married?" I asked Chris as Flea butted his head against Chris's elbow, demanding attention. "Because if you do, I'll find a ridiculously romantic place and time and ask you."

"No," he said but rolled onto his front, reclining half on my chest with his bare feet dangling off the end of the bed. "But tell me anyway where you'd take me."

I hummed and ran my fingers through his hair a few times. "I could take you back to Scotland," I said. "To Edinburgh."

"I'd like that," he agreed.

"There's plenty of romantic places there. I think I still hold dual citizenship. We could even get married there, in the registry office in the Old Town.

"Or Paris," I continued. "Because, you know, it's traditional. But you're not really that traditional."

"I'm not."

"Then maybe Hawaii. Or the Maldives, or Borneo."

"I could take you out somewhere and ask you under the stars," I said, and scratched my blunt fingernails through his hair. "I know it's cold at the moment, but the sky is pretty clear and you could keep me warm."

"I'm starting to regret saying no, now," he said softly. "You seem to be pretty good at all this romantic shit."

"I like romance," I said. "It's easy to tell someone you love them, and we've got the physical side of things down pretty good. But romance is showing someone how you feel for them, and it might be silly or not make much sense, but I think it's important."

"No one's ever done that for me before," he said. "I mean, fuck, Rob, you wake me up with kisses. I usually get a shove to the ribs and told that I need to get out."

I laughed and pulled him closer.

"One day," I said carefully, my fingertips dancing over his bare hip and the sensitive spot just below it, "not now, but at some point, would you wear a ring, if I bought you one?"

"A wedding ring?" He sounded dubious.

"No," I said, suddenly aware that I was not making my meaning clear. "Just a ring. You wouldn't have to wear it on your wedding-ring finger, you could wear it on your thumb if that's what you want. It would just be so I could look at it and know people could see something of mine on you."

"I think I'd like that," he said and pulled my mouth to his so we could exchange slow, searching kisses until my jaw ached and my face felt sticky with his spit.

"So," he said after an indeterminable amount of time. "Have I converted you? Will you bunk off with me all the time now?"

I could tell by the tone of his voice that "bunking off" was about to become a standard double entendre in his vocabulary. Instead of a proper answer, I mumbled something about him being a bad influence and rolled toward the shower.

CHAPTER THIRTEEN

WHEN it happened, I knew straightaway.

It didn't make any sense for me to know, but I did.

Dark had set in hours ago, and I'd finished all of the work I needed to do for the evening and had settled down on the sofa for a quiet couple of hours with a new book.

I heard his motorbike first of all. The sound of the engine was familiar to me now. He hadn't called or texted me to say he was coming—that in itself wasn't unusual.

The engine cut out, and I waited for the sound of his shoes on the stairs and his light knock on the door.

He didn't knock.

I heard his key turning in the lock and called out to him, hello or something similar, although his response was a silent removal of his coat and shoes by the door.

Then I knew for sure.

I set my book down on the coffee table and waited for his warm weight.

Still without speaking, he crawled onto my lap, straddling it with one leg either side of my own, pressed his face against my neck, and determinedly did not cry.

I held him close to me, rocking him gently, and ran my fingers up and down his back. The physical exhaustion seemed to roll off him in waves, flowing out of his skin and sinking into my own.

His hair smelled of my shampoo where he'd washed it last in my shower. It would only take a few moments of searching to see his effect on my life, and the clear effect I had on his. Some of it was etched in ink that was not going to wash off.

When he sniffed, I realized the effort it was costing him to not cry, which was sometimes more exhausting than actually crying in the first place. I wanted to give him permission to let it go, just let it all go, Chris, but if he didn't want to cry in front of me, that was okay too.

"When?" I asked after a period of time long enough to make my thighs go numb but not yet fall asleep.

"Not this weekend, the weekend after," he said. His voice sounded hollow. "One last goodbye gig and then out on Sunday morning."

"Okay," I said, because really, what else could I say?

"Tell me not to go," he said, pulling back from my shoulder and gripping my arms tightly. I got my first good look at his face since he'd come in, and he seemed wrecked. Totally emotionally wrecked. "Tell me to stay here with you and I will."

"I can't do that," I said gently. Removed his hands from my arms and set them back down by his sides. "This is your life, Chris, not holed up with someone who can only hold you back by the sheer nature of our relationship. How long would it take you to start resenting me?"

"I need you more than I need them."

"But do you need me more than you need your music?"

He couldn't answer that.

"You know where I am," I said softly. "I've got no plans to move. So if you ever need me, come back and find me."

He scrambled back and stood frowning down at me. "I can't believe you're not going to fight for us."

Standing too, I took his hands in mine. "If I thought there was any chance I could win, I would fight," I said quietly. "You need to go and do what it is that you're meant to do. And I'll do the same."

His voice was barely more than a whisper when he asked, "Can I stay?"

"Come on," I said, tugging him through to the kitchen. "Let's have a cup of tea."

IN THE week that followed, I helped four musicians load up a camper van and trailer that was surely disproportionate to their needs.

"The drums take up a lot of space," Lexi explained as I helped her wrap and box up their small amount of kitchen equipment. "And Chris won't ride his bike if it's raining too hard, so there has to be space on the trailer for that as well."

"Where did the camper come from?"

She laughed and pushed her red curls back from her face. "My grandmother bought it when she retired with the intention of traveling across the country in it. She'd never left Florida before. She got as far as New Orleans and decided she liked home best after all. Technically it's on loan from her until we get back home, but I don't get the impression she's too bothered if we keep it."

"Who drives?" I asked as I taped up another box.

"We take it in turns," she said. "There's only really sleeping room for three; a compartment over the driver's seat and the back bench pulls out big enough for two. If we stop for the night, then we draw straws for who has to sleep with the passenger seat cranked back."

We started on the next lot of drawers, carefully wrapping the breakables in newspaper.

"We can live out of the van for about two weeks before we start trying to murder each other in our sleep," Lexi continued. "We learned that going through Virginia."

The goodbye gig was well promoted. Several local bands played in support, and I almost got into the music, almost, until the significance of the night dawned on me and the fog of melancholy settled around me again. I was trying so fucking hard to stay upbeat, or at least normal, because Chris was taking our impending separation to heart.

Despite all my best efforts, there were moments when I looked at him and felt another little fracture spread through my heart.

That night I knew he ached from the way he held his arms, and I tried my very best to kiss the pain away.

Neither of us slept particularly well.

There was an urgency to experience everything that we possibly could before he left, our kisses soft and sweet and searching, hot and passionate and needy. He was going to leave bruises on me, of this I was sure but didn't care. I would wear his marks with pride.

We took it in turns to demand attention, our fingers ripping the sheets from the bed so at times we lay tangled in them, sleeping only on the bare mattress. Then we woke again and wanted something else, him in me, over me, riding me, under me until we were breathless and sore and hurting in an entirely different way.

The next morning he refused to shower.

"I want to smell like you," he confided in a hushed whisper.

The few things that were left to pack took no time at all. Lex and John took the van down to the club and packed up the last of the equipment while Danny and I loaded trash bags with bedsheets to be washed when they stopped next. Chris sat on the porch and chain-smoked, refusing to help. He had always excelled at sulking and making his point.

The van came back.

John loaded the bike onto the trailer.

And Chris stood on the front path, the house all locked up, and clung to me for dear life.

I wanted to comfort him, to whisper lies into his hair that would make our parting easier. *We'll talk every day. I'll see you again soon. You'll find someone else.* Or the things that weren't lies at all but still impossible to say. *I love you. I'll never forget you. Please don't forget me.*

To give them their due, his friends gave us our privacy as for the first time I saw him cry, his hot tears soaking the front of my shirt.

We had to break away eventually.

His kiss tasted of salty tears and the sort of pain that breaks you apart inside and cigarette smoke and Chris.

"I love you," he said, his forehead pressed to mine, his hand tightly wrapped around the back of his neck so he could tug at his own hair. His eyes screwed closed.

"I love you too." I didn't realize until that moment that I was crying too.

It was easier to keep my eyes shut as he kissed me again and, with a sound of absolute distress, pulled away.

I didn't want to watch him climb into the van and pull away, and then I did.

My last memory of him was seeing him curled up on the passenger seat of the van with his head on his knees.

And then he left.

INTERMISSION

IN THE weeks since he left, I've changed. Considering all the ways I've changed since first meeting Chris, this isn't such a surprise, but these are changes that only those closest to me have noticed.

I could have thrown myself into my lectures, but there was no passion there for me. Instead I picked up the battered manuscript that I'd been working on for nearly six years, the pages and pages of notes and scribbles and research, and poured myself into making something new.

Before he left I had just started to see myself in terms of him; I became Chris's partner, Chris Ford's boyfriend, even, and as terrifying as those terms were, I embraced them.

Without him I feel lost again, and the only way I can find myself is to redefine who I am, this time not in terms of Chris but in terms of myself and my own achievements. I want to be able to call myself a published author and a specialist in my field. From all the research I've done over the years, I know that nothing like what I'm working on exists out there. Maybe there's a reason for that; maybe no one wants to read it or buy it or sell it, but maybe no one has ever thought of putting it together before.

After six years of research, it takes me a little over six weeks of work to turn that pile of scrapbooks and notes into a tangible manuscript. I've considered asking the university for a sabbatical, but having something at home to go back to and work on is even more exciting, like I have a secret identity. Like Superman.

Only Superman never walked around in a daze. Superman never got to the grocery store and had no idea what food was in the cupboard and what he needed to buy. And I bet Superman never pulled over on the side of the road with a paper bag on the passenger seat full of cereal and cat food and cried until he thought his chest might break.

The missing him is intense.

But, as they say, life goes on. Mine certainly has.

Christmas came and went with the usual festivities that I felt strangely distant from. New Year. More snow. The big thaw. The inevitable flash floods. My daughter. Holding it together for Chloe. Because Chris had helped me to reestablish a relationship with her that I'd thought was nearly impossible.

Then I go home and miss him some more.

Tiptoe toward spring, tentative, baby steps as the days start to get lighter and my mood starts to lift, little by little, day by day.

I'm not ready to go back out into the big wide world again yet and start dating, as Marley has been suggesting I should. But I chance a night out at the gay bar, even though I know it will remind me of Chris. It's not as bad as I thought it might be. There are other people my age there, as well as the deluge of young, beautiful people.

The offer of swapping numbers with someone is enough to nudge me the next bit further along the path to healing, to moving on. I don't take it but buy him a drink instead. We agree that if we see each other again, it might progress to a dance.

Baby steps.

One Saturday afternoon, I agree to take Chloe and Cassie to the movie theater to see the new Disney film. It's getting me out of the house, according to Lu, and I know that she worries about me so I do it without too much fuss. Of course, I can't do it without any fuss at all or she'll ask me to do it all the time, and I'm definitely not yet ready for that.

Cassie asks if her Uncle Chris is going to come too, and I have to explain that Uncle Chris isn't here anymore. Children are so perceptive, and she comes and gives me a hug. I've never been quite so touchy-feely with her; we don't hug all that often, so it means a lot that she does it.

I spend more time with my sister. Attempt to reconcile with my parents, although that venture is dismissed after just one meeting with my mother. The miserable old hag.

The tattoo on my arm serves as a reminder, although not for what I thought it might. It's not a reminder of Chris, or of Edinburgh, although sometimes it does act as both those things. Instead it's a proof that sometimes when I step out of my comfort zone, good things can happen. It's a symbol of my own strength and an indelible way of telling my own story. *This is who I am. This is where I came from.*

There are moments when I think I'm managing, that I'm doing okay without him. It's okay, he was just one lover, I can move on from him like I moved on from Brett. It's bullshit, of course. Sometimes I cry so hard I can't breathe and the little capillaries under my eyes break, leaving tiny red splotches.

Bloody tears.

PART
TWO

CHAPTER
FOURTEEN

WHEN January melts into February, the pain in my chest starts to ease off. I'm not breathing easy again yet, but I am breathing.

I consider updating the car. Dismiss the thought. Look at taking a job somewhere not in Boston next year as a touring lecturer, in New York, maybe. Somewhere different, just for a year. The truth is, for all of my hard work trying to get over him, Chris is everywhere I look, and it's suffocating.

Not that I'd be able to move until the summer anyway.

That idea, too, is dismissed.

I find myself spending my evenings sorting through notes and scraps of paper, ideas for the book that were abandoned in the first draft. Most of them are good ideas, they just held me back on the direction I wanted to take at the time, and I've got a vague idea of reworking them into a second volume.

When there's a knock at the door, I very seriously consider ignoring this rude person calling at such a late hour; then, sighing, I gather all of my papers into a pile and stack them on the coffee table before going to answer it.

I open the door and he's standing there, his leathers covered in water and shaking as he trembles from the cold.

"What are you doing here?" I whisper.

"Can I come in?" he asks.

I step aside to let him in, completely baffled by his presence. We stand in silence, looking at each other, until I reach out and tug the zipper on his jacket. It seems to be the signal he had been waiting for to strip out of his protective clothing, although his shirt underneath seems almost soaked through.

"Where's your stuff?" I ask.

"Down on the bike," he says. His lips look almost blue from the cold.

"Get in the shower before you freeze," I say to him. "I'll go bring it in."

The wind is biting cold and the rain is still hammering down as I dash out to his bike and unload the bags he has attached to it. I'm soaked too by the time I get back to the flat, and I can hear the shower is running, so at least he's getting warm.

There's no precedent for this, and I have absolutely no idea what to do. So I lock up, bolting the front door and making sure Flea has food, then find two pairs of pajama pants from the drawer and set one pair out for Chris, dressing in the other myself.

It's still early, but the rain and black clouds outside are making it seem later than it really is—although it's always been dark in this flat. I don't want to go to bed, not really, but I want to talk to him about it all even less, so sleeping is a good compromise.

He's wrapped in my towel when he comes out of the bathroom, and I realize that all the others are in with my laundry. I'm not upset but once again reminded of his familiarity in my home and the way he seems to slot seamlessly into my life.

Chris looks down at the pajama pants with a little frown, then dries off his hair, and the last droplets of water from his skin.

I try not to stare.

I wondered if maybe he would have put on weight or lost it since I saw him last. His absolute normality is somehow more shocking than if he looked radically different. It feels like I've changed so much in the months since he left that it's left a tangible sheen on my skin, like a snake shedding the old and leaving something shiny and raw underneath. I'm shiny and raw now, but he looks just the same as I remember.

Or not the same. I've probably elevated him to godlike status in my memories. He's not as perfect as I want to remember him. He's still got chunky thighs, and his hair needs cutting, and... and... no. He's just perfect.

After he's pulled the pajamas on, I lift the duvet for him and he lies down next to me, still not saying anything about why he's here... why he's back. Why he's home. Chris is on "his" side of the bed, and I curve my body around his and slot my knees into the bend of his and quietly tell him to lift his head so my arm can pillow it.

He sighs deeply and snuggles back into my body, taking my hand and pulling my arm closer to his chest.

"I missed you so fucking much," he says.

"Don't," I tell him. "Not tonight. Let's just go to sleep."

After a few minutes he starts to shake, and even though his skin is warm from the shower, I think that maybe the cold has gone all the way down through muscle and sinew right into his bones. All I can do is hold him tighter until the trembling stops, and even then I keep hold of him tight until we're both deep in sleep.

THE next morning he's rolled over and his face is pressed right up against my chest, distorting his nose and making him snore. It makes me smile, and he grumbles as I start to pull away, desperate not to leave him, but I have to.

"No," he mumbles and reaches for me.

"I have a lecture this morning," I say to him.

Chris mumbles something else and starts to snore again so I go and take a shower, let the cat out, and make a cup of coffee because I think I'm going to need the caffeine kick for the day ahead. When I go back into our bedroom, he's sitting up and blinking at me, rubbing the sleep out of his eyes like a child.

"There's more coffee in the pot," I say softly.

"Rob," he says, then clears his throat. "We didn't get to talk last night."

"I'm sorry," I say. "I really do have to run, my lecture is at nine thirty. But I can get the TA to take the seminar so I should be home by twelve-ish."

He nods, then sneezes three times in rapid succession and shivers. "You look hot, Prof."

"And you look sick," I counter. He smiles warily at that.

"I've been on the road for a while."

I don't want to think about that quite yet, I'm not ready to face the possibility that he's driven halfway across the country to see me again and I'm not even sure if he's staying. I scratch my chin absently, then pick up a scarf from the chair next to the door and wrap it around my neck.

"Please… please stay?" I say. "I won't be long. But I have to take this lecture."

He nods again.

"Where else am I going to go?"

I don't want to think about that and determinedly don't as I head out into the damp, freezing morning toward the campus and my lecture hall. The only thing that saves me for the ninety minutes I'm delivering the lecture is the fact that I've spent the past few weeks working like crazy, either on the book or on my lesson plans. Due to that my material is exceptional, as are my notes, and I manage to hold at least twenty percent of the class's attention, which I consider a massive success.

I can only think that it would be nice if I could hold my own attention as well.

At the beginning of the year, the departmental heads and university gods bestowed upon me a reasonably competent TA, and I'm happy to leave her in charge of the seminar, especially considering the quality of my prepared material.

Kelly doesn't look particularly pleased to be given charge of the two-hour discussion, but that's her problem and not mine. I wish that my only problem was having to engage a class of bored freshmen, but mine is much more complex. I consider offering her the chance to swap and for her to deal with a sick maybe-ex-boyfriend while I take the freshmen, but she doesn't know Chris and she'd probably only try and steal him from me.

The skank.

"Skank" is one of Chloe's words and I've decided I like it, and in Kelly's case it's particularly apt.

The temptation to break all speeding and road traffic laws to get back to him is huge, but I force myself to Drive Like a Christian (another of Chloe's terms) and stop by Chris's favorite deli on the way home to buy him some chicken soup and a couple of sandwiches and fresh orange juice. The drugstore next door provides me with painkillers in case he needs those too, and I force myself not to buy anything else until I've properly assessed how sick he really is.

It's only a short drive back to the flat from the deli, and I nearly weep with relief when I see that his bike is still outside.

He's still in there. He hasn't left.

He's still in there. He hasn't left. Oh, shit.

Shit.

Foolishly, I hope he's sleeping when I get in, either on the sofa or in bed to delay our inevitably difficult conversation for just a little while longer, but he's awake. Sitting on the sofa, with the blanket from the end of the bed on his lap and the cat on the blanket and still wearing my pajamas.

I hold up the bag from the deli and say, "Chicken soup."

He smiles, and it's a smile I recognize as belonging to me, and it means maybe, just maybe, things will be okay.

"Chicken soup sounds great."

I don't want him to have to move, so I fix a tray in the kitchen with the soup and the sandwiches and the juice and coffee, just in case he's hungry, and kick Flea off his lap to set it down. I get a pout (from the cat) for that, but I couldn't care less.

Chris is home.

THE prospect of a conversation neither of us wants to have or will like hangs over us for a while as he eats his sandwich and soup and I sit in the armchair next to him, afraid to get too close. His appetite gives me the hope that he can't be that sick, really, he's probably just caught a cold.

More than anything else in the whole world, I want to take him back to bed and hold him again, to feel his weight in my arms so that I can know, without a doubt, that he's real.

When he's done, Chris puts the tray down at his side and looks over to me.

"Are you mad?" he whispers with his eyes low.

"What?" I demand. "No. Why on earth would I be mad at you?"

He studies his hands and shrugs. "Because I left."

"No," I say softly, the urge to go to him now overwhelming. "No, I'm not mad, baby. I know why you had to go. I'm just very confused as to why you're back."

"Is it too painfully cheesy to say that I missed you too much?" he says with what I now think of as his patented smirk. His eyes seem brighter now that he's eaten, his skin healthier.

"It's not cheesy," I say. "But it's not enough."

When he sighs deeply and looks away from me, I start to understand that this goes deeper than a fleeting whim to see me again.

"Have you been following us online?"

The band have been keeping a blog and a Twitter account going, as well as their mind-bogglingly frequent Facebook updates. For a while I would check in, telling myself that I just wanted to make sure he was doing okay. But that was more painful than just letting him go, so after a few weeks I stopped altogether.

"The last thing I heard was that you got to Chicago safely."

Mental calculation flashes across his face as he counts back to how long ago that was. Then he nods.

"Yeah. Chicago was good."

"Then?" I prompt him. I'm such a masochist.

"A couple of weeks ago, we started putting the word out that we were looking for a replacement drummer." Instead of looking apologetic, he looks defiant. "Sam called us a few days later, I spent some time with her teaching her the beats, then I started traveling back."

"Why?"

"I've never had this before," he says, gesturing to the space between us. "And I suppose I might find it again if I look hard enough. But I don't want to go looking again. I want you."

"The band, though…."

"The band won't make it," he says bluntly. "We're good but nowhere near good enough. They're my best friends and my family, and I love them to bits. And this whole thing, touring the country and playing every city on the way, yeah, it was a dream.

"You know Lexi and John are having a baby?" he says suddenly. I shake my head. "Yeah. She's only just, you know, knocked up and whatever. But he's already put a ban on her crowd surfing."

"So he should," I say with a smile.

"They're going to come back here to have the baby. Lex loves the area, and John's grandparents are here."

"What about Danny?"

"Danny's good enough that if he wants to make it, he will."

I'd always wondered if Danny was the odd one out from the group. He sort of stood on the fringe a little bit, and although the chemistry was there when they played, he never seemed as close to the others. It made sense that he would maybe try to go solo or join another group.

"I've had a lot of road time to think about this," Chris says carefully. "It wasn't an easy trip back. If I didn't want to be here, I've had plenty of time to turn around."

"I'm really grateful you didn't," I say.

"Rob, I don't think we should live here," he says in a rush. "Not that there's anything wrong with your apartment, but it's sort of… small."

"Okay." The word is long, stretched out to make up for its inadequacy.

"We should look for a house together. Somewhere with enough space for you to be able to work and for me to be able to practice and play without us killing each other. And if we get a house, then we can look for somewhere with enough bedrooms that Chloe can come and stay sometimes."

It starts to dawn on me that he wants for us to live together. It takes a while for this thought to settle in my head; it runs through the different parts of my brain like treacle—rational, emotional, instinctive, subconscious….

"And because it's going to take a while to sort all of that out, moving, I mean, by the time we're ready, then John and Lexi will probably be just about ready to move back. So I thought they could sublet this place."

"I own the apartment," I say, as if that's relevant.

"Then you could rent it to them. Your office isn't that big, but it's big enough for a nursery, and they won't want a massive place at first anyway."

"Hang on," I tell him, raising my hands. "I need to get this straight. You want to live with me, move out, get a house, and have your friends live here."

"That's part of it. Yes."

"You want to live with me," I repeat, since this is the crux of the matter.

"I want to spend my life with you," he says in a quiet, scared voice. I realize that all of my dithering has probably scared the boy into insanity, and I feel pretty bloody close to breaking point myself.

"Oh, God."

Too late, it dawns on me that I'm probably having a panic attack, and at the most inopportune moment. Chris throws back the blanket from his lap and falls to his knees in front of me, guiding me to put my head between my knees in a calm, gentle voice.

It takes a few minutes for me to stop hyperventilating, and during that time Chris's hand never stops its movements through my hair. From this close I can smell him and can tell that he hasn't showered again yet. He still smells a little bit like me, from the shower gel he used last night, but more than that he smells like him.

My heart hadn't just broken when he left. It had shattered.

Finally I start to come back to my senses, and he's still there, watching me with his pretty eyes that are full of equal parts amusement and worry.

"Are you back in the land of the living?" he says, teasing me, and I love him even more for it.

"I think so."

Clearly not, because when I try to sit up, I get an almighty head rush.

"Woah."

Chris leans in and presses his lips to mine. It's unexpected, this kiss, with his hands braced either side of me on the arms of the chair. I respond almost explosively, wrapping my hand around the back of his neck and pulling him close to me. I can't stand not touching him anymore, and even though we're not done with this conversation and there's still a lot for me to get my head around, at least I know that he's not about to leave.

He's smiling against me as I pull him up onto my lap and laughs brightly as I figure out the best way to keep him balanced there. He wriggles a little bit, then rests his head against my chest and sighs.

"Sorry about that," I murmur into his hair.

"The freak-out or the kiss?"

"Both. Neither."

He laughs again and turns his cheek. I recognize the move, which places his lips right in alignment with my own, and there's no harm, no harm at all with leaning in and brushing my lips over his.

"So, are you up for it?" he asks.

"Yeah," I tell him. "Let's do it."

He scrambles from my lap with a stupid grin on his face that just makes me love him more, if that's even possible. When he reaches for my hands, I let him tug me to my feet and lead me through to my bedroom, which I better start thinking of as ours now.

Chris pulls of my pajama pants, and of course he's not wearing anything underneath them, so when he lies back on my too-small bed, it's just him, perfect and naked and waiting for me.

I've left my shoes at the front door and can't be bothered to take anything else off; pouncing on him and pinning him to the bed while we kiss seems far more important. And it's somehow very erotic, me being fully clothed in my work clothes while this man, this impetuous, amazing man, is nude beneath me.

"Are you sure this is okay?" I ask him. "You're not catching a cold, are you?"

"Rob," he says in that voice that no one else is allowed to use, with the nickname only he can ever get away with saying, "I wanted you to fuck me last night and you didn't. If you don't fuck me now, I might actually die."

I laugh and kiss him again, and the warm slide of his tongue on mine, his soft, wet lips caressing mine so sweetly is all I need. All I need right now and forever and ever because he's mine.

His body is warm. Not so warm that I'm still worried about being sick; more the type of warm that comes from sleeping in and then curling up on the sofa with a blanket and watching TV for most of the morning and not doing anything else. The lazy bugger.

"This is mine now," I tell him, running my hand possessively down his side. "No one else gets to touch you."

"No one has touched me since the first time you did," he whispers to me. "Ever since I had you, I didn't want anyone else."

There's a part of me that still questions if it's all real—that is, until I'm all the way inside him again with the feel of his breath on my cheek and his hand on my hip, the other in my hair. All of this is home.

And I know now that my home is where he is, not this little apartment that has been too small for me for years but a real home where we can make it ours.

After, he's quiet, and the late afternoon sunshine warms the room. When Flea jumps onto the bed to join in our snuggle, Chris welcomes him without any hesitation.

"He missed you, you know."

"Of course he did. Me and Flea, we have a connection."

"You're the only person on the bloody planet he likes."

Chris snorts and kisses the top of my head. I lose one of his arms to the cat, who is demanding scratches behind his ears.

"Chloe misses you too," I say, deciding that this is an okay topic of conversation.

"Really?"

"Yeah. She asked if you were going to be home for Christmas."

"I'm sorry I missed it," he says. "She texts me sometimes."

"I didn't know that."

"She tells me about her competitions and I tell her about our gigs. Then a couple of days later, I text her to ask her how she got on, and she texts me to ask how the gig went. That's about it really. Sometimes she mentions you."

This catches my interest. "Really? What does she say?"

"That would be an invasion of her privacy," Chris says, and I can tell he's smirking. "She was worried about you for a bit."

I think back. I probably gave them all cause to worry at some point over the last few months. It feels like a lot to admit how badly I failed at keeping up appearances while he was away, and by the sounds of it he's already been filled in by my daughter. I decide it's something he doesn't need to know.

"It's better now you're back."

"For me, too."

My head naturally finds a dip on his chest, and I allow my cheek to settle there, listening to the regular *thump-thump* of his heartbeat and drifting on the warm feelings that come with good sex with beautiful men. From this vantage point, I can see his penis. I haven't really studied it flaccid before, and it lies heavy on his thigh, gently snuggled in a nest of light blond hairs. I'm not nearly as comfortable with my nudity as Chris is, and I like to have a blanket pulled up to my waist, but he just lets it all hang out, unafraid. I envy that about him.

I must drift more than I intended to as I wake with a start.

"Hmm?" I demand. "What time is it?"

Chris shushes me and runs his fingers through my hair.

"You were only sleeping for about twenty minutes," he says in a soft voice. "I couldn't bear to wake you up."

I settle again, my cheek now feeling hot and sticky from being pressed so tightly against Chris's skin. Sighing deeply is just an excuse to bring his scent back into my lungs.

"Ready to go again?"

"You are joking," I tell him.

"Not at all."

His cock is stirring with interest, and I let my fingertips stroke its length cautiously, exploring to test its responses. Chris rolls onto his side, reaching out to grab his Boy Butter and taking another generous scoop of it, easing it into himself.

I slide my index finger in alongside his, surprised to find that he isn't as tight as when I prepared him the first time. Then I wonder why that surprises me, since he has already been fucked once. I didn't even know I've got this kind of recovery time, but I'm nearly hard again, and his kisses and my finger tangling with his just inside his anus is enough to take me all the way there.

Chris tucks his knees up to his chest.

We sleep in this position with me cradling him back against my body; the echoes of that most intimate position resonate as I line my body up with his and once again push into him.

The second time it's different.

This time it feels like we have all the time in the world, and really, now we do. I'm no longer questioning if this is real. And although there are still so many things that need to be answered, they can all wait.

This is much more important.

My hand closes around his, and together we take hold of his cock, stroking it in time with my easy rocking inside him. There's no pressure, no rush, no time for anything but this beautiful connection between us.

I feel like I could spend all day, or maybe forever inside him.

"We have a lot of making up to do," he says, giving my hand a squeeze and unconsciously echoing my thoughts.

"I can't believe how much I need you. Missed you so much."

"I missed you too. Tell me."

"I love you."

I can feel him melt at my words. It's like he has nothing left to give me and lets me take what I need from his body. That doesn't mean he stops moving, or seeking his own pleasure too; instead it's a different kind of submission.

It feels like we haven't kissed in hours, and the gentle brush of my lips over his makes my heart thump painfully in my chest. His tongue slides easily into my mouth, and I want him so badly, want more even though it's impossible, I'm already inside him as far as I can go. The taste is him and me and the something unique that will only ever exist between us together.

When my second orgasm is torn from my body, everything hurts, and I cry out his name, over and over, safe in the knowledge that this, too, is only ours. No one else can ever have a piece of it.

"Rob." My name is on his lips too as his sticky release floods my hand, and I press my face into his back.

I am never, ever going to let him go again.

CHAPTER FIFTEEN

THERE'S something about the atmosphere in my home office that is far more conducive to working than my office at the campus. And since it was at this desk that I wrote my manuscript, with the cat sitting on my feet and an endless supply of tea and biscuits to keep me going, it feels right that this is where I should sit to edit the damn thing.

Although it's yet to land a publishing contract, my name and reputation and impressive resume have been enough for an agent to agree to represent me. That's enough, for the time being.

From this room I can hear the front door to the building slamming shut and the sound of Chris's distinctive, heavy footfalls as he races up the stairs. It feels good to expect him home, even if he seems to completely keep to a schedule of his own making.

"Rob!" he yells as he closes the door behind him. I roll my eyes. The apartment is small enough that he doesn't need to shout.

"I'm in here," I say in a perfectly reasonable talking volume.

"Oh." He sticks his head around the door and grins. "Are you working? I can come back later."

"It's not important." That's not strictly true. But it can wait. "What's up?"

"I have something for you. Well, for me, really. For us."

"Oh?"

He comes through and hands me a sealed envelope. While standing behind me his arms wrap loosely around my neck, and his chin rests on my shoulder as I slip my thumb under the seal and pull out two typed sheets of paper.

It takes a few minutes for me to interpret the list of abbreviations and numbers, but his name at the top of the sheet, and the name of his doctor, gives me some indication.

"Are these… blood tests?"

"Yup."

I check the date. "From six months ago."

"Just after we met."

"And… from last week."

"I'm clean," he whispers in my ear. "I was clean six months ago, and I got checked again to make sure there was nothing nasty lingering. You're the only person I've been with since then."

It dawns on me, and I laugh. "You're still hung up on the bareback thing."

"Damn right I am," he says emphatically. "I knew I'd be okay, I've always been careful. But this is the proof so you've got more to go on than my word."

"I would have trusted you," I say, feeling a little stung. "This wasn't necessary. And you should know I can't reciprocate."

He kisses the side of my neck wetly. "Okay. When was your last test?"

I think back. "About eighteen months ago?"

"Was it all clear?"

"Yes."

"And how many people have you slept with since then?"

A long pause. "One."

"Is that one person me?"

"You're not beyond being put over my knee for another spanking," I say, but he's already laughing, and I can't help but join him. Chris manages to slide around onto my lap, and I search out a kiss. Our lips are like magnets these days. If we come within a certain distance of each other, kissing is inevitable.

"So will you do it?" he asks, and I have no reason to say no.

He straddles me, and even though his jeans are ridiculously loose, there's still a strain across the front of them. In these and a plain white shirt, he's more handsome than ever, and of course I can't keep my hands off him. He's beautiful and he's mine.

When he starts to unbutton his shirt, I realize that he means right now, and the thought makes me smile. He's so damn impatient, impetuous, and it's going to get him in trouble one of these days. I can't say that I mind, though. He's been making my life interesting for far too long for me to care.

His shirt is tossed over my monitor, effectively cutting me off from my work, which is all the excuse I need (did I need an excuse in the first place?) to ignore the work I should be doing and focus all my attentions on him instead. And Chris is a much, much more interesting subject than editing.

I could spend hours on him.

"Come on," I gasp, pulling back from his kisses. "Let's go to bed."

"No." He is quite effective at pinning me to the chair. "Right here."

"Kinky," I manage before he bites my earlobe and makes me gasp. "Kinky bastard."

"Yeah. Oh fuck, yeah."

The thought—fucking in my office—is all I need to make the space in my jeans uncomfortably small. There's no way we can do it in my office at work—and if I know Chris, which I think I do, that's probably what he wants. This is a good substitute, though.

"Lube," I say. "It's in the bedroom."

But he's already shaking his head. "No. Bare. Rough. Like this."

"No fucking way," I tell him. "I've got no interest in making you bleed, Chris." I adopt my Scary Teacher voice. "Turn around, put your hands on the desk, and spread your fucking legs."

"Yes, sir."

A pair of jeans, not mine, get flung across the room, and a cat disappears out the door in a blur of grey fluff. It's his own fault for getting between us.

Chris is still toeing off his socks, and somehow he's naked again while I'm fully dressed. I rectify that situation and leave him waiting for me as I carefully remove the last of my clothes, folding them and placing them on the desk next to his right hand. It's a test—to see if he'll disobey me. Part of me hopes he does, just so I have an excuse to spank him again.

Unfortunately he's being incredibly well behaved, and as I sit down again, the leather feeling nice against my thighs, his ass is now at the perfect height for me to get to work on him. Since I know what's coming next and that this has the potential to not only hurt him but do some damage, I take the responsibility of adequately preparing him very seriously.

My tongue laps him from his balls to the base of his spine a few times; then I close in on his hole and lick it with soft little jabs. He's making noises that aren't quite whimpers but almost, his hips rocking back to me as I knead his cheeks in time with the rhythm of my tongue. I can tell when he's almost ready to come. I've listened to those sounds a countless number of times and ease off a little before he gets there.

"Shit. Shit." He's laughing as he straightens up. "You're going to make me come before we even get started."

One look at me makes his eyes darken and the smirk drop from his face. I'm not sure what he's seeing in me, but it makes him drop to his knees and take my cock in his mouth.

It's moments like these when I know I'll be the only man to ever feel Chris's lips around his cock ever again, because there's no way in hell I'm letting him go. He's mine now, and this feeling belongs just to us.

Spit isn't really good enough to use as lubricant, and in nearly every other situation, I would insist on using the real stuff. But this is something that he's wanted for a long time, and clearly something that he's waited to share with me. And on some level, I understand his need.

"Are you sure you're ready?" I ask as he resumes the position astride my thighs.

"Yes," he says, cupping my cheek in his palm and kissing my lips softly. "I've waited so long for this. I'm so glad it's you."

"I'm glad it's you too," I whisper.

Since he got back, making love more than once a day has become the norm for us, like we actually are trying to catch up on the time spent away from each other. Of course, there are other ways we're reconnecting too, but nothing quite brings forth the rush of warm, fuzzy, loving feelings like sex.

He keeps one hand on my face and reaches back with the other to guide my cock into him. I hold his hips, keeping them steady and maybe gripping too hard as he sits back on me.

As the first inch slides home, I wrap my arm around his waist, wanting him to feel loved and cared for while this happens. He's incredibly tight, and I force him to go slow. There's no rush; we can spend hours doing it if necessary.

Our eyes are locked together, and I need that, I need to keep a close watch on him because God knows I love him and I really desperately don't want to hurt him. He seems to understand that even though I'd count having sex in my office as slightly kinky, that doesn't mean I won't make sure I'm making love to him.

"Fuck," he whispers, and I immediately grab his hips.

"If this is hurting you, we should stop, right now," I tell him. And I mean it. Nothing is worth him being hurt, and we can always try again later.

"I'm okay," he promises, although his eyes are a little glassy. "I'm okay. You're just stretching me. It feels good."

"Yeah?"

"Oh God, yeah."

Despite this, I force him to go slow with my hands tight around his waist and slow, lazy kisses setting the pace. When he sits down and his ass hits my thighs, he throws his head back and groans unashamedly, his fingers now gripping my arms so hard it hurts.

"All the way," I say with a little breathless laugh.

As his fingertips cup my cheek, I kiss his palm, and we seem to find our rhythm moving together. At a glance down, his cock is thick and heavy against my belly, red at the tip and swollen. I can feel his heartbeat rushing, his breath now shallow and urgent.

For all the times we've had sex in the past, this is the first time we've done it in this position, and it does take a few minutes for me to find the right angle for him. When I do, that brush against his prostate that draws curses and whimpers from his throat, my cock twitches deep inside him.

There is nothing, nothing quite like watching him like this. There's already a red flush spreading through the black ink on his chest, and he's too tight, too perfect, and I'm close....

"Chris."

And I'm there. His fingers reach back behind himself to feel where we're joined, and I take over the job of stroking his cock with a grip erring on the side of too hard to get him over the edge with me.

I can feel that this is an emotional release for him just as much as a physical one when he lays his head down on my shoulder. Although there's no sound apart from his breathing, his shaking shoulders tell me all I need to know about the ragged sobs in his chest.

I'd love to carry him through to bed, to cross the threshold with him in my arms, but my knees, back, arms are too weak. Our clothes stay scattered around my office as we silently make our way through to my bedroom, where we collapse on the bed in a tangle of liquefied limbs.

"Chris," I whisper.

"Mm?"

"Can you remember, back ages ago, when I asked you if you'd wear my ring?"

"Yeah."

"This is probably a bad time to ask...."

He twists his shoulders so he can look me in the eye. "Rob, did you buy me a ring?"

I blush and shrug. "Maybe. Do you want it?"

"Yes. Of course."

"Are you sure?"

"Rob. Give me my fucking present."

"I can't reach it from here," I say, secretly loving that he's still exactly as I remember him. "You can, though. Top drawer."

I'm silently blessing my tiny bed as he reaches for the drawer and retrieves a small suede pouch.

"Is this it?"

"Yeah."

I prop myself up on my elbow so I can better see him as he tugs open the strings and pulls the silver ring out.

It was bought when I was Christmas shopping months ago. I was in the mall with Chloe, helping her pick things out for her brother and sister and Lu and Mike, when we passed the jewelry store. In the window was a display of men's rings, and my eyes were immediately drawn to a selection of wide silver bands inlaid with strips of beautiful dark wood.

The contrast appealed to me, and when we were done and I'd dropped Chloe home, I went back and bought one for him. Even though he was miles and miles away. That didn't seem to matter for some reason.

While Chris runs his thumb back and forth over the ring, I suddenly feel a spike of rejection in my stomach. It was the wrong time to do it. He feels like I was pushing him back into the relationship. It's too soon.

"Oh, Rob," he whispers and rolls over into my arms.

"You like it?" I dare to ask.

"It's perfect."

"You don't have to wear it all the time," I rush to explain. "I won't be upset if you don't want to."

Silently, he hands me the ring. "You put it on," he says.

And now it's up to me. I took a guess when picking the ring size, but I was thinking of his fourth finger when I did. All I want to do is be a part of him again, so as I nudge him back onto his side, I take his right hand in mine and slide the ring onto his finger.

Then the rush of worry comes.

"Are you sure this is okay? I don't want to be the one who ties you down...."

"You're not tying me down," he says, rolling the ring around on his finger with his thumb. "Why would you think that? And if you say it's because I'm young, I might have to smack you."

I wonder for a moment if he really will. "But you are young."

When it comes, it's a stinging slap to my ass. Not that I mind.

"I'll do absolutely anything for you," I vow. "If you want the moon, I'll get them to gift wrap it."

"You're such a romantic," he says, and I can hear the smile in his voice. "Thank you. For all of it."

"Anytime."

And I mean it.

CHAPTER SIXTEEN

THE conversation about getting a new place together turns into consulting with a realtor much sooner than I had anticipated. Still, I want to show Chris that I'm serious about us making a life together, and the agency seem to be more than competent, so really there's no reason for me to delay anything.

"We should take Chloe with us," Chris says after I've set a date for some viewings. "I want to make sure wherever we move to, she's happy there as well."

"Sure. I'll call her."

"Hey—does she know I'm back?"

I shake my head. I've selfishly been keeping him to myself.

"Don't tell her. Then it can be a surprise."

I call Lu, just to make sure she doesn't have plans and to see if Chloe is even at home. Apparently she has homework, but Lu is happy for us to take her out for a couple of hours.

"You know Cassie will want to come too," I say as we drive out. "She missed you like crazy."

"I don't mind."

Clearly my plan for a romantic afternoon looking at possible love nests needs to be adjusted. Still, I can't really complain about how much Chris seems to care about my daughter and her happiness.

The house seems quiet and calm when we pull up outside, and I'm sure this is merely a front for the chaos inside. We decide to ring the bell rather than let ourselves in, and it takes a good few minutes until there's a response.

I can hear Cassie thundering down the stairs screaming, "I'll get it, I'll get it!" and I look to Chris with a smirk.

The door clicks and swings open, and Cassie stands there, openmouthed for a moment. Then: "Uncle Chris!"

In a move they don't seem to have forgotten how to execute, she jumps into Chris's arms and he swings her around, laughing.

"Oh, I missed you, Pumpkin Pie," he says, tickling her ribs.

"I missed you too," she says seriously. "Are you back for good?"

"For good," he promises.

We take a few steps inside, and I shut the front door. The noise of someone else rushing down the stairs reaches us as I do. Chloe stops much as her sister did but affects a calm nonchalance the polar opposite of Cassie's reaction.

"Hey, Dad. Chris. You're back."

"I am," he says.

"For good," Cassie adds.

She smiles. "Good. Does Mom know you're here?"

"I called her earlier to let her know we were coming. We've got an appointment this afternoon with a realtor to look at a couple of houses. Do you want to come with?"

Her eyebrows rise up to her hairline. "Are you serious? You're moving out of the moldy apartment?"

"It's not moldy," I protest, stung. "But yes. We're going to look for a new place."

"Can I come?" Cassie asks.

I catch Chris's eye over her head. She's still balanced on his hip.

"If you can promise to be a very, very good girl," he tells her.

"Pinkie promise," she says, holding out her little finger. Chris hooks it with his own, and they shake on it.

"Come on, Cass," Chloe says. "You need to get changed if we're going out."

The little girl seems to be in play clothes, a pink tracksuit, and although I don't have a problem with it I know Lu has high standards of how her children look in public.

"Can I choose?" Cassie asks as Chris puts her down and Chloe takes hold of her hand.

"Sure. Mom's out in the garden with Carter," Chloe says as they head back upstairs. "I'm sure she's dying to see you."

I know my daughter well enough to interpret that her mom is going to want all the gossip about Chris's return to Boston, and I'm not disappointed.

Now that Carter is older and far less breakable-looking, I'm happy to take him as Lu and Chris "catch up." She gives him the obligatory "Don't you dare ever hurt Rob again or I'll kick you in the nuts" speech, and I let her, partly because I know she loves me and it'll make her feel better.

I've arranged to see four houses, one not too far from where Lu lives, and fortunately that's the first one on the list. I get Chris to call ahead and let the realtor know we're running slightly behind schedule. In allowing Cassie to choose her own clothes, we have a three-year-old in tow wearing pink cowboy boots, green, reindeer-patterned leggings, and a T-shirt with Elmo printed on it. Never mind. I live and learn.

Jessica—the realtor—doesn't seem to mind as I introduce the fairly ragtag bunch of people she didn't know I was bringing with me.

"Are these your children?" she asks.

"Chloe is my daughter," I say. "Cassie is… extended family."

Thankfully she doesn't push the issue. It's far too complicated to try and explain.

The first house is slightly bigger than I expected after looking at the pictures online. It's a new property, brand new; no one else has lived here. We follow Jessica around, nodding at all of the features she points out, but I can't help but feel like the place is too cold. Too clinical.

When we get to the bathroom, which is just… white, everywhere… white toilet, tiles, shower, bath, floor, towel rail, the towels on the towel rail, the toilet paper… I decide that this isn't the place for us.

"I'll let you have a look around by yourself," Jessica says and heads back down the stairs. The white-carpeted stairs.

"Don't touch anything," Chris whispers to Cassie. "You'll get fingerprints on it."

Chloe leads us back through to the master bedroom.

"Don't take this the wrong way, Dad," she says slowly, turning in a circle with her arms outstretched. "But I don't think this is the right place for you."

"Yeah," Chris adds. "There isn't any mold anywhere."

"Watch it," I warn him. And sigh. "You're probably right."

"Next place?" she suggests.

The next place is better. It's another house, slightly older but with a huge back garden and a tire swing hanging from a large tree. Chloe takes Cassie down to swing on it as Jessica gives us the lowdown.

"There's work to be done on it," Jessica warns us as we watch the girls from the patio deck. "There's only electricity on the ground floor at the moment. And you're probably going to want to redecorate most rooms."

"A real fixer-upper," Chris mumbles. I take his hand and squeeze.

When I finally get Cassie to come back to us, she's panting hard.

"That," she says, "is a very good swing."

"Thank you," I tell her. "These things are very important."

Never mind the fact that the kitchen needs to be completely ripped out and reinstalled, or that there's damp coming up through so we'd need to fit new carpets, and the bedrooms are actually on the small side. There's a swing in a tree, so the child approves.

In reality, we're never going to take the place, and Jessica apparently gets this vibe as we leave relatively quickly. I can't blame her. When we spoke on the phone a few days earlier, she asked a fairly detailed list of questions as to what we were willing to look at, and places that "needed work" I'd agreed to. Just... not quite that much work.

With two houses down and both being big no's in my book, and Chris's too if I can read him well enough, I'm starting to feel a bit discouraged. We drive back into the city into one of the more "up-and-coming" neighborhoods, where Jessica starts to enthuse about the quality of the schools nearby.

"It's a real family area," she says with a sunny grin.

I don't have the heart to tell her that we have no intentions of expanding the family or having the girls come and live with us full time.

Still.

The next house is the only one I actually seriously consider. It's very clean, tidy, clearly currently owned by a family who have made themselves scarce. There's a playroom, which I mentally earmark as an office, and a well weather-proofed garage where Chris could set up his drums.

The whole place could do with a good clean and possibly some redecorating, but they would be little jobs that could be done as we go along. Chris lets Cassie explore the garden again, and I tug him to one side.

"It's the best place we've seen so far," he says reasonably, and I agree. "It's not *the* place, though."

I sigh and pull him closer to me. "If we look for perfection, though, who's to say we'll ever find it?"

"Doesn't mean we stop looking," he says.

The sound of little feet on the floor distracts us, and Cassie comes in to what should be a dining room but is being used as storage by the current owners.

"The yard isn't so good here, Uncle Chris," she laments.

"Ah, well." He scoops her up. "One more to go, eh?"

For a moment, just a tiny, little moment, I let myself fantasize that Chris and I have a child together, a house in a nice neighborhood with good schools and a backyard with a really good tire swing. When he looks at me, I get the impression he can see right inside me, down to these silly ideas that I really truly don't want to act on, but it's always nice to spend time in someone else's life. Especially when it's so easy to shrug it off again.

"Cassie, cover your eyes," Chris says seriously.

"Why?"

"Because I'm about to kiss your Uncle Rob."

She giggles but does as she's told, smacking her hands over her eyes as Chris leans in and kisses me with an aching softness that liquefies my bones and sends butterflies from my stomach to my throat.

God, I love this man.

"I've only got one more place to show you," Jessica says as she locks up behind us. "It's actually only a couple of blocks over. If you don't mind walking, you won't lose your parking space, and we can see some of the area at the same time."

"Sounds good," Chris says, and we follow her up the street.

It really is a nice area. There's a park just a few more blocks over, just a small one but somewhere to go chill out when the weather is nice. And it's not too far from a street of nice restaurants, coffee shops, and convenience stores. And a Chinese takeout place. These are all very important points.

Cassie takes my hand as we walk, in between me and Jessica with Chris and Chloe behind us. I don't mind too much. They're catching up on some soap opera that I don't watch. I'm lost in my own thoughts and don't catch what Cassie is saying until I force myself to pay attention.

"Uncle Chris is gay," Cassie tells the realtor with relish.

"Really," Jessica says, a polite but amused expression plastered on her face.

"Cassie, shut up," Chloe whispers furiously from behind us, but she is ignored.

"Mhmm," Cassie says. "That means he doesn't like girls. He likes boys instead. My mommy says that's okay, though. You can like whoever you want to like."

"Is that so."

"Yes. So when I grow up, I'm going to marry a penguin."

At this point Chris can't hold in his laughter any longer and presses his face into my back. I can feel his shoulders shaking with silent giggles. At least he's hiding it from Cassie, who would surely be upset if she thought he was laughing at her.

"Is there any particular reason why you think a penguin will make a good husband?" Jessica enquires, and I decide right then and there I'm going to buy a house from this woman because she's working really bloody hard for her commission.

"Yeah," Cassie says in the same tone of voice one would say "Duh." "'Cause they live in Antarctica."

"Antarctica" is a big word, and I'm more than a little impressed that she knows it, and so much about the endemic nature of the habitat of a penguin.

Fortunately at this point we reach the next house and poor Jessica is spared any further dealings with Cassie. For the moment, anyway.

From the curb, I fall in love.

Not with the man next to me—I've been in love with him for ages. But with the house.

It's a classic Boston brownstone with steps up to the front door, enclosed with wrought-iron handrails. The door is painted a bright, shiny red.

"It's a split-level condo," Jessica is saying, and I force myself to tune in to her voice and pay attention. "This street was developed in 1890, and these houses were originally all one unit. Nearly all have now been split into two spaces. Shall we have a look inside? The apartment we're looking at today is actually the top two floors."

"There's no need," Chloe mutters as we walk up to the shiny, shiny, pretty front door. "Dad wants it already."

She's right, of course. That childish sense of *want it, now, make it mine* doesn't diminish one bit as she leads us through a black-and-white tiled entrance hall to the second floor to the apartment door, and through that into a warm, bright, living space.

"I thought you might appreciate that this space is slightly quirky," Jessica says. "On this level is the kitchen, bathroom, master bedroom, and an office space. Upstairs, in what was once the attic, there's a second bedroom and a large living area."

I want it, I want it, I want it.

"I'll let you explore," she says with a little wink in my direction. She pulls an iPad, of all things, out of her extraordinarily large handbag and starts tapping away on it.

The apartment is decorated and furnished, although sparsely, indicating that there's no one living here at the moment. Thick cream carpet and sage green walls lead us down to the kitchen, which is at the end of the hall directly opposite the front door. In here we find dark wood countertops and cupboards, light walls, and dark red, blue, and green glass tiles on the walls, giving the entire space a magical, bejeweled feel.

I mourn the lack of a dining area until we climb the stairs and it becomes apparent that there's room for a large dining table and chair set to be placed at one end of the long living room while leaving plenty of space for a sofa and a couple of chairs to go at the other end. Breaking the two spaces is a huge window with a sill large enough to turn into a window seat.

Kneeling on it, I can see out onto the street below.

The others are following me around and talking amongst themselves, clearly respecting my desire to explore this place myself. When we turn to the second room in the attic, Chloe smiles.

"My room?" she asks, and I nod. "It has skylights."

"Is that a good thing?"

"Yeah. It's cool."

Cassie seems to be flagging a little bit, and I'm reminded that she is only three years old and we've done a lot of dragging her around the city today. Chris picks her up again, and she rests her head on his shoulder, her thumb tucked securely in her mouth.

The office space has an entire wall of built-in, deep mahogany bookshelves that make me almost whimper with pleasure as I run my hand across them. There's also an oddly placed door, which Jessica tells us was something the current owners had to install as a fire escape, but all I can think of is that it's the perfect place for a cat flap.

The garden below isn't ours (I can't force myself to break it to Cassie just yet) and I hope the people downstairs won't have any objection to Flea.

I want to see the master bedroom again, and we stand in the room for what feels like a long time, absorbing the space and what it has to offer.

Soft, blue-grey walls, white trim, more of that luscious thick carpet. No attaching bathroom, but I can live with that. Another window out onto the street—it's right below the living room upstairs.

"There's nowhere to keep your drums," I say, looking for the negatives now. "No off-street parking either."

"Not high on my list of concerns," he says. "There's a corner of the family room where I can set up the drums. And it's the attic so it won't disturb the family below us."

My dining table, I think wistfully.

"You can keep the drums in my room," Chloe says, leaning on the door frame in a pose very reminiscent of one Chris might adopt. "Get a futon, I can sleep on that."

"You're not having a futon, you're having a bed," I say firmly.

She rolls her eyes. "Stop looking for problems, Dad," she says. "This place is perfect. You love it. So does Chris."

"Do you?" I ask, afraid that I'm being desperately selfish now. This is supposed to be a home we're building together, making a family of the two of us. There's no point in choosing somewhere we're going to want to move out of in a few years' time.

"If you want a proper house, we can get one," I rush to continue, not giving him time to agree just to make me happy. "I know you wanted a house, and I'm okay with that, I really am. This is more of a bachelor pad sort of place anyway. Not a family home."

"Do you two want kids?" Chloe asks with a note of panic in her voice.

"No," Chris says calmly. "We want a place where you'll be comfortable to come stay sometimes, and Cassie too, when she's old enough. And like your dad said, somewhere where we can have a home together."

"So?" Chloe and I say at the same time.

He laughs. "I really, honestly love it," he says. "I love it for me, because it's beautiful and classy and it feels like a home. And I love the way it makes you light up. So we should get it."

"Really?" I say, and he nods.

"Really really."

He lets me kiss him, quickly, softly, but a kiss loaded with meaning.

"Jessica," I say as we walk out of our master bedroom as a family. "I think we'd like to put in an offer."

OF COURSE, nothing is as easy as that when it comes to buying houses, and unfortunately there are other people who are equally as enamored with the gorgeous split-level condo as we are. Rather than the days I was expecting, it takes weeks of bartering back and forth before our offer is considered by both the bank and the seller.

There are too many complications. I have a mortgage on the flat I've lived in alone for the past few years and have to make sure that any rent I charge on it will cover that initial loan. All the annoyances and legal shit of being a registered landlord. And taking out a second, joint mortgage on a rather expensive second home.

But there are things that stand in our favor.

My job, for one, which leads nicely to my reputation within the academic community, for two. Chris's occupation as a musician is slightly more problematic as it's far less steady work, but he gets a great reference from the Boston Symphony Orchestra, which helps a lot. And finally, thankfully, I have enough in my savings that the move isn't going to hit us too hard financially.

The process of sitting down with Chris and working out exactly what we both earn and our outgoings isn't easy. I have a child and a college education, neither of which came cheap. I was expecting for him to not have much in the way of savings, but I'm slightly humbled to find out he's been working his cute little bubble butt off since he was sixteen years old. Apart from the expense of the motorbike, he's been saving like crazy and has enough set by to be an equal partner in the house.

We have a few conversations with John and Lexi to find out when they're planning on moving back to the city, and manage to plan the move to mean that there's not too long a period of time when my flat will sit empty.

I agree to rent it to them furnished, since all they've really got in the way of furniture can be packed up into a camper van and trailer to be dragged up and down the country. This means shopping. Lots and lots of shopping.

There are moments when I seriously consider giving Chris, Chloe, Luisa, and Jilly a list of things we need and just sending them off on their own; surely this is a better idea than being dragged around furniture store after furniture store and trying to agree with all three of them, which is possibly the most impossible, fruitless task in the given universe. Especially since Jilly and Lu are prepared to double team against me.

With poor Mike left in charge of Cassie for the afternoon (he has plans to take her to the Boston Children's Museum) and Carter strapped to his mother's chest, Chris and I take them back to the condo so we can look at it again and Lu and Jilly can see it for the first time.

Both women *oooh* and *ahhh* in all the right places, and Lu takes pictures on her camera phone in the desperate hope that this shopping trip will go better than the last one. It couldn't possibly be any worse. Forcing myself to put the experience out of my mind, I begin to make a mental list. Apparently everyone else is doing the same thing.

"Right," I say in my decisive, man-about-the-house voice. "Where are we going for coffee? Because I'm damned if I'm going to wander around without a purpose again looking for bloody candlesticks to go on the mantel that we don't have and cushions to match the sofa that we haven't bloody bought yet."

Luisa looks amused. Chloe looks shocked. Jilly rolls her eyes.

Chris grabs hold of my sweater and pulls me to him for a hard kiss.

I'm entertained enough to flick my hand at the girls in a vague *shoo* motion as I let him kiss me. He hums against my lips and pulls away, only to kiss my cheek with a loud smack.

"Love it when you're all commanding," he says in a low voice.

"Let's just go home and have sex," I whisper once I'm sure the girls, my daughter in particular, have left the room. "They don't need us there. They definitely don't want us there. And they can probably do a better job than we can anyway."

"Nope." Chris kisses me quickly on the lips and takes my hand to drag me from the room. "Come on, we're gay men. Interior design is supposed to be something we're good at."

I forgive myself for not believing him.

CHAPTER
SEVENTEEN

THERE isn't a lot to do in the way of decorating since the new apartment has been so well kept by the previous owners, but once the sale has completed and the place is officially ours, I decide I want to repaint my office. When we first visited, one wall was a deep, rich orange, which was nice, but I want something more relaxing for the space. And apparently Chris has agreed to help Chloe redecorate her room "however she wants." This decision has been made entirely without my knowledge or prior approval, and by the time I find out about it, I can't say no without looking like the bad guy.

I have visions of lurid pink and purple swirling in my head as Chris takes her down to the hardware store to go buy paint. While they're gone, I slap warm, coffee-colored paint on the walls in my office and sulk.

When my phone rings, I seriously consider not answering it. I know that it's Chris because he has his own ringtone. He seems to be the only one who doesn't know this, since he's never next to my phone when he's the one calling it.

"Hello?"

I'm such a loser.

"Hey, Rob. Do you know how to hang wallpaper?"

I have visions of '60s psychedelic swirls.

"No. Sorry."

"Ah, well. No worries. See you in a bit." He rings off. My heart sinks further for my beautiful, beautiful apartment. It's okay, I tell myself. We can just keep the door closed up there. No one need ever know.

When they return, I'm resigned to the horrific.

And am forced to eat humble pie when Chloe shows me tins of paint in cream and gold.

"It looks nice," I say, trying to keep the surprise from my voice and failing.

"Thanks," she says, flushed and excited. "Chris said that I could paint the walls a different color to the windowsill and stuff. I'm going to get matching linens for the bed, too."

"Did he, now," I mutter darkly. "Go on and change and we can get started."

She grins and bounds up the stairs. Thankfully, since the room is white already, there's no need for base coats or anything like that. I raise an eyebrow at Chris once she's out of earshot.

"Oh, you owe me one," he says. "You owe me an hour-long rimjob while I eat ice cream and watch *Gossip Girl* with no sarcasm."

"At the same time?"

"Fuck, yeah. I can multitask."

He rummages through the bags and extracts the other cans of paint, rollers, brushes, and trays. "We went through pretty much the entire spectrum of girlish, nauseating color schemes. I'm serious, at one point she wanted to paint the ceiling blue with white fluffy clouds on it."

"Jesus."

"Damn straight. There's no fucking way I'm having white fluffy clouds in my house. Then we moved on to wallpaper, and she wanted this gold brocade shit because it was 'elegant', so I jumped on that and talked her into the gold paint."

"An hour-long rimjob? Sure you can last that long?"

He's laughing as he pulls me down into a messy kiss. "I love you."

"Love you too, you silly bugger."

THE new furniture arrives in dribs and drabs, meaning one or the other of us is constantly speeding across town to let the delivery guys in. We end up dumping most things in the living room on the top floor, because it's easier to get the bigger things up there to begin with and take them back downstairs after rather than having it all on the first level and having to haul it up the stairs.

When our official "moving day" comes, it's something of an anticlimax, since we've been doing so much stuff in the apartment already. Nearly all of our clothes, the pieces of kitchen equipment we're keeping, and my books and DVDs and photographs have all been taken across town in the back of my car. The last few things that we've been living with are easily packed into a couple of suitcases. Then it's just Flea in his carry box (which he *hates*), and it's time to say goodbye.

Which is ridiculous, when I think about it, because it's not like I won't still get to see the place. My name is still on the deeds, and I'll probably be the one called out to fix the blocked sink or whatever. But this was the place where I fell in love.

The making love "one last time" in our bed starts sweetly, tasting all the memories behind us of doing the same thing so many times before. Then Chris slaps me on the ass and forces me to fuck him hard, and that's better, somehow.

Lexi and John arrive right on schedule while Chris and I sit out on the front step waiting for them. Laughing, Chris surges to his feet and runs to greet them with warm hugs, and I realize that it's been a good few months since he last saw his closest friends.

I, too, envelop Lexi in a warm hug and obligingly pat her tummy, which is still impossibly flat, although she claims a bump is starting to poke out.

"I'll take your word for it," I tell her with a smile. We force her to sit down and not lift a finger to help as Chris, John, and I haul their boxes in from the trailer, although almost immediately she starts to sort things by where she wants them to go.

When the others go back down again for the last load of boxes, I catch Lexi standing in the doorway to my office. To the room that used to be my office. She has a little smile on her face as she sees me watching.

"Your nursery?" I ask, and she nods.

"I don't think I've said thank you yet for letting us have the place. And at such a reasonable rate."

"It's my pleasure," I say genuinely. "Chris and I were never going to stay here forever. I'm just glad it meant you could come back to Boston."

She tucks red curls back behind her ear, then hugs me again. "You're so perfect for him."

"I know," I whisper. "But he's so perfect for me, too."

John agrees to load up my old desk and take it across town in their trailer, which is a blessing because I hadn't quite worked out how I'm going to move it, and Lexi clearly won't need it if she's turning the room into a nursery.

We follow in my car, Chris holding Flea on his lap, who I swear is sulking at being locked up and refuses to listen to my promises to let him out just as soon as we can.

"Just think, Fleabag," Chris says to him through the bars of the cat box. "No more coming in and out through a window anymore. You get a real cat flap."

"Mmrow."

"I don't think he's too impressed," I say, signaling to turn onto our road.

Of course, getting my antique desk up several flights of stairs, through the front door, down the hall, and into my office is about as easy as the entire operation sounds. When it's done I'm sweating. But that's it. The last piece moved in.

We thank John, lock the front door, and let Flea out to explore his new house.

Chris sighs heavily. "What first?"

Books, the little selfish voice in my head demands. *Unpack and arrange all your books.*

"Bed," I say—surprising myself.

Chris grins impishly, as if he knew I was going to say something else and stopped myself.

"The frame and the mattress are already here," he says. "We just need to assemble it."

"Sheets?"

"Are in the box marked 'sheets'. You should know, you packed them," Chris says, taking my hand to drag me down the hallway. The bed was the only thing I managed to direct to the correct location when the delivery people were here. I didn't much fancy having to drag it back down the stairs again.

Much to Luisa's amusement, on our epic shopping trip, Chris and I chose another small double bed, the same size as the one in my old flat. I claimed, at the time, that this was because it was easier to keep the same sheets that I already had rather than having to replace them all with new. She saw right through me.

I'm not surprised that when we're assembling the thing, we end up in a debate (not an argument, definitely not an argument) about the position of the furniture in the room. Unfortunately, when we viewed the apartment for the first time, this room was completely bare, so we had no guide on how best to place things.

I want it on the wall facing the window so we can watch the sun rise every morning.

Chris wants it on the wall facing the door so he can protect me from scary intruders.

Yeah, right.

Of course, this leads to us needing to locate all the other furniture for the room and put that in place as well, so we can work out where's best for everything to go. I don't want to argue with him, I desperately don't, but I can't help but think that if we're going to have this debate in every room we come to, we're going to need a lot more than the long weekend we've planned to get everything unpacked.

When I give in to him, Chris only throws another strop.

"What?" I demand.

"I don't want you to let me get my way because you love me, I want you to let me get my way because I'm *right*."

"Oh, fuck's sake," I mutter, sitting down on the edge of the bed (that's facing the door) and rub my hands over my face.

He somehow manages to squeeze his way onto my lap between my elbows and knees and wraps his arms around my neck.

"We have a house together," he whispers.

"A flat," I correct.

"An apartment," he contradicts.

I flick his ear.

"Rob?"

"Hmm?"

"Can we have a bath?"

"Don't see why not."

There's a big tub in the bathroom as well as a standing shower unit, and for the size of the flat, it's larger than one would expect, which is good. I like a big bathroom.

From somewhere, God only knows where, Chris locates a bottle of shower gel, which will have to do in place of bath bubbles because we don't have any. I'm aware not to over-fill the bath since two of us are going to be getting in it and, you know, Archimedes's principle of displacement.

I get in first, and Chris naturally settles in front of me with his back to my chest. I idly think that the light in here is too dim and I'll need to replace it to make sure I don't cut myself shaving in the mornings, especially during the winter.

My hands trail up and down Chris's arms and over his chest as our feet and legs twine together. For once he seems to be completely relaxed, not buzzing about something or another or hyped up on caffeine. Usually the only times he's like this are after we've had sex— or when he's asleep.

I carefully take one of his hands—his left one—between both of mine and start to massage his long fingers. There are calluses from years of gripping drumsticks, and I rub them gently, surprised at the intimacy of this act.

Chris drops his head back to my shoulder and hums in deep, deep contentment.

"Another first," he murmurs.

"What was that?"

"I've never done this before."

"Taking a bath with someone?"

"Yeah. It's nice."

I slipped his silver ring off his right hand and put it on his left thumb for safekeeping while I turned my massage to his other hand.

"Will you fuck me later?" I ask suddenly.

As Chris tilts his head back to my shoulder, I can feel the blush creeping up the side of my neck. Outbursts are usually his domain, not mine.

"Yeah," he says, sounding amused. "Of course. Any reason in particular? Or just christening the new bed?"

"Bit of both," I say and attempt a nonchalant shrug.

"You're strange."

There's a sentiment I can agree with.

Unpacking, as I predicted, takes a good three days to do, and even then we don't get everything done. My initial confusion quickly turns to annoyance as I realize that I'm not going mad, and yes, Chris is following me around and rearranging stuff. It takes a lot of self-control not to snap at him. I've lived alone for far too long and have had everything just the way I like it, which admittedly is not the same way things would make sense to other people.

As I carry another box of books destined for my office down from the lounge, I almost trip over Chris sitting on the bottom stair. He's talking on his phone rapidly to someone and gesticulating wildly with his free hand. I maneuver the box around him, and he grins up at me impishly. He's turned me into such a sap.

In my office, I set the box down on my desk and start to methodically stack books on shelves. The task is calming, and I hum to myself as I do it.

"Hey," Chris says, leaning on the door frame.

"What's got you grinning like a Cheshire cat?" I demand as he meanders over for a kiss.

"That was my brother."

"Which one?"

"Drew."

"The one with the kids?" I ask. My box is nearly empty now, so I lay the last few books on the shelf. They'll get propped up with the next one.

"No, Jacob has the kids." When I turn back, he's sitting in my desk chair, still grinning away at me. "Drew is the one who is going to send The Box up here."

I take the bait. "The box of what?"

"Not the box, The Box," he corrects, and the second time I hear the capital letters.

"Okay, The Box of what?"

"Porn," he says delightedly. I roll my eyes and disassemble my very standard box, taking it back upstairs for the next one. Chris follows me.

"I find it hard to believe you have no porn with you at all," I say.

"Well, I do," he concedes. "But The Box is epic. It's not just porn, really. There's butt plugs and lube and this gorgeous, massive bright-red dildo...."

His sigh, when it comes, is one of deepest longing.

"I had no idea you were such a little pervert." I did, of course.

"Yes you did." He knows me too well.

He's still following me as I take the next box down, and I don't realize until we're back in the office that he's brought the last one with him.

"Give me kisses," he demands. I'm happy to oblige him. "I've got something else to tell you."

"Go on."

"I've got a job. A proper, regular job. It's not full-time hours or anything, but it's good."

I can't for the life of me figure out why the box of porn was more important than this, but I've long stopped questioning anything to do with Chris and sex.

"That's fantastic," I tell him. "Where is it?"

"At the ballet," he says.

"The Boston ballet?"

"Yeah. They use a drummer instead of a pianist for a lot of their rehearsals, especially for the contemporary crap. But for the big classical numbers as well because it's easier to keep in time with a drummer than some floaty music, especially when they're learning new pieces."

"How did you get that on a contract?"

"I told them I was happy to take the job but I needed at least a six-month deal because I want to stay in Boston and I can't unless I have something more secure."

"And they bought that?"

"I can be very persuasive when I need to be, Professor."

"Don't I know it," I mutter under my breath. He throws a pencil at my back, which Flea immediately pounces on. I hadn't noticed that he was watching our conversation, probably from "his" windowsill.

"So you got six months?"

"Nope." He pauses, for dramatic effect, I'm sure. "A year."

"That's really great. Well done, baby."

He appears under my arm, insinuating himself into my embrace.

"This could lead to good things, you know?" he says softly. "I could get some good references and be able to play for the bigger orchestras."

"That would be great. You're really starting to build your portfolio, you know?"

His smile lights up his face.

"Yeah. That's the idea."

"Do you want me to take you out to celebrate?"

"Nah. That's okay. Do you want help with your books?"

I shudder at the thought. "Thank you, but no."

"Okay. I'm going to go set up my drums."

Before he leaves, I kiss him again. Because I can.

I WILL inevitably rise before Chris in the mornings and pad around the house, making breakfast and getting dressed while he's still passed out, spread eagle on the bed, leeching whatever warmth is left from the sheets I've abandoned. It's okay. Despite the fact that my job calls for early mornings, I'm much more productive after midday and don't particularly want to talk to him once I've rolled out of bed.

I'm brushing my teeth in the bathroom when he comes in behind me and flips the lid up to use the toilet.

"You didn't kiss me this morning," he mumbles, his voice scratchy-rough from sleep.

I spit.

"Hmm?"

"This morning. You didn't kiss me."

"Yes, I did."

I didn't even know that he knew I did that. Before leaving our little sanctuary of too-small bed and warm skin, I always, *always* kiss him. Usually on the shoulder, but really, any patch of skin will do. It depends on the position in which he's sleeping.

He still looks grumpy as he flushes and nudges me out of the way to wash his hands. When he's done, I angle his face into a minty kiss.

"Promise," I whisper to him. "Go back to bed, sweetheart."

He nods and pads out of the bathroom, and I decide he's probably still at least half-asleep.

By the afternoon he's clearly forgiven me.

Dropped the bike off for a service, his text reads. *Can you pick me up from the studio? Finish at 7. Love yoooooou xxxxx*

For some reason this reminds me of Chloe's "Dad can you pick me up" texts, and I wonder whether to be disturbed or amused. I go with amused. I can vaguely remember him telling me about the service the night before when we were curled up on the sofa, but I was tired and probably drifting.

I text him back in the affirmative.

The night is clear and not quite as dark as last night, indicating our journey toward spring has taken another step. I park the car on a side street and wander up to the front of the ballet company's rehearsal space, straining my ears for any sound of Chris's familiar drumming, but I can't hear it.

When the first few dancers start filtering out through the door, I guess he'll soon be on his way.

For some reason I can't place my finger on, he looks subdued as he comes through the doors and heads straight for me, falling into my embrace.

"What's wrong?" I ask him, my fingers lightly combing through his hair.

"Nothing," he says, then corrects himself at my glare. "I'll tell you in a minute. Tell me?"

Now I'm worried. "Tell me" is for bed, for sex, and sometimes for showers. Not the middle of the street on a Tuesday evening.

"I love you," I tell him and bring him back closer to me. When he searches for my kisses, I give them to him willingly, despite the fact that we're on the middle of the street on a Tuesday evening, or maybe because of it.

When we break apart, another group passes us, and this time one of them stops.

"Chris," she says pleasantly, and I search my brain for a moment to figure out how I know her. "And Professor McKinnon. I'll admit, I didn't know the two of you were an item."

"Celina," I say, finally placing the woman as someone I met at an AIDS benefit back in December. She's one of the creative directors at the ballet, if I remember correctly; a tall woman with a soft brown cap of hair. "Nice to see you again."

"And you."

"Rob is the reason I came back to Boston," Chris supplies. "I did some work for Celina before, but it was difficult for me to do anything more because of the band."

"Well, it seems I should thank you, then," Celina laughs. "He's been a great success here. Very popular."

For some reason this makes Chris look sick. I decide to make our excuses, and we leave.

"What's up?" I ask as we head back to the car.

"Nothing," he says absently. I grab his hand. He's clearly upset about something, and as much as I don't want to push or pry, I can't help but feel like it's my duty to look after him.

"Let's go for dinner," I say. Chris looks at me as if I'm mad. I just shrug. "What are you in the mood for?"

"Oh, Rob, I'm not hungry," he says with a sigh. I grit my teeth and decide to battle it out.

"Please? We don't get to do this very often."

He nods, and I sense victory.

Since it's the closest thing to where I'm parked, I take him to Nando's. The last—and only—other time we were here, I watched him eat chicken wings like they had just announced a global chicken crisis and this was his only chance to eat it for the rest of ever. My dramatic side is born of having a teenager.

My choice of restaurant, such as it is, draws a small smile from him at last.

I let him order and resign myself to Coca-Cola. Then the waitress brings me iced tea, and I realize that I've underestimated him once again.

"I got you the unsweetened kind," he says and slurps his Coke. "It's probably still too sweet for you...."

"It's good. Thank you."

I purposefully don't talk until the silence between us is heavy with unspoken words. This silent pressure is much more effective at coercing him into spilling his troubles than yelling at him would be.

"I know what you're doing," he says.

"Hmm?"

"Bully," he mutters. "One of the guys at the ballet hit on me, okay?"

I frown at this complete nonconfession. Then my stomach drops. "Okay. That must be such a rarity for a beautiful and devastatingly sexy man like yourself. However did you cope?"

He blinks at me.

"You're not mad?"

"Did you act on it?"

"No!"

"Sure?"

Now he's mad. "Of course I'm sure, Rob. You know what you mean to me."

"Ditto," I say and gesture to his ring. His eyes linger on it for a minute.

"You're really not mad?"

I laugh now. "No, Chris. I'm really not. If you didn't act on it and politely told him no, then that's fine. These things will happen over the course of our relationship. You just have to deal with it."

"Oh. I didn't exactly *politely* tell him no."

This makes me snort with laughter. "Was he being a pest?"

"Shit, Rob, that's an understatement."

Our food arrives then, and we spend a few minutes rearranging the table and starting to eat.

"I'm slightly confused as to your reaction, though," I said, picking up the conversation several chicken wings later. "Why would I be mad at you?"

Chris carefully wipes his fingers and takes a long pull on his drink. Then his eyes level with mine, and he grips the edge of the table—apparently unconsciously—as he chews his bottom lip.

"Because someone before used to get mad at me."

Oh, fuck. There's no precedent for this; we haven't ever discussed Chris's previous partners. I'm in uncharted territory and unsure of my footing.

"Oh," I say. "Did they hurt you?"

He nods silently.

"In more ways than one?"

A pause, then another, shakier nod.

"Fucking hell, Chris." I sigh and lean back in my seat. After a moment I pick up my fork again and spear a fry. "So, who are we going to talk about first? Ballet boy or mean boy?"

He smiles and shrugs, selecting another wing. "Ballet boy?"

"Works for me."

"His name is Nathan."

"Okay."

"He's one of the principals. And gorgeous. You know, from a subjective point of view."

"Of course," I said drily.

"And half the guys in there are gay. If I were single—" He breaks off at my glare and hastens to add, "Which I'm not, obviously, but if I were.... Anyway. He was just a bit friendly at first, you know? Asking me where I learned to drum and stuff and where I'm from and my family. I told him about you, and he seemed interested. Nice. And I thought it would be nice to have my own friends in Boston, other than my friends I met through you or Lexi and John."

He pauses to finish eating, slurps his drink, and waits for my silent signal for him to continue.

"Then he just started getting really touchy-feely, and not in the good way. And I was constantly moving away from him—stepping back or whatever, trying to get my personal space back. 'Cause he was always up in it. Then he sort of... I dunno. Said we should go out together, and I said sure, I'd check when you were free, and he laughed and said no, he didn't want my boyfriend to come with us. And I should just go over to his place.

"And since I said no, he's just being a bastard to me. Complaining to Celia that my beats are out, which they're fucking not, Rob. I'm good at what I do. Or that I'm too fast or too fancy or whatever. Jerk."

I agree with him. The guy sounds like a complete jerk. And this is one of those moments when I need to protect what's mine, in the most loving and nonscary way I know how.

"Do you want me to kick the shit out of him for you?"

He laughs. "No, baby, I don't. But thanks for the offer."

I shrug and make it clear that it's his loss.

"So that's ballet boy out of the way. What about mean ex?"

Chris, for the first time in all the months I've known him, looks almost apprehensive. Then I realize it's not apprehension at all. It's vulnerability. And somehow that's much, much worse.

"You're not the first guy I've dated who's older than me," he says, then stops speaking to finish eating.

"I guessed as much," I supply, to fill the silence as much as anything else.

"I don't have a kink," he protests. "It's just that—in my experience—guys who are older than me generally treat me better. They're done with all the crazy drugs and bullshit you get in the gay community wherever you go. Most of the time they don't live with their parents." He smirks. "But there are always exceptions to that rule."

I consider his words and decide they make sense. "But," I reason, "there's a much higher chance that older guys will come with baggage."

"Like kids?" he says. "Chloe isn't a negative point against you, Rob. I do genuinely like her."

"And she likes you too. But you have to admit there were a few tense moments there at the beginning."

He shrugged. "You were worth it. Still are."

"How much older than you was he?" I ask, knowing now that there was someone in particular who hurt him.

"About twenty years? Maybe more."

"And how old were you?"

"Nineteen?"

He said it like a question, and I wanted to go back in time, locate a nineteen-year-old Chris Ford, and kick his motherfucking ass.

"Just tell me, Chris," I sigh.

"He was a leather daddy," he says. "Proper old-school top, you know? Gnarly, mean guy with tats and a leather harness and nipple rings. I thought I was in love."

I snort. He ignores me and cleans another chicken wing to the bone, which he then uses to gesticulate with. "He liked to spank me, and, well, you know that I like that. And he liked to call me his "property," which I thought I liked at the time. When we were out, I wasn't supposed to speak to anyone else without his permission. He bought my drinks, he told me when to dance and with whom. Did you notice I just said *whom* correctly?"

"I did. Well done."

"Thanks, Professor." He smirks. "And then it got to a point where I was being punished more than I was being loved. He started to use stuff on me, paddles and whips and stuff, and beat me until I cried. I never knew about safe words or anything like that. He never gave me one. Then one night he went at me with his belt because I went out without him and another guy hit on me. I was punished for letting him buy me a drink. That night he made me bleed. Never saw him again."

"Fucking hell, Chris." That's all I can come up with. Fucking hell.

"I guess, other than you, he's the only other person I've had a long-term relationship with. So I'm sort of still learning what's okay and what's not, you know, in a normal relationship." A long pause. Then: "Tell me what you're thinking."

It's not a request.

"I feel bad for spanking you," I admit, and he's shaking his head before I even finish the sentence.

"Don't be. I wasn't lying when I said I'm into that. He was just into really hardcore S&M stuff. You love me, Rob, you don't control me."

"Couldn't if I tried," I say softly, attempting to joke with him. He smiles.

When we finish eating, Chris lets me pay for dinner and we hold hands as we walk back to my car. It's rare for us to do it in public, but I think we both need the reassurance tonight. When the sky cracks open, the rain is immediately torrential, and we duck into a covered alley to wait it out.

It's not particularly cold out despite the rain, but we still end up snuggled together. Then he kisses me.

I back him up against the wall and loosely pin his wrists to the brickwork either side of his head, making my exploration of his mouth a thorough one. I know his taste so intimately, the way he fights back for more of my tongue and demands the rough, slow, needy slide of tongue against tongue, teeth and lips and the curve of his neck down to his shoulder.

The alley smells of wet cement and a little bit like trash, but I don't care. He's hard; I can feel it poking my thigh, and when he whispers, "Suck me," it's a raw demand rather than a request.

"Here?"

"Fuck yeah. There's no one around. Do it. It won't take long."

And then I'm crouched down, my face level with his button fly as I push metal through denim, and his fingers are in my hair as I pull his cock out. He wasn't lying—he's more than half-hard already.

For reasons completely unfathomable to me at this point, I don't suck his cock very often. Sex between us seems to focus on his main source of pleasure, which has always been his ass. He smells so fucking good, though, like man and musk and Chris.

I take him to the back of my throat, and in seconds he's wet and thick against my tongue, and I can feel that he's all the way hard now. Not huge, but big enough.

He hisses at the cold air on his damp skin as I pull back, then let him slide back into my throat. My fingers hold his hips steady, forcing him to stay fucking still and not thrust, because to be honest I'm not good at having him push it in. It's something I need to control.

Soon I'm bobbing my head back and forth with a slightly firmer suction than what I'd normally use, my fingers rubbing at the responsive spot behind his balls that seems to have a direct, zinging connection to his prostate. He's muttering something under his breath, but I can't hear him over the sound of the rain.

A slight tug on my hair is all the warning I get that he's about to come, and then heat floods my mouth, and I'm forced to swallow quickly to stop it choking me.

When I straighten up, he's still laughing and pulls me in for a kiss. Although I've swallowed all of it, I'm sure he can still taste himself on my tongue, and *fuck* if that isn't one of the hottest things I've thought in a while.

"Tell me," I say when he pulls away, his fingers combing though my hair, which is now slightly damp from the rain in the air.

"Love you," he says. "You miserable bugger."

I throw my head back and laugh.

THE mornings are starting to get lighter as we creep toward spring. Still, Chris rarely wakes before I do, so I have something of an uncomfortable moment finding an empty bed and a light bedroom, and the smell of tea and hot, buttered toast coming from the kitchen.

I find a pair of boxers on the floor and deem them suitable and sufficient to wander through the flat to look for him. In the kitchen, my cat is curled on one of the chairs and Chris leans back against a counter, one of my white, wide-bowled china teacups with the blue willow patterns cradled in his hands.

In the early morning light, I can see the ring I placed on his finger glinting softly. He notices my eye line and looks down at his hand, then back at me. It's so right, so absolutely fucking right that he's wearing it. Nothing could be more perfect.

He, too, is barely dressed in the blue-and-white striped shirt he bought for me, the buttons done up all wrong and the sleeves rolled up to his elbows. Underneath he's managed to coordinate with tight white boxers that only serve as a reminder of what he keeps in them.

"Tea," he says, lifting the cup and nodding to the pot that matches the teacups. He made tea in a pot. My heart skips again. If he keeps doing things like this, then I'm going to end up in the emergency room having a heart attack.

"Thank you," I tell him. The toaster pops, and he turns back to the counter, retrieving our breakfast and spreading the butter liberally. Cuts the toast into triangles. I love him even more.

He has one triangle in his mouth and crunches it loudly when he turns back to me, grinning widely. I brush his hair out of the way of the toast so he doesn't accidentally chew on it.

"I never drank tea before I met you," he says.

I kiss buttery toast crumbs from the corner of his mouth, unsurprised when he turns his face against mine and demands a hot slide of tongue over soft, pliant mouth. My hands hold his hips steady while we search for confirmation, then find it on each other's lips. *Mine*, I think. *You're mine.*

"And now?" I ask.

His eyes hold a touch of amusement as he returns my kiss.

"Tea is good."

ANNA MARTIN is from a picturesque seaside village in the southwest of England. After spending most of her childhood making up stories (early versions of her illustrated tales starring her stuffed animals should be available on eBay shortly), she studied English literature at university before attempting to turn her hand as a professional writer.

Apart from being physically dependent on her laptop, she is enthusiastic about writing and producing local grassroots theater (especially at the Edinburgh Fringe Festival, where she can be found every summer), travelling, learning to play the ukulele and Ben & Jerry's New York Super Fudge Chunk.

Anna claims her entire career is due to the love, support, pre-reading and creative asskicking provided by her closest friend, Jennifer. Jennifer refuses to accept any responsibility for anything Anna has written.

You can find Anna at her website, http://www.annamartin-fiction.com/, or on Twitter @missannamartin.

Dreamspinner Press
For more of the
best M/M romance,
visit
Dreamspinner Press
www.dreamspinnerpress.com

CPSIA information can be obtained at www.ICGtesting.com
Printed in the USA
LVOW130840080712

289128LV00002B/14/P